RETURN

of the

HIGHLANDER

Julianne MacLean

BOOKS BY
JULIANNE MACLEAN

The American Heiress Series

To Marry the Duke
An Affair Most Wicked
My Own Private Hero
Love According to Lily
Portrait of a Lover
Surrender to a Scoundrel

The Pembroke Palace Series

In My Wildest Fantasies
The Mistress Diaries
When a Stranger Loves Me
Married By Midnight
A Kiss Before the Wedding
(A Pembroke Palace Short Story)
Seduced at Sunset

The Highlander Series

The Rebel – A Highland Short Story
Captured by the Highlander
Claimed by the Highlander
Seduced by the Highlander
Return of the Highlander
Taken by the Highlander

The Royal Trilogy

Be My Prince
Princess in Love
The Prince's Bride

Harlequin Historical Romances

Prairie Bride
The Marshal and Mrs. O'Malley
Adam's Promise

Time Travel Romance

Taken by the Cowboy

The Color of Heaven Series

The Color of Heaven
The Color of Destiny
The Color of Hope
The Color of a Dream
The Color of a Memory
The Color of Love
The Color of the Season
The Color of Joy
The Color of Time

Praise for Julianne MacLean's Historical Romances

"MacLean's compelling writing turns this simple, classic love story into a richly emotional romance, and by combining engaging characters with a unique, vividly detailed setting, she has created an exceptional tale for readers who hunger for something a bit different in their historical romances."
—BOOKLIST

"You can always count on Julianne MacLean to deliver ravishing romance that will keep you turning pages until the wee hours of the morning."
—Teresa Medeiros

"Julianne MacLean's writing is smart, thrilling, and sizzles with sensuality."
—Elizabeth Hoyt

"Scottish romance at its finest, with characters to cheer for, a lush love story, and rousing adventure. I was captivated from the very first page. When it comes to exciting Highland romance, Julianne MacLean delivers."
—Laura Lee Guhrke

"She is just an all-around wonderful writer, and I look forward to reading everything she writes."
—Romance Junkies

Scotland, 1730

For as long as she could remember, Larena Campbell had possessed an unnaturally keen sense for impending danger. She could feel it in the air, like a whisper of warning, brushing lightly across her skin. Strangely, however, on the day that changed the course of her life forever, she'd had no notion of any unexpected threats. She hadn't felt the danger when she rose from bed that morning, nor during those critical moments leading up to the skirmish.

Instead, she had come close to falling asleep in the saddle numerous times, her head bobbing forward repeatedly as her horse, Rupert, plodded leisurely, shifting her from side to side in a rocking motion as they moved across lush green glens and shallow burns, where the water flowed clear as polished glass.

Perhaps it was the heat that dulled her senses. It was unusually humid for an August afternoon in the Highlands, and there wasn't a single stitch of wind. The dense and heavy stillness of the air—marked only by the incessant buzzing of insects on the pale purple heather of the moors—was soothing and hypnotic. She felt as if she were floating on a summer haze. Floating away...far, far away from the anguish and chaos.

Or perhaps she had simply let down her guard. She was, after all, traveling with an escort—a highly skilled and disciplined brigade of English soldiers in tidy scarlet uniforms. They had been commissioned with the task of delivering her home to Leathan Castle in one piece.

But *that* was no excuse. She should have known better than to allow herself to feel safe and secure with *anyone*, especially under the circumstances.

Though she could hardly blame herself for what happened next. She'd been assured that the soldiers were competent and well trained in the arts of war and rebellion. They were also well rested—a significant advantage in situations such as these—while Larena had hardly slept a wink over the past seven days. How could she, when she'd just been shot like a musket ball, straight into the fires of hell and back?

She blinked heavily as she recalled the terrifying sounds of the battle—the thunder of charging hooves and musket fire, steel clashing against steel, the violent cries of death and aggression. In hindsight, it was clear now that everyone would have been better off if her father had simply surrendered himself to the English, but he was a proud and courageous laird. He had done his best to repel the attack, but it was no use. He was now a prisoner in his own dungeon, charged with a number of treasonous Jacobite crimes, and his castle had been confiscated for use as an English garrison.

Hence the reason for her lack of sleep over the past six days, for she had snuck away in the night and ridden hell-bent to Fort William to meet with the King's representative there—with whom she had a personal connection.

To plead for her father's life.

Surprisingly, everything had proceeded like a dream from that moment on, for he had listened to her plea with sympathy and understanding. She was now returning home with a company of armed English escorts and the King's official pardon in her saddlebag.

Sweet Mary and Joseph. It all would have been ideal, if only her luck had held. But as soon as she and her protectors entered the shade of the forest, the whole world erupted into a violent explosion of gunfire.

And that's when the *real* trouble began.

Two

They came out of nowhere—those reckless, dirty rebels—just looking to stir up trouble. It had become a problem lately, ever since the unexplained disappearance of the famous Butcher of the Highlands—a fearless giant of a warrior who fought for Scottish freedoms and the Jacobite cause by ransacking entire camps of British redcoats at night. His attacks came without warning, always under the cover of darkness. According to folklore, he appeared like a phantom in the mist—with blood dripping from his gleaming battle-ax, his eyes filled with murderous rage—and committed morbid acts of villainy. He drove terror, like an iron spike, into the heart of every English soldier on either side of the border. For a time, the mere knowledge of the Butcher's existence had crippled the King's military strength in the North.

Many, to this day, insist that the Butcher was naught but a ghost. Others believe he was true flesh and blood. Dead now, most likely.

Though, in recent months, new bands of hooligans had begun to rise up and wreak havoc throughout the Highlands. According to rumor, they had taken up the sword to finish what the Butcher had begun—which was nothing good. At least not in the eyes of the British army.

As soon as the first shot whizzed by Larena's shoulder, her heart crashed like thunder in her chest and all the blood rushed to her head, but she was hardly the swooning type. Raised with three older brothers—all groomed to be warriors—she was suitably scrappy for a woman. More important, she knew how to use a bow and arrow better than most.

Within seconds, another shot struck the senior officer square between the eyes. Down he went, out of the saddle like a felled tree. Then the shouting began. The soldiers scrambled for their weapons as a motley crew of ruffians came screaming out of the bush, brandishing swords and axes.

Larena kicked in her heels and wheeled Rupert into the trees, dismounted, and withdrew her bow from the saddle scabbard. She found her footing, adjusted her stance, reached over her shoulder, and slid an arrow from her bow sack. The whole world went quiet as she positioned her fingers on the string, looked down the length of the arrow and aligned it with her target—a rebel Scotsman who was just about to swing a mortal blow to one of her escorts.

Relaxing her grip on the string, she let the arrow go.

It hit its mark, dead center. The rebel's eyes went wide. He peered down at his chest, dropped his sword, and collapsed to the ground.

While the British soldier rose to his feet and scrambled to reload, Larena fired off three more arrows in rapid succession. Meanwhile, the violence of the skirmish was escalating to an alarming degree. The soldiers were leaping off their horses and fighting the kilted rebels with knives and sabers.

No, this cannot be happening.

Larena's mind screamed with images of her father swinging from the noose if her protectors failed to deliver her to the castle in time. She reached faster into her bow sack and took aim to end the skirmish as quickly as possible.

Another shot rang out and Rupert spooked beside her. He reared up on his hind legs, pawed the air, and let out a high-pitched squeal. Larena was knocked off balance just as she let loose another arrow that twanged into a tree.

"Easy now!" She tried to reach for Rupert's halter, for she couldn't let him run. He carried the King's pardon in the saddle bags.

It was no use. Her horse bolted into the wood.

"*No, Rupert!*" she cried. "Come back!"

She ran after him, but only managed a few steps before another shot was fired from the road and a searing pain reverberated inside her skull. She grimaced and pressed her palm to the side of her head. When she looked at her hand, it was covered in blood.

Nausea welled up inside her.

Fighting to resist an oncoming wave of dizziness, she staggered to the side, made an effort to grab onto something, but her knees buckled beneath her. She dropped her bow and the next thing she knew, she was tumbling down a steep embankment. Twigs and branches snapped noisily while foliage cut into her flesh and bruised her flailing body as she crashed into a grove of saplings, grunting with agony the entire way.

Suddenly the world stopped spinning. All was quiet except for the chatter of a squirrel somewhere in the treetops. Larena could do nothing but lie on her back on a cool bed of moss, blinking up at the swaying canopy of leaves overhead, listening to a creek babble nearby, while pain throbbed in her bones.

Get up, Larena. You must.

But alas, her body would not respond.

She heard no more sounds of combat. The fighting must have stopped. Who was the victor? she wondered dimly. Perhaps they would come looking for her.

For a long while she lay among the trees, contemplating her fate until another fog rolled through her mind and she couldn't keep her eyes open.

This can't be how it ends, she thought with terrible, aching regret.

She had come so far.

I'm sorry, Father. I wanted so badly to save you.

Finally, she let her eyes fall closed and wondered if the stories she'd heard about death were true. Would she see a bright light? Would it take away the pain? And would her mother be waiting there to welcome her?

Relaxing back in the saddle, Darach MacDonald couldn't help but wonder about the strange dream he'd had that morning, just before dawn. He'd dreamed he was a hawk, soaring high over the mountains, flying home again.

Later, when he rose from bed and gathered up his weapons for the day, something had felt different. He couldn't quite put his finger on it, but he'd sensed that everything in his life was about to change.

Had it been a premonition? Or just a meaningless dream to remind him of his regrets?

Either way, it did not diminish his surprise six hours later when he was combing the forest on a routine scouting mission with his brother Logan, and heard shots fired in the distance.

Darach reined in his mount and turned to Logan who rode beside him. "Did you hear that?"

"Aye, I did," Logan replied, stopping as well.

They sat quietly on their horses. It had been a stagnant and uncomfortably muggy day, but suddenly a breeze whispered through the treetops. Darach closed his eyes and lifted his chin to savor the coolness on his neck as he listened carefully.

Nothing happened for a few seconds, then another shot rang out in the distance, followed by the angry shouts of men.

"Sounds like a monster of a brawl," Logan said.

"Aye," Darach replied, gathering up the reins. "It's coming from the old cart road, back that way. We'd best have a look."

It was their duty as scouts for their laird, Angus the Lion of Kinloch Castle, to keep watch over his lands. Most days were tedious and uneventful as they circled the distant perimeter—around and around continually, day after day—as these were peaceful times. Not much happened at Kinloch.

But something felt different today...

Urging their horses into a canter, they rode through the forest for half a mile or so to reach the road. By then the gunfire had ceased and the forest had gone quiet again.

"Which way?" Logan asked as they paused on the road, their horses tramping around skittishly. "I don't hear anything."

Darach looked north, then south. For a brief moment they lingered, listening for some indication of the direction of the skirmish. Then finally something broke through—a sound, far away at first, then it grew closer.

Darach raised a hand. "Do you hear it?"

"Aye."

It was the rumble of approaching hooves. They both turned as a riderless black horse dashed around the bend, galloping toward them as if the devil himself were on its heels.

At the sight of Darach and Logan on the road, the harried beast skidded to a halt and reared up.

"*Whoa!*" Darach vaulted lightly off his horse, dropped to the ground, and took hold of the dangling reins. "Easy now, soldier. Settle down. Trouble's over."

The gelding stomped around and snorted anxiously, tossing his head while attempting to flee, but Darach held tightly to the leather reins.

"There now," he said in calming voice. "Don't worry, friend. You're safe with us."

As the animal gradually gentled, Darach took note of the empty scabbard and saddle bags the horse carried.

"At least we know which direction," Logan mentioned, gesturing toward the south.

"Aye." Darach fetched a rope out of his own saddle pouch and tied a bowline to lead the gelding behind them. "Let's see if we can find out who you belong to," he said to the animal. "What do you say to that?"

The horse tossed his head and nickered.

Darach stroked his neck before remounting his own horse. A moment later, they were on their way down the road to investigate.

⚜

"What do you make of this?" Logan asked as they dismounted and walked toward the morbid display on the road. A few loyal horses remained nearby, seeming oblivious to the carnage, nibbling at leaves in the woods. "Redcoats and Scots alike. Do you recognize the tartan?"

Darach knelt on one knee to look more closely at one of the fallen Highlanders. He couldn't have been more than eighteen—with an arrow sticking out of his chest. "This one's a MacDuff," he said. "I suspect they were having some fun, imitating the Butcher. Angus won't take kindly to them stirring up trouble like this."

"What about the Redcoats?" Logan asked, bending forward to pull a small knife out of a soldier's leg. He wiped it clean on the dead man's trousers and slid it into his own belt.

"They're a long way from Fort William. Do you think something's brewing?"

"Like what?" Darach asked with displeasure as he rose to his full height, still gazing down at the face of the fallen MacDuff.

Logan gave him a knowing look. "You must know what I'm talking about."

With a heavy sigh, Darach stepped over the body of an English soldier and took note of the fact that he hadn't had a chance to draw his sword or pistol. He'd been shot between the eyes.

"Another Jacobite uprising?" Darach replied. "Aye, it could be that, or maybe just the foolish antics of a few of young troublemakers, looking for something to brag about." He stopped and surveyed the damage. "What isn't clear is whether or not there were any survivors. None of these men, on either side, were stripped of their weapons."

"A strange thing, that," Logan replied. "Maybe there was only one survivor and he was wounded. Couldn't carry anything."

Darach scanned the edge of the road on both sides for evidence of a retreat. His eyes narrowed in on a trail of broken foliage that led into a dense section of the wood.

"Stay here with the horses," he said, drawing his sword and stepping into the bush. "And keep your wits about you."

"Always do," Logan replied.

With quiet movements, Darach followed the trail to a spot where he found a mangled section of low-lying ferns and evidence of hoof prints on the soft ground. He knelt down to look more closely at the prints. Reaching down, he touched what appeared to be the imprint of a small-heeled boot.

Odd, for a company of British soldiers in the wilds of the Highlands. This was no ballroom.

Rising to his feet, he carefully pushed his way through the brush and continued a short distance until he found a bow on the ground. He bent to pick it up.

Holding it in his hand, he tested its weight and strength. It was Scottish workmanship, no doubt about it. But where was the archer? he wondered, glancing all around. The trail seemed to go cold in the spot where he stood.

Pausing a moment to listen, he heard the sound of rushing water from somewhere and peered to his right, down over a steep overhang to a creek bed below.

Bloody hell. There was a woman down there.

⋘⊹⋙

"Logan!" he called out over his shoulder as he dropped the bow on the ground. "I found a woman!"

Digging his heels into the soft ground to slow his descent, he relaxed his body and slid most of the way down to the bottom.

Rushing to her side, he knelt over her and saw that she had suffered a serious blow to the head, for her flaxen hair was stained and matted with thick, dark blood. Upon closer scrutiny, it appeared to be a gunshot wound.

Was she English? he wondered as he pressed his fingers to her soft neck, just below her jawline, searching for a pulse.

He examined the features of her face—the soft freckled complexion, the small upturned nose and full lips. She was a beauty, no doubt about it. Quickly he moved the pads of his fingers from one spot to another on her neck, and there—*at last*—he found a pulse.

Darach turned on his knee and looked up the slope to where Logan stood at the top. "She's alive!" he called out.

"Look out!" Logan cried.

Whack! Pain reverberated at the back of his head and down the length of his spine. He saw stars, then fell forward onto his hands and knees.

Moving swiftly, he rolled onto his back. The woman stood over him holding a large stone over her head. With wild, murderous eyes, she drew her hand back as if she were about to smash his face in.

"*Ach!*" he bellowed as he caught her slender wrists and forced the rock from her hands. In a flash of movement, he flipped the crazed hellion onto her back and pinned her hands to the ground above her head.

"Let me go!" she cried, kicking with her legs and fighting to free herself.

"I'll do no such thing, lassie. Not until you apologize."

"For what!" Her cat-like green eyes flashed with fire.

"For thumping me on the head just now. I suspect that'll leave a mark."

She grunted with frustration and continued to struggle, pumping her hips like a bucking filly while Darach straddled her firmly.

Logan descended the slope and moved to stand over them. Seeming unconcerned by their tussle, he withdrew an apple from his sporran and crunched into it while he watched the woman wiggle and squirm.

"Who is she?" he casually asked while chewing.

"None of your damn business!" she yelled, but her accent revealed that she was Scottish.

Logan bent forward over her face. "You're on MacDonald lands now, lassie, so that makes it very much our business." He took another bite of the apple.

"Get *off* me!" she ground out, then she let out a frustrated huff and finally relaxed.

For a few critical seconds, Darach's brain seemed to stop functioning at the sensation of their joined hips. He couldn't remember the last time he'd had a woman, and this one was as comely as any he'd ever met.

"That's better, lass," he said, mentally shaking himself out of any lusty thoughts about the woman who had just tried to bash his head in. "You're hurt. You shouldn't be exerting yourself."

Chest heaving, she shut her eyes and took a moment to catch her breath, which allowed Darach time to examine her features more closely.

She was young and small—rather waiflike, in fact, except for a lush bosom that caused his blood to course a little faster through his veins. She wore a blue bodice over a simple white linen chemise and dark skirt. There was no sign of any tartan, which was why, at first glance, he'd thought she was English.

The lass took a deep steadying breath which drew Darach's attention again to her bosom, where he lingered a moment. Then his eyes returned to her flushed cheeks, soft open mouth and disheveled, blood-stained hair. Tangled and messy, it reached nearly to her waist, splayed out on the forest floor beneath her.

"Tell us where you come from lass," he said, "and why you got into a scuffle with the Redcoats."

She frowned up at him, as if she were bewildered by the question, then she blinked a few times. "I don't feel very well."

He stared down at her with some concern as her eyes grew empty and unseeing. Then she bucked again for a few alarming seconds, as if possessed by some sort of demon, and passed out.

Darach released his hold on her wrists, leaned forward, and tapped her on the cheek. "Lassie, are you all right? Wake up. *Wake up!*"

"Is she alive?" Logan asked, kneeling down beside him and tossing the apple core away.

Darach found the pulse at her neck. "Aye, but she's in a sorry state. We need to get her back to the castle. Angus will have questions about what happened here, and she's the only one who can answer."

Logan's eyes lifted and grew dark with unease. "There may be others."

"Aye." Darach considered that. Then he stood up and looked around. All was quiet.

He surveyed the grade of the slope. "She can't weigh much. I'll carry her up over my shoulder. You go ahead and gather as many weapons as you can from the dead. Check the saddle bags and pockets of every horse and soldier. We need information."

Logan nodded and climbed back up to the road while Darach gazed down at the unconscious beauty at his feet.

She had spirit, to be sure, but who *was* she? And what part had she played in the ambush?

Wasting no more time thinking about the hows and whys, he squatted down, slipped his hands beneath her small, fragile frame, and hoisted her up over his shoulder like a loose sack of grain.

A short while later he was grunting and sweating, nearly to the top of the woody slope, when Logan appeared above him.

"Maybe I ought to wait for you to reach the top before I tell you this," he said.

Darach wrapped a hand around the trunk of a small tree and paused a moment to catch his breath. He hugged the lassie's lush little bottom against his cheek. "Spit it out, Logan."

His brother hesitated. "The woman you're hauling up the hill is a Campbell."

A Campbell?

Darach froze, then shifted her awkwardly on his shoulder. "Don't tell me she's from Leathan Castle."

Logan made a face. "Sorry brother. Looks like that's where they were headed. But it gets worse."

"How?" Darach asked, still pausing at the crest of the rise.

"She's the chief's daughter."

Every muscle in Darach's body strained hotly under the added weight of the woman draped over his shoulder, and he couldn't help but wonder about the dream he'd had that morning. Maybe it had been a premonition after all...

But Lord in heaven, he didn't want anything to do with what that implied.

"She's the daughter of *Fitzroy* Campbell?"

Darach felt a stab of disillusionment as he recalled how he'd been struck dumb by her beauty moments ago and aroused by her fighting spirit when she rose up to brain him with the stone. Then she'd fought valiantly against his hold, bucking and wiggling beneath him. He was twice her size and possessed at least three times her strength, yet she had been fearless and undaunted.

A small shudder traveled down his spine, for she was a Campbell.

Worse...she was Fitzroy's daughter.

Young and tantalizingly pleasing to the eye.

Ach...Bloody hell.

Glancing over his shoulder at the creek bottom below, Darach wondered if he and Logan would be better off if he simply dropped her and never mentioned a thing about this to anyone.

M any hours later, Larena woke from a murky pool of darkness to the sensation of a cool cloth dabbing at her forehead. Her head pounded mercilessly, ringing like a heavy mallet on an iron anvil. Confusion flooded her mind, and she had no notion of where she was or even what day it might be.

She fought to lift her heavy eyelids. It took immense effort for them to respond. At last they fluttered open, and she found herself gazing up at a man.

He was a Scot, dressed in tartan, with compassionate green eyes and long, golden hair tied back with a leather cord.

Larena tried to speak, to ask where she was, but she couldn't seem to form words. Everything seemed hazy in her mind, as if her brain were full of cotton.

"There, now." The Scot spoke softly in the flickering glow of the candlelight. "You'll be all right now, lass."

But where am I?

The Highlander dipped the cloth into a porcelain basin by the bed and squeezed it out. She listened feebly to the sound of water dripping out of it. Then he gently stroked her cheek and dabbed at her parched, cracked lips. Larena continued to blink up at him, helpless and perplexed.

A loud clang of metal jolted her into a sharper state of awareness, and the sound of a bar lifting on a door helped her to realize that she had been imprisoned somewhere.

With growing panic, she lay very still, glancing around the room. It was small, sparsely furnished and without windows. There were half a dozen candles burning on a candelabra next to the bed. The walls were constructed of stone.

The door swung open and another Scotsman entered, his strides heavy and purposeful across the stone floor. He had thick, dark, wavy hair and eyes black as night. He stood over the bed and glared down at her with menace.

The door slammed shut behind him with a terrifying echo of finality. The dark Scotsman hooked a thumb into the leather sword belt that lay across his broad chest. "What's yer name, lass?" he asked.

Still not sure if she could form words, Larena blinked up at him and beheld muscle-bound arms and massive, dangerous hands. She could only imagine the rippled brawn of his hips and abdomen beneath the loose white shirt and heavy tartan.

This one was a warrior, no doubt about it, built like an iron-tipped battering ram. Her gaze rose to his face—a shockingly beautiful display of masculine features, sculpted with clean lines and compelling angles. Yet there was softness in those full, moist lips...lips strangely familiar to her, as if she'd encountered them in a dream.

"I asked you a question." One dark eyebrow lifted. "Do you remember striking me in the head, lass?"

Suddenly it all came rushing back to her...the ambush on the road, the violent deaths of her British escorts, and Rupert galloping off with the King's pardon that was meant to save her father's life.

Dear Lord. Her father...

Heart suddenly pounding with apprehension, she attempted to rise up on an elbow, but a wave of dizziness swirled through her head.

The golden-haired Highlander urged her back down on the pillow. "Not yet, lass. You're not strong enough."

"Where am I?" she asked.

Her first words, spoken at last.

"Kinloch Castle," the darker one replied.

Frustration sparked in her veins. "Kinloch..." *Please, no.* "Am I being held prisoner here? You have no right."

"Aye, we have every right," he replied, his voice husky and low. "You're a Campbell, are you not?"

"Aye, but—"

"No buts, lass. The MacDonalds of Kinloch have long standing issues with the Campbells of Leathan. You know it as well as I do, so I'm not sure what you were thinking, crossing onto our lands in the company of British soldiers."

She struggled to think clearly but her brain was still a fuzzy, tangled up mess. She covered her eyes with a hand. "I didn't realize we'd entered MacDonald territory." Heaven help her, it had been too hot and humid. She hadn't slept in days. "Please accept my apologies for that, but I really need to go. I must return home."

"What's your hurry?" the dark one asked. The antagonism in his eyes and the threatening note of suspicion in his deep, smoky voice was enough to send a bolt of alarm straight into her heart.

She tried to sit up again. This time the golden-haired one made no move to stop her. He rose from his sitting position on the edge of the cot to stand beside the taller one.

Side by side—one dark, one light—they were an alarming sight to behold.

Larena touched her bare feet to the floor. "I must leave. I've lost too much time already. Oh, God, what day is it?"

Nausea poured into her stomach. She had no choice but to pause and grip the edge of the hay-filled mattress and wait for the wooziness to pass, for she wasn't certain she could rise without falling over.

"You won't be going anywhere, lass," the dark one said. "Not until you tell us what you were doing with the Redcoats and why they're all lying dead on our laird's road."

She scoffed. "You're asking *me*? Aren't *you* the ones who ambushed us?"

Her two captors exchanged a curious look.

"Nay, lass," the golden one said. "We had nothing to do with that, and you're lucky we came upon you when we did, or you'd still be out there on your own. Dead most likely."

Larena studied their expressions. "It wasn't you who attacked us?"

"Nay."

Still not sure if she believed them, she exhaled heavily and strove to remain calm. If she had any hope of leaving here peacefully, she had to keep things affable.

"Well, then, I apologize for the misunderstanding and I thank you for your assistance. But I must leave now, and I need my horse." Then she recalled that Rupert had spooked during the conflict and run off into the forest.

Feeling defeated, she cupped her forehead in a hand. "Please tell me you have him?"

"Why does it matter, lass?" the dark Highlander asked with narrowed eyes.

She raised her chin. "Because he's carrying an important document. If you didn't find him, I must go and search for him." Neither of the men responded to that, so she elaborated. "He was spooked during the conflict and galloped off. I tried to stop him and that's when I fell into the ravine. *Please.* It's a matter of life and death. If I don't find him and return home straightaway—"

The dark-haired one reached into the folds of his tartan and withdrew a rolled letter. "Is *this* what you're looking for?"

Larena stared at him with wide eyes, leaped to her feet, and tried to snatch the document from his hand.

He shoved it behind his back. "Easy, now," he said, giving her a fierce look of warning. "First you're going to tell us what this is all about and who you are. And we'll need your full name, lass—especially the part that ends in Campbell. Then we'll see about letting you go."

Without hesitation, she said, "I'll tell you everything you need to know. Truly, I'll do anything you want—*anything*—if you promise you'll return that document to me."

Something darkly sensual danced across his face, and he took a step closer, crowding her up against the bed. "That's a very tempting offer, lass. I can think of all sorts of interesting ways you could deliver on that promise, but I'll have to respectfully decline, because you'll be coming with me now."

For a few heart-stopping seconds, Larena's muddled brain couldn't process the meaning behind his suggestive reply. She was too overcome by his physical nearness, the impossible bulk of his sheer brute size, and the sultry, outdoorsy scent of his body.

He wrapped his big hand around her elbow, which effectively yanked her out of her confounding stupor.

"Where are you taking me?" she asked as he led her to the door.

He banged on it three times with the edge of his big fist. The bar lifted and the heavy oaken door swung open.

"You're about to be presented to the Laird of Kinloch," he replied.

Good God.

"You plan to hand me over to Angus the Lion?"

She'd heard the stories. Angus was the most fearsome, ruthless laird in the Highlands. Some even speculated he might secretly be the infamous Butcher.

"I don't intend to simply hand you over, lass," her captor replied. "I plan to be right there at your side, listening to every word that comes out of your comely little Campbell mouth."

With that, he thrust her forward into the torch-lit corridor, while the golden one remained behind.

⫷⟫

Larena had heard many frightening and gruesome tales about Angus the Lion and how he had taken Kinloch Castle by force a decade earlier, reclaiming it for the MacDonald clan. He had seized it from his enemies, the MacEwens, who had been awarded the ancient MacDonald stronghold through Letters of Fire and Sword from the King, in return for their service to the crown.

When Angus broke through the gates and staked his claim, not even the English army wished to retaliate and wage war upon the great Scottish Lion. The MacEwens, as a result, had been forced to take oaths of allegiance to their conqueror, who had claimed the fallen chief's daughter as his wife.

And so it remained today—MacEwens and MacDonalds, united by warfare and marriage.

In recent years, it was said that the Great Lion of Kinloch desired peace for his clan. At least Larena hoped that was the case. Her father rarely spoke of the MacDonalds, for there was bad blood between them, ever since the massacre at Glencoe many years back.

"Don't be shy, lass," her captor said as he walked behind her up the circular stairs of the North Tower to the solar, where the Lion awaited her arrival. "He just wants to know what's been going on at Leathan Castle, and why your father's head is destined for a spike."

The cruel words spoken about her beloved father sent an icy chill down her spine. "You are horrid to say such a thing to me."

"I'll say whatever I please, lass," he replied as they reached the top, "for he's a Campbell and so are you."

Together, they strode through an arched entry into a brightly lit hall with a wide bank of leaded windows. Larena was forced to shade her eyes from the blinding light of the setting sun. An enormous tapestry covered one curved tower wall, but otherwise the space was sparsely furnished.

She sucked in a breath just then at the sight of a large warrior to her left. He stood with his back to her at a sideboard, pouring whisky into three glasses. His silvery-blond hair hung loose down his back, almost to his waist, and he carried a massive broadsword in his belt.

A scalding rush of anxiety coursed through her blood at the mere notion that she was about to meet Angus MacDonald—a man her father had warned her about as a girl.

He is ruthless, without a heart. He despises the Campbell clan and would see us all dead if he could. Stay away from Kinloch, Larena. Never set foot there...

According to the gossip she'd heard at Leathan Castle, the Lion was monstrous and frightening, horribly disfigured with battle scars, and he bore the look of the devil in his eyes.

But then he turned and regarded her with a pair of ice-blue eyes that made her breath catch in her throat—partly because she was on edge, but mostly because he was not ugly or disfigured at all. In truth, he was astonishingly handsome.

He sauntered leisurely toward her with a glass of whisky in each hand, held one out to her, and spoke in a polite tone. "Welcome, Larena Campbell."

At the sound of her name on his lips, her ragged nerves snapped and she backed into what appeared to be a brick wall behind her. It turned out *not* to be a brick wall, however, but the dark Highlander who had escorted her to the tower.

Feeling her cheeks flush with heat, she cleared her throat and glanced back at him over her shoulder.

"Take the whisky, lass," the dark one suggested in that quiet, smoky voice that rode over her like velvet. "You look like you could use a drink."

Wetting her lips, she searched for some composure and stepped forward to accept the glass from her host. "Thank you."

The Lion handed the other glass to her captor, then studied her with steely, narrowed eyes as she raised the whisky to her lips and sipped, hoping that it wasn't poisoned.

Maybe it was, for it burned like a roaring bushfire down her throat. It took every ounce of self-control she possessed not to cough and sputter, because she'd never tasted anything like it.

Fighting to recover, she swallowed hard and met the Lion's gaze directly.

"So..." he said, returning to the sideboard to pick up the third glass he'd poured. "Darach tells me you got into a little scuffle with some Redcoats not far from here."

Larena glanced over her shoulder again, realizing she now knew the dark Highlander's name. *Darach.*

"That's not what happened," she explained, facing forward again. "If you would permit me to relay the truth of the situation..."

Angus raised his arm, as if he were about to conduct an orchestra. "Please, feel free."

Though, on the surface, his words and actions appeared to be cordial, he struck Larena as dangerously unpredictable, a man whose mood could turn in an instant. She imagined him handing her a drink one second and breaking her thumb the next.

Drawing in a deep breath to steady her nerves, she tossed back the rest of the whisky in a single gulp and grimaced in agony. "That's strong," she croaked.

"Aye, it's Moncrieffe Whisky, the very best the Highlands has to offer."

Still working to recuperate, she allowed Angus to take the empty glass from her trembling hand and lead her by the elbow to a chair.

"Why don't you sit down, lass?" he said. "You look a little pasty."

Aye. She certainly *felt* pasty. Not to mention dizzy from the bloodied lump on her head, the strong whisky, and fatigued and worried for her survival—as well as her father's.

Aware of Darach, following like a shadow beside her, she sat down on the wooden chair and watched Angus pull up a stool to sit down before her.

"Better?" he asked.

She nodded her head, but her heart still pounded heavily in her chest.

"Now tell me everything," Angus said in an encouraging tone that made her hope he might prove to be understanding.

"It may surprise you to hear this," she told him, "but I was not involved in the attack on the Redcoats. I don't know who was responsible for that, for I was on the receiving end of it. You see…the British soldiers were acting as my escorts back to Leathan Castle."

"To deliver the King's pardon that would save your father's life?" Angus clarified.

"Aye."

He studied her eyes intently. "Tell me more, Larena. How did this come to be?"

She swallowed hard. "I had ridden all the way to Fort William to meet with His Majesty's representative there...to plead for mercy on my father's life. I was very fortunate that he awarded it to me, and for that reason I must leave here and return home as soon as possible."

"To save your father from the executioner," Angus added.

"That's right."

"But why was your father sentenced to death?" he asked. "That is what I am most curious about, for I was under the impression that the Campbells of Leathan enjoyed kissing King George's arse."

Perhaps another woman might have been shocked by the Lion's coarse turn of phrase, but Larena had been raised with four older brothers who were crude in their youth. In fact, she was just as curious about—and confused by—her father's motives when it came to his recent indiscretions.

"It appears that my father did not entertain the same political views as our former chief."

She was keenly aware of Darach circling around to watch her more carefully. Her eyes lifted and she was immobilized by the intensity of his stare.

"Are you referring to former Chief Ronald Campbell?" Angus asked. "He was a Hanoverian, from what I recall. Very loyal to King George."

"Aye," she replied, "but as it turns out, after he died without any heirs, and my father took his place as chief, my father began a secret campaign to support the Jacobite cause and put the Stuart king back on the throne." She lowered her gaze to her hands. "I believe he was taking steps to raise an army."

Both Angus and Darach frowned at her in bewilderment.

Angus leaned forward. "You mean to tell me that your father, Fitzroy Campbell, is a Jacobite? Good Lord. Now I've heard everything."

Angus turned to look up at Darach who was standing beside him. "What do you make of that, Darach? Are you shocked?"

"Aye," he replied, gulping down a deep draft of his drink and wincing at the flavor. Or perhaps it was disgust at the information she'd just conveyed.

Larena sighed heavily. "Believe me, I was as shocked as you are—even more so when the English soldiers broke down our gates to arrest my father. I swear I knew nothing of his plots against the King. That's when I slipped out and rode to Fort William as fast as I could to plead for his life."

Darach's head drew back in disbelief. "And they agreed to spare him? Why? How in God's name did you convince the King's representative in Scotland to offer your father a pardon?" He paused, then his eyes raked over her body. "Unless…"

"No, it wasn't *that*," she firmly insisted. "And I am insulted by your insinuation, sir."

Angus slapped Darach's arm. "Look what you've done, man. You've scandalized the poor Campbell lassie, and after everything she's been through…Apologize to her at once."

"My apologies," Darach said reluctantly, and took another swig of whisky.

Larena sat up straighter in her chair. "If you must know, I have an old family connection with the King's man, Lord Rutherford. I thought perhaps he might feel sentimental about Leathan Castle and agree to help me."

Angus inclined his head. "Why would Rutherford feel sentimental toward Leathan?"

"It's complicated. Please, if you would simply give me back the pardon and release me so that I may deliver it in time."

The two Highlanders stared at her in silence. Then Angus shook his head. "Sorry, lass. Complicated or not, I must know everything. Why did Lord Rutherford agree to spare your father's life?"

Seeing no way around it, Larena tried to explain things as plainly and efficiently as she could, because she needed to leave this place as soon as possible, before it was too late.

"Because he sired a bastard son who is half Campbell," she told them. "That son was raised by his mother at Leathan Castle until he was sixteen or so, but then she died. The boy and I were good friends…although I haven't seen him in many years, not since I was a young girl, when Lord Rutherford came to collect him and raise him in London. I was only eleven at the time."

Darach strode closer and squatted down before her. She found herself distracted by the flecks of silver in the inky blackness of his eyes.

"What is this bastard son's name?" he asked.

She lifted her chin and spoke proudly. "Colonel Gregory Chatham."

Darach's eyebrows pulled together with dismay and she wondered if he knew the name.

If he did, he revealed nothing.

"I find it difficult to believe," Darach said, "that mere sentiment would cause Lord Rutherford to spare the life of a Scottish traitor, just because his own bastard son had fond memories of his childhood in the Highlands."

There was something fierce and indomitable in Darach's expression. It sent icy fingers of fear twisting around Larena's heart. "You are correct," she replied. "There is more to it than that."

Again, with a show of pride and defiance, she lifted her chin and folded her hands together on her lap.

"Are you going to tell us, lass? Or keep us in suspense?" Angus asked, rising from the stool.

Darach rose as well and she tried not to feel intimidated by their elevated statures before her.

"Fine," she replied. "In exchange for the pardon on my father's life, I agreed to marry Lord Rutherford's son."

"*Marry* him," Darach said with a look of surprise.

"Yes. Evidently, those feelings of fondness his son, Chatham, had…." She paused and cleared her throat. "It was not a fondness for the Highlands, per se, but rather a fondness…for *me*."

Stunned, the MacDonald chief and his warrior scout stared down at her for what seemed like an eternity, then Darach abruptly turned away and strode to the windows where he looked out at what was left of the setting sun—a mere sliver of blinding fire over the horizon.

Angus paced, as if considering the situation at great length. Larena noticed that he glanced often at Darach.

Before long, her heart began to pound like a hammer. Had she made a terrible mistake just now? Perhaps she shouldn't have revealed her marriage arrangement to these fighting MacDonalds. Perhaps they would view it as a threat to Scotland or themselves—to have a half-Campbell, half-English chief ruling at Leathan Castle.

"Are you at all familiar with this man you are pledged to marry?" Angus asked, stopping in the center of the hall. "What do you know of his character today?"

"As I told you," she replied, "I haven't seen him in years. I was only a child when he left Leathan."

"What sort of child was he?" Angus pressed.

Larena thought back to those long ago days when she used to run and play with her brothers in the bailey, fighting each other with wooden swords, pretending to be warriors. She had taken part as well and it was with them that she had learned to shoot arrows with remarkable accuracy for a girl.

Chatham had been nothing like her brothers.

"He was intelligent," she told them, "which was why I enjoyed his company. He was different from the others."

"How so?" Angus asked with a slight frown.

"No one could read like Chatham could," she replied. "No one had the interest. And he was quiet, I suppose. Sometimes the older boys bullied him." She looked down at her hands on her lap. "My brothers included."

She had not been proud of how they treated Chatham. But her brothers were all gone now—fallen heroes at the Battle of Sheriffmuir, many years back. She was the only one left. Her father's only child—the only hope left to carry on his legacy at Leathan.

"At least this way," she heard herself saying to Angus, "my father's grandchildren will be lairds of Leathan one day. If I don't marry Chatham, the castle will fall to the English as a garrison and the members of my clan will have no home." She looked up. "For that reason, please, sir, I beg of you...I realize you do not owe me anything. I am a Campbell and we've always been at each other's throats, but I pray that you will find it in your heart to let me go, so that I may deliver the pardon to save my father's life and fulfill my promise to Lord Rutherford."

Angus considered her plea. "That was quite a speech, lass. No wonder Rutherford couldn't resist your offer."

"It wasn't my offer," she said. "The marriage was his idea."

Angus's golden eyebrow lifted.

"So you'll hand yourself over to an officer of the British army," Darach asked, striding toward her, "to save your father's life?"

"Of course. What other choice do I have? Wouldn't you do the same in my place?"

"I can't answer that, lass," he replied. "My father's dead."

Tension rolled into the room, but Larena kept her gaze fixed on his. "I'm sorry to hear that."

He gave no reply, but his eyes were dark and insolent.

"Well then," Angus said, finishing his drink and striding to the sideboard to set down the glass. "I thank you for your candor, Larena Campbell. You've been most forthcoming. For that reason, I will honor your request and return your father's pardon to you. I will also arrange an escort to deliver you safely to Leathan Castle immediately. I will send word to Rutherford at Fort William to inform him that his soldiers were attacked by a young band of MacDuff rebels, but that you are now safe under my protection. In return, you will explain to your future husband that Angus MacDonald of Kinloch desires peace between our clans and also with the English. Assure him that I have no interest in another rebellion. I wish only for the people of Kinloch to live with freedom from strife."

Larena stood up—surprised, relieved, and more grateful than ever. "Thank you, sir. You are most generous."

He turned to Darach. "And you will be the one to escort the lady home. Take your brother Logan as well."

Darach bristled noticeably, and Larena suspected she did the same, for the mere idea of traveling through the Highlands with this dark and menacing Highlander sent her heart into a spin.

"That's not necessary," she blurted out. "I am perfectly capable of traveling on my own."

"I'll hear no such thing," Angus jauntily replied. "You are not yet recovered from your wounds. You must allow me to offer protection."

"I don't need protection."

She was not surprised when Darach interjected. "Perhaps another clansman would be more suited to the task. Clearly the lass is not fond of me."

"I can see that, plain as day," Angus said. "What did you do to her, Darach?"

"Nothing," he replied defensively. "I didn't harm a single hair on her head, not even when she tried to brain me with a rock."

Angus faced her. "Is that true, lass? Did you try to brain my scout?"

A sickening lump formed in Larena's belly and she prayed he would not retract his earlier offer. "Aye," she replied, "but only because I thought he was one of the attackers who killed the English soldiers. I had been unconscious. I didn't know where he had come from."

"So it was self-defense, then," Angus concluded, "and a misunderstanding. In that case, I see no reason why you cannot be friends." He gave Darach a look. "I'll hear no more arguments. Go and make preparations. You will leave tonight. Good-bye Larena Campbell. If we meet again, I hope it will be under improved circumstances."

"As do I. Thank you, sir." She curtsied and walked out, but stopped for a moment outside the door to close her eyes and let out a deep breath of relief. *Thank the Lord.*

She started off again and Darach followed. As soon as they reached the top of the curved staircase, she turned to face him. "Do you still have the pardon?"

He patted his sporran. "Aye, it's right here."

She held out her hand. "Then I will have it now, if you please."

A slow, intimidating grin curled the corner of his mouth, but he shook his head. "Nay, lass. I am assigned to protect you until we reach Leathan Castle. So I'll protect this document as well."

"I am perfectly capable of guarding that document myself," she told him.

"Like you guarded it on the road with the Redcoats when musket balls started flying and your horse took off with it?"

She lowered her hand to her side and thought of how Rupert had bolted. She had never seen him so terrorized. "Where did you find him?"

"He found us," Darach explained. "He was in a mighty hurry, too. It wasn't easy to calm him. It took some careful finessing and a few soft words."

Larena scoffed. "Then it must have been your brother, Logan, who accomplished that feat." She picked up her skirts and descended the stairs. "Because finesse doesn't seem to be one of *your* finer qualities."

Darach followed her down. "I can be charming when I wish to be, lass. I just haven't felt the inclination around you—not since I learned you were a Campbell."

Her feet tapped lightly down the stone steps. When she reached the bottom, she stopped and looked left and right. "Where are we going? I have no idea."

He took hold of her arm and led her down a vaulted stone corridor. "Back to your cell until it's time to leave."

"Surely you don't intend to lock me up again," she said with exasperation, hurrying to keep up with his brisk, long-legged strides. "Your chief said you were to be my protector, not my jailor."

"That's the thing, lass. I don't trust you not to bash me over the head again to get your hands on this pardon, and I certainly can't protect you if you ride off alone into the night."

"Would it really be so bad if I did?" she challenged. "Wouldn't it spare you the unpleasantness of having to endure the next few days in my company? I am a Campbell, after all, and clearly you are not fond of the name."

They descended another set of stairs that led to a narrow, torch-lit corridor below ground level.

"But then my chief would be displeased with me," Darach replied, "and I cannot have that. I took an oath, lass. I owe him everything."

"Yes, yes," she said, "I understand. You're a MacDonald and loyal to your chief."

They arrived at her cell door, which had been left open. An armed clansman stood guard. Candles still burned inside, but Logan, the gentler one, was gone.

Darach nudged her through the doorway. "I'll be back to collect you in one hour," he said. "I suggest you try and get some rest because the moon is full. We'll be traveling until midnight at least."

"Will you give me back my own horse?" she asked, thinking of Rupert and feeling a rush of panic as Darach moved to close the door.

"Aye, you can have him." He began to back out.

Feeling suddenly apprehensive and not wanting to be left alone, Larena took a quick step forward. "And you're certain that Logan will come with us?"

Darach paused with his hand on the latch. "Why do you ask that?"

"Because..." she paused. "He was kind to me. And you have been...*less* than kind."

Darach regarded her with narrowed eyes. "Logan has that way about him, especially when it comes to lassies in distress, but don't expect him to be your nursemaid."

"I won't. I'm only glad it won't be just the two of us."

Darach inclined his head and grinned at her with devious amusement. "Ah...I see now. You're afraid to be alone with me."

Her sense of pride reared up violently. "I most certainly am not. Why would I be?"

"Because maybe you don't trust yourself to resist the powers of my overwhelming masculine appeal."

Larena let out a laugh. "Hah! Go ahead and imagine that, Darach, if it makes you feel pleased with yourself."

"It does indeed." He began to close the door. "Now sit tight lass. I'll be back to fetch you in a wee bit."

With that, he slammed the heavy oaken door and lowered the bar with a deafening clang that made her jump inside her skin.

Then, quite unexpectedly, the bar lifted again and the door opened a crack. He peered in at her with a teasing smirk.

"Don't feel guilty, lass. It's not a crime to find another man attractive when you're betrothed to one you barely know."

Before she had a chance to reply and put him in his proper place, the door slammed shut again, and she found herself lunging for the pillow to pitch it at the door.

B y the time they left the castle and crossed the drawbridge to the meadow beyond, the full moon was on the rise. Crickets chirped noisily in the grasses while a gentle breeze whispered through the treetops in the forest, just ahead. The sound of Rupert's hooves plodding over the ground was strangely comforting to Larena after her separation from him earlier that day. She was relieved to be out of the damp prison cell and on her way home, at last.

There were still many miles to cross, however, with these two MacDonald clansmen as escorts. She hoped they would prove to be good men and worthy of their laird's trust. She also hoped Angus the Lion was worthy of *her* trust, for these were uncertain times. Pray God he had not given orders to destroy her father's pardon—or worse, slit her throat—as soon as they crossed onto Campbell lands, for what did the Lion have to gain from the survival of her father, chief of an enemy clan? Wouldn't he gain some personal satisfaction if the Campbell stronghold fell to the English?

Either way, she could not stop to question any of that now. She had to believe she was on her way home, and if she kept her wits about her, she would arrive in one piece, in time to save her father's life.

It was midnight when they finally stopped to set up camp on the banks of Loch Loyne. Stubbornly, Larena had wanted to continue on, but the horses needed rest and water. Besides that, she was hardly in top condition herself, having been shot in the head that very morning by rebel Highlanders.

Well…perhaps "shot in the head" was an exaggeration. The musket ball had merely grazed her scalp, but it had been enough to cause a significant loss of blood. It was the fall shortly thereafter that had nearly killed her.

"Are you feeling all right, lassie?" Logan asked as he dismounted. "You've not looked well these past few miles."

"You've been keeping an eye on me, have you?" she asked as she, too, attempted to dismount. She felt slightly dizzy, however, and had to pause.

"Let me help you." Logan reached up to assist.

Laying her hands on his broad shoulders, she slid down from the saddle and came to rest lightly on her feet before him. He was not as tall or muscular as his older brother, and certainly not as darkly menacing. His hair was the color of honey and his eyes were blue, but there could be no doubt about it. He was equally handsome.

Logan's hands still rested on her hips as he looked into her eyes. "Are you sure you're feeling all right?"

"I'm fine, truly."

Slowly, he shook his head. "I don't think so, lass." He untied a rolled up woolen blanket from the back of his saddle and took hold of her hand, then led her away from the water to the dark edge of the forest.

"Plant yourself right here." He spread the blanket out on the ground under a large sycamore.

"Thank you." Larena sat down, stretched her legs out, leaned back on her arms, and closed her eyes. "That's better."

Logan dropped to one knee before her. "The surgeon at Kinloch said you might feel a bit woozy for a few days, on account of the swelling in your head."

"I have a swelled head, do I?" she asked, opening her eyes and giving him a look.

Logan returned her smile. "You'd have every reason to suffer with that affliction, lass. You must receive many compliments, from men and women alike."

She raised an eyebrow at him which only encouraged him to continue. "Surely you know how beautiful you are. You have fine cheekbones, hair like a summer sunrise...and the most friendly eyes. They make a man feel at ease."

She regarded him uncertainly in the moonlight. "Are you flirting with me, Logan? I hardly think that's wise. Aren't you supposed to loath all Campbells?"

"It's my brother who cannot let go of the past," he replied.

Just then, Darach's big black warhorse trotted onto the pebbly beach. They both turned their attention toward him as he rode straight to the water's edge and waited for his horse to drink his fill before backing up and dismounting.

Logan spoke with a hint of apology in his tone. "I should help set up camp. Will you be all right here for now?"

"Of course. Thank you."

"I'll take care of Rupert and bring you something to eat," Logan added. "Just lie back and rest."

As he left her side, Larena was uncomfortably aware of Darach watching his brother take up his duties. Then Darach turned his dark, steely gaze to meet hers. He held her transfixed for a tension-filled moment before he looked away and began to unsaddle his horse.

⟨≈⟩

A short while later, they were all seated around a small campfire eating bread, salt pork, and cheese. Darach was stretched out on his bedroll on the opposite side of the fire, leaning back on an elbow with his legs crossed at the ankles, while Logan sat beside Larena on a fallen tree.

"How long will it take us to reach Leathan Castle?" she asked, directing her question at Darach.

"Five days," he replied as he tipped his leather flask up to take a swig of whatever was inside—that swift-kicking whisky, no doubt. "Six if the weather is poor and the rivers swell."

"Don't worry, lass," Logan said, leaning close. "We'll be there in plenty of time to deliver the King's pardon. Your father will live. No matter what it takes, we'll make sure of it. Would you like some more wine?"

"That would be very nice, thank you." She held out her cup which he refilled from the bottle he'd brought along in one of his saddle bags.

For the next little while, Logan engaged her in conversation about her upbringing. He asked questions about her brothers and how she'd learned to shoot a bow and arrow with such deadly efficiency. He also enquired about her mother, who had died from a sudden fever when she was a girl. Logan was sympathetic and understanding when she described how the loss had affected her.

Throughout all of this, Darach offered nothing to the conversation. He sat across the fire, staring at Larena through the flames, listening to every word spoken, watching her inter-actions with his brother with what appeared to be extreme aversion.

When it was time to let the fire go out and get some rest, Logan stood up and offered his hand to help her rise from her seat. "If you find it chilly, lass, you can have my bedroll in addi-tion to your own. I have my tartan to keep me warm."

"That's very generous of you, Logan, but I'm sure I'll be warm enough."

He escorted her to her bedroll and knelt beside her. "Do not worry about a thing, lass. We'll stay close and keep watch."

"Thank you," she replied. "You've been very good to me, Logan."

He rose to his feet and left their small camp.

Larena lay down and tried to go to sleep, but it wasn't easy with Darach sitting broodily on the other side of the fire, watch-ing her with what appeared to be suspicion and displeasure. He raised the whisky flask to his lips and sipped it, never taking his eyes off her while Logan whistled a tune at the water's edge.

Tension seemed to grow thick as muck, causing Larena's heart to pound. Feeling a sudden concern for her own welfare during the night—and that of her father's—she glanced around at all the saddle packs and finally spotted her own. Trying not to arouse too much attention, she stood up and moved to fetch the pack that contained the King's pardon. Carrying it back to her bedroll, she lay down and slid it under her head like a pillow.

Before she closed her eyes, she met Darach's looming gaze and felt a shiver of apprehension in her bones. "Why are you staring at me like that?" she boldly asked. "I don't like it."

"There's not much else to look at," he coolly replied.

She let out a frustrated breath and labored to fall asleep to the eerily cheerful sound of Logan's whistling.

⟨⟨⟨⟩⟩⟩

She wasn't sure what woke her. It couldn't have been more than an hour after she'd drifted off, for what was left of the fire was still glowing red-hot on a bed of ash. She stared at the pulsing cinders in a groggy state of bewilderment.

Was she dreaming? No, sadly not. She remembered everything—the attack on the road, the gunfire, Rupert galloping off, and the violent, painful tumble down the hill to the creek bed below. She pressed two fingers to her temples, wishing all of it was naught but a bad dream. If only she could go back to the life she had known a fortnight ago, before any of this had begun.

It was impossible, of course. She had no choice but to accept the current situation, and travel through valleys and forests with two MacDonald clansmen who might or might not be worthy of her trust. She had yet to learn the answer to that.

Leaning up on one elbow, she rubbed her eyes and was surprised to see two empty bedrolls around the fire and no sign of either Darach or Logan.

Had her worst fears been realized? Had they abandoned her already and stolen her father's pardon?

With a rush of panic, she checked the pack she'd been resting her head upon and found the document inside. She was relieved also to spot Rupert and the other two horses tethered to a nearby tree. But where were the Highlanders?

Rupert nickered softly in the night. Then she heard it—the sound of voices in the distance, speaking in hushed, heated tones. Larena tossed the coverlet aside and crawled around the fire to look further down the beach.

There, she recognized the shadowy figures of Darach and Logan, standing at the water's edge under the ghostly glow of the moon. Logan was gesturing wildly with his hands, as if he were angry about something, though he kept his voice low.

She wished she could make out what they were saying to each other. Did it have something to do with their mission to deliver her to Leathan Castle? Perhaps Angus the Lion was a villain after all. Perhaps he had given them orders to dispose of her, or take steps along the way to prevent her father's pardon from reaching him in time.

But Logan had been so kind to her. Perhaps he was trying to prevent that from happening.

Or perhaps this disagreement was something else entirely—something personal between the two brothers. She'd noticed the way Darach had watched her converse with Logan that evening. There had been a constant, burning hostility in his eyes that caused the hairs to rise up on the back of her neck.

Perhaps he simply didn't approve of his brother showing her kindness, for she was a member of an enemy clan. The chief's daughter no less.

As they continued to quarrel, she predicted one of them would soon storm off and return to the fire. Deciding it would be best if they knew nothing about her eavesdropping, she crawled back to her bedroll, lay down, and drew the cover up to her ear. Closing her eyes, she feigned sleep as she awaited their return.

CHAPTER

Eight

The following morning, the Highlanders rose early with the sun and shared the task of cooking eggs and coffee over the fire. Though Logan made a few polite attempts at conversation, Darach made no effort to do the same. His irritable silence caused an uncomfortable tension to hang in the air, heavy as the rolling mist across the lake. He spoke not a single word to his brother, or to Larena.

Later, after packing up the camp, they trotted the horses into the forest in a single column and rode for many hours. When at last they emerged from the cover of the trees onto a wide moor swathed in purple heather, Larena urged Rupert into a quick trot to catch up with Logan.

"When will we stop again?" she asked, though it was not what she really wanted to know.

"Soon," he replied. "There's a narrow river just beyond that outcropping in the distance."

They rode on in silence, and Larena couldn't resist glancing over her shoulder at Darach, who was far enough behind them to remain in sight, but not close enough to hear what she was about to say to his brother.

"May I ask you something?" She faced forward again.

"Anything, lass."

Breathing in the fresh summer fragrance of the moor, she watched Logan's profile with interest. "Last night, I woke up and heard you and Darach arguing on the beach. I'm sorry. I wasn't my intention to listen in on a private conversation, but—"

He glanced at her with concern. "Did you hear what words were spoken?"

"No," she replied, perhaps too hastily. "You were far away, but it was obvious that you were quarreling."

Logan's shoulders rose and fell with a deep sigh of defeat. "Aye. That we were."

When he made no move to elaborate, she pressed a little more firmly for information. "Did it have something to do with me, or this mission to take me home? Darach made it clear that he feels no fondness for me. He didn't want to help me, not even when Angus asked him to. I'm sure he would have preferred to toss my father's pardon onto a fire and let me rot in the Kinloch dungeon."

Logan swayed to and fro in his saddle, squinting across the distance. At last he turned his gaze to meet hers. "Pay him no mind, lass. He can be thoughtless sometimes. As for the two of us...Well...we don't always agree on certain things."

"Such as?" A bold question, to be sure, but she wanted to know. "You both seemed quite cross."

Logan took a moment to consider how best to reply. "Darach may be my brother, but sometimes he sticks his nose where it doesn't belong."

"How so?"

Logan slanted her a look. "He's not pleased by how I've been paying you so much attention, lass. Ever since we left Kinloch, I've been asking you questions, making an effort to get to know you."

"There is no crime in that," Larena replied "The way things stand, we have no choice but to spend the next few days together in close proximity. I see no reason why we can't at least be cordial."

"That's exactly what I told him," Logan agreed, "but he's my big brother and he can't help but be overbearing—although he thinks he's being protective. To be honest, I think he's worried I'll lose sight of our purpose. He thinks I'll fall arse over teakettle for your charms and make a fool of myself—which *would* be a problem, considering you're betrothed to another, not to mention that you're a Campbell. I'm not sure which bothers him more. The second thing, most likely."

"That's absurd," Larena said. "I'm sure you are perfectly capable of fulfilling your duty to your chief, and I'm not *that* charming."

"No?" he added with a grin. "Maybe I am in danger, lass. You are a bonnie young thing, if you don't mind me saying so."

Larena couldn't help but shake her head and blush a little, for she wasn't accustomed to such blatant praise from a man. "You are a shameless flatterer, Logan."

"Aye, I am a smooth one," he replied with a playful smile. "But I only say these things because they're true." He inhaled deeply, closed his eyes and turned his face toward the sun. "But have no fear, my bonnie lass. I won't lose sight of my duty." His eyes met hers again. "I'll deliver you to Leathan, no matter what it takes."

Larena quavered under the heat of his stare. "I do appreciate that," she replied, then she glanced over her shoulder again. "But I am not so sure about your brother. With the looks he gives me sometimes, I fear he's imagining a good time to shove me off the edge of a steep cliff."

Logan laughed. "Nay, lass. He may be a bit hardhearted sometimes, but he would never do that."

They were quiet for a moment, listening to the grasshoppers and bees on the moor, feeling the cool, swift breezes on their cheeks.

"Not that it's any of my business," Logan mentioned eventually, "but I hope the man you're pledged to marry is a good man, lass, and that you won't ever feel as if you'd made a mistake. If I am to be your protector, I could use a bit of assurance, because I wouldn't want to deliver you into a bad situation. So can you tell me...*is* he a good man?"

Larena regarded Logan carefully in the late morning sunshine. "I believe so. At least from what I remember of him."

She couldn't deny, however, that she was struggling with crushing doubts and concerns about marrying a man she barely knew. A man she didn't love, when she'd always dreamed of a great, passionate romance for herself.

At least Gregory Chatham was half Campbell. That was something. And her father would live because of Chatham's lifelong affection for her.

In the end, she knew it was the right thing to do, so she was determined to be content with it.

"I thank you for your concern," she added, shaking herself out of those thoughts. "It touches me that you care."

"Oh, I do, lass," Logan replied, tilting his head thoughtfully, holding her steady in his deep, green-eyed gaze. "Do not ever doubt it."

She smiled at him as they broke into a canter toward the river. All the while, she was keenly aware of Darach, dark and silent like an ever-present shadow behind them, as he broke into a canter as well.

CHAPTER

Nine

For the rest of the day, Larena made no more mention of the argument she'd witnessed the night before, though it was never far from her thoughts. She was curious about these MacDonald brothers and the obvious friction that existed between them. Though she did not presume to understand it, she suspected there was something in their past that had driven a wedge between them and continued to plague them.

At the same time, they seemed immensely loyal to each other, for they scouted together every day, and Darach *did* appear to be protective of Logan.

Although, from her vantage point, Logan was hardly in need of anyone's protection. He was a highly skilled and formidable warrior all on his own. She knew this because when they stopped for lunch at the river, Logan ate quickly, then politely excused himself to practice swordplay on a flat patch of grass a short distance away.

While Larena removed her stockings and dipped her feet into the fast-flowing water to cool them, she couldn't help but watch Logan move through the exercises with tremendous strength, speed, and agility.

Of course, there was no opponent taking part in the exercise, but Logan was clearly well trained in the arts of hand-to-hand combat, and if there had been an opponent, she suspected he would have been quite thoroughly bested.

Logan's footwork was sublime. He was fit, trim, and lean. Incredibly virile and in top form.

As she watched him, the noonday sun beat down upon her head and the heat caused her to perspire beneath her snug bodice. Growing uncomfortable, she was reminded of her injuries. Soon her head began to ache.

Taking in a deep breath to fight off a sudden unexpected queasiness, she lay down on the grass, closed her eyes, and covered them with an arm to block out the sun. Her heart raced but she strove to focus on the sensation of the cool water rushing past her feet and the sound of birds calling out to one another overhead.

Before long, a voice cut through all the sounds and sensations of the natural world. "Are you feeling all right, lass?"

Sucking in a breath, Larena removed her arm from her face and squinted up at Darach, who stood over her, silhouetted against the sun. He cast a cool shadow across her face.

"I have a headache, that's all," she replied.

"Can I do anything for you?"

Surprised by the first evidence of kindness on his part, she managed to form a polite reply. "No, thank you. I don't believe there's anything that can be done. I must simply endure it."

He gazed down at her for a long moment. "We'll make camp early tonight so you can get some rest." Then he turned and walked away.

Once again, the hot sun beamed down on Larena's face. It was accompanied by a sudden feeling of unease over this uncomfortable situation, so she sat up to make sure Rupert—and her saddle bags—were still in sight. Thankfully they were. Everything appeared to be in order.

Larena lay down again, shaded her eyes, and focused her attention on the fresh, clean water at her feet.

⊰⊱

"Are you absolutely certain, lass?" Logan asked with raucous laughter, nearly tipping over sideways onto his elbow. The moon was high in the night sky. They had just finished eating supper by the fire in a small glade in the forest—but clearly Logan had consumed too much wine, and perhaps so had she. "Maybe he was just confused."

"I am positive!" Larena replied, laughing. "The grooms-man walked straight into that big pile of steaming manure and stomped on it like it was a barrel full of grapes."

"But why?" Logan asked, still laughing.

"I don't know," she told him. "Maybe he enjoyed the warm, squishy feel of it between his toes. It was a cold night, if I recall." She laughed again. "Oh, Logan, stop. My stomach hurts!"

"I'm not the one telling the story!" he shouted. "You only have yourself to blame for that belly ache, lass."

Fighting to recover from her indelicate convulsions of laughter, she sat up. "Oh, that rabbit was delicious, by the way. Where did it come from?"

With grinning eyes that twinkled in the firelight, Logan glanced across the fire at Darach. "My brother got lucky this afternoon. Isn't that right, Darach?"

"That's right," the dark Highlander coolly replied as he reclined against his saddle packs with one knee raised. He'd been keeping himself occupied for the past hour by using the blade of his knife to shave the bark off a number of sticks, which he then simply tossed into the fire.

Larena felt the silliness drain out of her body as she regarded him intently, for he was watching her and Logan with his usual dark and broody eyes.

"It was very good," she told him.

He shrugged a shoulder, as if it were nothing. "How's your head?"

"Much better tonight. Thank you for asking."

He offered no reply.

Suddenly drawn in by his apparent boredom, Larena sat forward and asked curiously, "Did you not find that story about the groomsman amusing?"

"It was bloody hilarious," Darach replied flatly, reaching for his flask and tipping it up. He kept his eyes fixed on hers the entire time.

For a long moment Larena stared at him, then something peculiar bubbled up inside her. For some reason she couldn't begin to understand, his drab response wrenched at her funny bone. She lowered her gaze and began to chuckle.

"What's so funny?" Darach asked.

"I'm not sure."

"It must be the wine," Logan mentioned to Darach, "because we both know you're no jester."

"I apologize," Larnea said, looking up. "I think it must indeed be the wine. If you will excuse me." She gathered up her skirts and rose unsteadily to her feet, realizing that the wine must have been stronger than she'd thought because she felt sillier than a tipsy goose. "I must make use of the necessary—if only there *was* one." She swayed slightly to and fro as she looked around. "If I can put one foot in front of the other, I'm sure I'll be perfectly fine."

Staggering away from the fire to a nearby thicket, she found a private spot in the darkness to take care of business.

An owl hooted somewhere in the treetops. She looked up, wondering if she could see it in the moonlight, but it remained out of sight.

When she finished, she began to make her way out of the bushes, but had to stop a moment to search for her bearings while the ground swayed beneath her feet.

Pressing the heel of her hand to her forehead, she shook her head, for she should have known better than to drink that third glass of wine. Or was it four? Heaven help her. Her nerves were stretched tighter than the string on her best bow. Not only did she have her father's fate to consider, but she was struggling to navigate through a tricky situation with two MacDonald scouts who were both handsome and alluring and terribly dangerous in different ways. One was dark and full of lethal loathing for her because she was a Campbell, while the other was far too charming for anyone's good.

Oh Lord… She truly *had* consumed too much wine. It would be best if she went straight to bed with no supper. Except that she'd already eaten supper…a delicious meal of roasted rabbit, provided by the surly one who looked at her as if she were a creature he'd like to trap, skin, and cook over a hot fire—then devour her whole.

Suddenly, she didn't feel so well.

Approaching the moonlit glade, Larena dropped heavily to sit on her heels on the grass. The world spun circles in front of her eyes, whirling so fast she couldn't keep the dizziness at bay.

She strove to focus on the campfire which was in sight, but it appeared to be duplicating itself, so she wasn't sure which one was the real fire. Squeezing her eyes shut and opening them again only made the world spin faster.

Eventually she became aware of a dark figure prowling toward her in the shadows then kneeling down in front of her.

"Are you feeling all right, lass?"

She peered at Darach, who placed a steadying hand on her shoulder. "I think I'm drunk," she said.

For the second time that day, she saw a spark of compassion in his eyes, and she was strangely befuddled by how it touched her.

"I *know* that you are," he replied. "But at least you're a funny drunk." He began to rise. "Up we go, now."

"Do we have to?" she asked dizzily. "Can't we just stay here?"

"Nay, lass," he replied, standing firm on the issue. "I must keep an eye on you. Come with me now." He held out a hand.

Larena finally took hold and couldn't help but notice how large and warm his hand was, also callused and rough. Her own hand felt very small and fragile inside his.

"Where did Logan go?" she asked as he drew her to her feet and she followed him to the fire.

"He's taking the first watch. He went to look around, but I suspect he's also taking a *very* long piss."

Larena's eyebrows lifted. "You shouldn't say things like that, Darach. It's vulgar."

"Did I offend you?" he asked, sounding sincerely apologetic.

She thought rather drunkenly about her answer. "I suppose it's no more vulgar than my story about the stomping grooms-man. And that makes me a pot."

"I beg your pardon, lass?"

"I am a pot calling the kettle black," she explained.

He gave her a small, barely perceptible grin that thrilled her in the most astonishing way.

They reached their bedrolls and he let go of her hand. Larena decided she wasn't ready to lie down yet, however, for the world was still spinning. Instead, she moved to sit up against the saddle packs—but not before digging around inside them, in search of the King's pardon.

"You needn't worry," Darach mentioned at the precise moment she laid her hands on it. "I've been keeping an eye on it for you."

She pushed the rolled up document back down to the bottom of the pack, lowered the flap, buckled it, and leaned back against it.

"I wasn't worried," she lied. "I just drank too much wine tonight and I couldn't remember where I'd put it."

"You're just anxious, that's all," he replied, forgivingly.

She closed her eyes and tipped her head back. "I suppose there is much to fret about, with my father sentenced to death if we don't arrive in time to deliver his pardon."

"I'll make sure that we do," Darach said. "But that can't be the only thing you're anxious about, lass. You're also facing a lifelong sentence of marriage to a total stranger."

Larena opened her eyes, lifted her head, and stared at him. "You make it sound as if that were an equally perilous fate."

"Isn't it?"

"I don't believe so," she said with a whisper of indignation, even though she'd been tossing and turning over the idea ever since she'd left Fort William. "I see it as a very small sacrifice to save my father's life."

Darach inclined his head doubtfully, as if he could see through her, straight into her soul. "It's your whole life, lass, until you draw your last breath. I respect your sacrifice, truly I do. Clearly you are very loyal to your family, but I wouldn't call it a *small* sacrifice, because I'm sure you must have had other plans for your future. Happier ones."

Yes, I most certainly did have plans. I once imagined myself falling madly in love with a handsome, devoted Highlander who would adore me from the first moment we met and love me until the end of time.

Perhaps Gregory would turn out to be that man. Larena had whispered a silent, wishful prayer to that end when she'd agreed to the arrangement in Lord Rutherford's chambers.

Nevertheless, breathing deeply, she attempted to explain herself to Darach. "Whatever I had planned doesn't matter anyway, because I couldn't very well refuse Rutherford's proposal and allow my father to die."

Darach poked at the fire with a stick. "Nay. That, you could not do."

"Unfortunately," she added, staring into the fire, listening to it snap and crackle while sparks flew about wildly, "alternatives become scarce with so little time to explore other potential courses of action. Believe me, when I watched them drag my father down to the prison, I tried my best to think of anything I could do to stop it, but the British army can be very intimidating."

"And you're about to marry one of their officers," he reminded her.

She pondered that reality. "It is my hope that I won't be intimidated by Gregory. From what I remember of him, he was a gentle-hearted boy."

"He cannot be that gentle if he rose to the rank of colonel here in the Highlands," Darach warned her. "Are you sure you're remembering the right person?"

"Absolutely. Look." She dug into her cleavage to withdraw the locket that hung around her neck on a long chain. "Rutherford gave this to me when I accepted his proposition. It shows that Gregory is the same boy I remember—only quite a bit older, of course. Come and see him."

Darach stood and circled around the fire to sit down beside her. He took hold of the locket, which was still strung around her neck, and examined the miniature portrait inside.

"He's not bad looking, I suppose," Darach casually commented, then he snapped it shut and lifted his gaze to meet hers.

She was unnerved suddenly by his nearness, transfixed by his dark features in the dancing firelight, his face so close to her own. She couldn't seem to take her eyes off the elegant line of his nose, those soft-looking, full lips, and that strong, unshaven jaw.

Letting her eyes wander down to his broad shoulders and the tartan draped across his shoulder and chest, she focused on the MacDonald clan badge at his belt as it reflected the firelight.

"Still," she added, lifting her gaze to his face rather than letting it dwell on his magnificent lounging form, "it's going to be strange to marry a man I barely know. I have to keep reminding myself that women do it all the time. Political marriages are hardly uncommon."

Darach frowned, then he faced the fire and leaned back against Logan's saddle. Reaching into his sporran for the flask he carried, he uncorked it and offered her whatever was left inside.

"No thank you," she replied, holding up a hand. "I think I've had quite enough for one night."

"I won't argue with you there." He raised it to his lips and sipped. "But I must warn you, lass. Be careful not to lose your head around my brother."

"What do you mean?"

Darach scanned the perimeter of the glade and listened carefully for a moment, then he spoke in a low voice. "When it comes to the lassies, he's a flirt. He knows how to charm them, so don't fall for it."

She inclined her head at Darach. "Are you implying that he might try to seduce me?"

"There is a danger of that if you're not sensible."

Larena's head drew back in surprise. "Not sensible... Darach, I am insulted. I may have had too much wine tonight, but I am pledged to another man and I do not take that promise lightly, especially when my father's life is at stake." She looked away in the other direction. "Besides, your brother has been a perfect gentlemen since the moment we left the castle, which is more than I can say for you."

"How have *I* not been a gentleman?" Darach asked, taking genuine affront at her tone. "Didn't I help you back to the campfire just now when you didn't think you could get up?"

Yes, he had indeed come to her aid, so she had no choice but to reconsider what she'd just said. "I suppose that was courteous of you. But that's not what I was referring to. I was talking about before."

"Before *what*?" he asked, still sounding offended.

Larena wondered uneasily if she had overstepped her bounds, but it was too late now. He was demanding clarification and she couldn't simply say "never mind."

Turning her face toward his, she wet her lips and spoke frankly. "I am referring to how you marched into my prison cell with my father's pardon which you refused to hand over to me, even though it was my property. Then you dragged me through the castle to speak to your laird. If I am to be perfectly honest, Darach, you were boorish and mean."

"Boorish."

"Don't you remember how you were?" she asked, turning her whole body to face him more squarely. "You reminded me countless times that I was a dirty Campbell and not fit to lick your boots—"

"Now see here, lass, I never said *that*."

"Well, perhaps not *exactly* that...but the implication was there. And ever since we left the castle, you've been quiet and moody, almost as if you're sulking about something. Probably the fact that your brother is far more charming than you could ever dream of being, and the fact that you don't know how to laugh."

"I do know how to laugh," he argued in that quiet, husky drawl that made something inside her tremble. He sat forward slightly and turned his body to face hers as well. "And I told you before, lass. I can be charming when I wish to be."

"I'll believe that when I see it," she replied, realizing that sometime during this conversation, she'd sobered up completely. She felt entirely clearheaded and sharp-witted enough to recognize that her heart was racing with exhilaration. "And please be informed that I have no use for your so-called 'helpful' warnings about your brother. I suspect you're just jealous because he's more pleasant than you are, and you simply can't keep up. And I am not foolish enough to be taken in by a charming seducer—if that's what Logan is. As I mentioned before, I think you're just jealous, and may I remind you again that I am betrothed? The way I perceive it, Logan is merely fulfilling his duty to your chief. I see nothing untoward in his attentions. If I drank too much wine tonight and behaved out of turn…that was my own fault because it's been a difficult time…with all that's happened lately."

Darach stared at her intently. "I'm not jealous."

He continued to look into her eyes, then down at her lips, his face mere inches from hers. Eventually, she could do nothing but stare down at her lap.

"Of course you're not jealous," she conceded. "I don't know why I said that. Clearly I'm still a bit inebriated."

Although it had nothing to do with the wine and everything to do with the dangerously intoxicating way his voice slid over her like soft velvet, rippling across her skin.

"Just keep your head on straight as far as my brother is concerned," Darach said in a commanding tone. He rose to his feet and returned to the other side of the fire. "Get some rest, lass. Tomorrow will be a long day. We'll be spending many hours in the saddle."

Nodding her head, she inched down into her bedroll, closed her eyes, and tried to think of nothing but her arrival at Leathan.

⊰≋⊱

Darach shouldn't have been surprised that the lassie curled up in her bedroll and fell asleep within minutes of closing her eyes. She'd had far too much wine to drink, and besides that, she had no notion of the danger she was in with him and Logan as her escorts back to Leathan.

It was just his luck that Logan was taking his good old time scouting the surrounding area, which left Darach with nothing to do but sit by the fire and watch over Larena. It was not a task he relished, for she was a Campbell—Fitzroy's daughter no less—and this whole situation had stirred up an angry hornet's nest full of problems, especially where Logan was concerned.

Darach bowed his head and shook it slowly with regret, for he'd once believed that the past was long dead and buried, and he and his brother could go on to live relatively normal lives. It had taken Darach many years to push certain memories into the ground and stop checking over his shoulder at every turn. He'd not woken up in a cold sweat in almost a decade, yet here he sat tonight, plagued with wretched torment as he watched Larena Campbell sleep soundly a few short feet away from him with no knowledge of the men who had been assigned to protect her. She knew nothing of their past or the extent of the antagonism they felt toward her father, Fitzroy Campbell of Leathan.

For two years ago, he had murdered *their* father.

At least that's what they suspected.

It was difficult for Logan. He had a fierce and reckless fire in his blood that Darach had never been able to put out, no matter how hard he tried. Ever since that day on the battlefield at Sheriffmuir, fifteen years ago, Darach had suspected that his baby brother would always feel as if he had something to prove. It was no secret that he blamed Darach for everything, including how their lives had turned out.

Over the past two years, however—since the death of their father—it had gotten much worse. Logan had always imagined he would return to make amends and somehow win back their father's approval, but that dream was snuffed out now. It was impossible to seek approval from the dead.

Sometimes Darach caught Logan staring absently toward the horizon, flexing and squeezing a fist while a muscle flicked hard at his jaw. In those moments, Darach knew exactly what he was thinking…where he wanted to go, what he wanted to do….

While all Darach wanted to do was forget the past and move on.

But ignoring the past wasn't easy on this night when the daughter of their father's killer slept across from him, her lush curves tempting and inviting beneath the tangled woolen blanket that had become wrapped around her shapely legs. Darach had felt a fierce and greedy lust for her from the first moment he saw her, helpless and unconscious in the woods, mere seconds before she rose up like a wild creature and struck him in the head.

She was brave and defiant, a sizzling spitfire, and perhaps that's what continued to stir his passions more than anything. He'd never had much interest in shrinking violets, and she was nothing of that sort. Ever since he'd flipped her onto her back and felt the strain of her hips against his heavy loins, he'd been fighting to ignore his body's desires and his intense awareness of her as a woman—even after he found out who she was. All day, the rise and fall of her ample bosom beneath that snug bodice had presented all sorts of stimulating diversions from the endless monotony of their journey. It was pure torture, because he had to remember that she was Fitzroy's daughter and engaged to an English colonel—therefore as off-limits as any woman could possibly be.

Not to mention the fact that his brother Logan had scheming designs of his own that Darach needed to keep an eye on—and talk him out of—or else they could both end up as dead as a couple stones on the moor.

Ten

L arena woke the following morning to a low rumble of thunder in the distance and the scent of rain on the air. Sitting up with concern for the oncoming weather and how it might affect their travels, she noticed that Logan was still asleep in his bedroll. Darach, however, was nowhere to be found, and all his possessions were packed up and gone.

With a white-hot flash of alarm, she quickly rifled through her saddle bag. Relieved, she found the critical document still inside.

Rising to her feet, she glanced around the empty clearing, which looked remarkably different in the light of day. Logan stirred and sat up.

"Morning, lass," he said blithely, rubbing the heel of his hand over his eye. "How are you feeling?"

"Moderately well, all things considered," she replied, distracted by the fact that Darach was gone. "I'm a bit parched, though."

"As am I." Logan stood up and adjusted his kilt, then seemed to take notice of her distress. "Darach's probably just gone to fetch some water from the creek," he said. "It's south a ways."

"I see." Making an effort to relax and wait patiently for Darach's return, she glanced toward the thick grove of junipers where she'd found privacy the night before...and made off in that direction, but not before she picked up the saddle bag to take with her.

When she returned, she spotted Darach on his horse within the trees on the far side of the glade. Oddly, Logan was gripping the horse's halter, holding him there. They appeared to be engaged in another heated discussion about something.

A twig snapped under her boot. They both shot irate looks at her.

Releasing his grip on the bridle, Logan stepped back and strode toward the fire, while Darach turned his horse into the clearing and dismounted.

"We need to get moving, lass," Logan said. "You'd best pack up. No time for a hot breakfast this morning as bad weather's coming in from the north. And unless you want to stop along the way to take shelter—which I assume you don't—you might want to prepare to get wet."

Without so much as a word to each other, Darach and Logan set about packing up the camp. The tension was thick as mud.

⟨⛤⟩

Rain began within the hour—a gentle mist at first, followed by a heavy downpour that swept a cold chill straight down the center of the Great Glen.

In light of the unusual humidity during the past few days, Larena found it a welcome respite at first, but by noontime, her teeth were chattering. Though she was wrapped in a blanket, she shivered incessantly beneath her gown and wished the rain would stop and the sun would break through the heavy cover of cloud.

The weather, however, was not the only chill during the journey that day, for Darach and Logan traveled apart. Logan rode at the front of the column while Darach brought up the rear, both of them wearing their tartans drawn up over their heads to keep dry. Not one word of conversation was exchanged all morning, and eventually Larena could suffer the silence no more.

Briefly, she considered galloping ahead to ride beside Logan, but she chose instead to slow her pace and wait for Darach to catch up with her.

"Is something wrong, lass?" he asked with concern as his horse trotted up beside Rupert.

"No," she replied. "I'm just bored."

"And you think I can remedy that?"

Rupert nickered and tossed his head.

"I don't wish to be entertained," she told him. "I only wish to talk."

Darach's eyebrows pulled together in obvious unease. "About what?"

While the cold rain continued to fall hard, Larena paused to consider how best to approach the subject. "If you must know, I'm curious about what you and your brother have been arguing about over the past few days. And please don't pretend you don't know what I'm talking about. I heard you on the beach the other night and I saw you again this morning. Based on our discussion last night, I can only assume it has something to do with me."

"Isn't that a bit vain, lass?" he asked. "To assume our private quarrels are all about you?"

She raised an eyebrow. "Point taken, but when I spoke to Logan about it, he told me you didn't approve of him flattering me with his attentions, and based on what you said to me last night, I see that it's true. But I feel there is something more you're not telling me."

He looked away with impatience. "What makes you think that?"

"Because something about this arrangement has you both on edge."

"Of course it does," he conceded at last. "You're a Campbell and I'm a MacDonald, which makes this whole situation a thorny one."

"Logan doesn't seem to have a problem with it," she reminded him, "which leads me to believe that the problem lies with *you.*"

Darach shook his head with frustration. "What does it even matter, lass? You'll be rid of us soon enough."

She pulled the blanket more snugly about her shoulders. "It troubles me because I am carrying an important document that means everything to me, yet I am not certain I can trust you."

His gaze burned into hers. "Of course you cannot trust me, lass. Or Logan, for that matter. You shouldn't be trusting *anyone.* Not in your current situation."

Larena scoffed. "Unfortunately, I have no choice, for I am at everyone's mercy." She faced forward to contemplate all the problems that lay ahead of her. "I must also trust that Lord Rutherford will keep his word about sparing my father's life if I marry his son. And I am required to trust that Gregory will be a good husband to me and a fair chief to the members of my clan. Also that we will all be able to go on and live in peace with the English."

"That's a lot of trusting, lass," Darach said skeptically. "You may want to rethink some of it."

A fierce gust of wind blew across the moor and blasted her cheeks with stinging raindrops. She shivered anew and found herself growing increasingly curious about the man Darach truly was beneath the cool, aloof exterior. "Clearly you do not have a trusting bone in your body. Why is that?"

He shook his head at her, as if she should know better than to ask him that question. "You don't know me, lass, and if you're as smart as I think you are, you'll be content to keep it that way."

With that, he urged his mount into a gallop and rode off to scout the forest ahead, leaving her behind, feeling disconcerted and bereft.

The voice of reason in her head told her that he was right. She should not wish to know him. She should simply let him go and make no further overtures of friendship—because what would be the point in that?—but her emotions were becoming restless and willful. Something intense was drawing her to him. She was constantly aware of his presence, near or far, and wasn't sure she could heed his warnings and resist the urge to learn what he was about.

◈

That night, further tension persisted around the fire, though it was mostly Darach who was to blame. While Larena made a few attempts to include him in conversation, he remained unresponsive. He instead focused his attention on the task of sharpening the long, pointed blade of his knife.

Logan, on the other hand, was his usual charming, jovial self, but nothing could alleviate the sense of ill feeling in the air.

"I apologize for my brother," Logan said eventually, speaking loud enough to reach Darach's ears across the fire. "Sometimes he lacks good manners."

Darach's eyes lifted. They were dark as Lucifer in the firelight. He gave his brother a hostile look of warning, then lowered his gaze and resumed the task of scraping stone over steel.

"Looks like we're on our own tonight, lass," Logan whispered close in Larena's ear while reaching for the wine jug. He held it out to offer her some, but she covered the rim of her cup with her hand. "No more for me. I want to be able to think clearly in the morning."

They were only three days' ride from her home. Between now and then, she couldn't afford to make any mistakes.

"That's probably wise," Logan replied, replacing the cork and setting the jug on the grass. "And how about that bump on your head. Is the pain gone?"

"It's much better now," she told him. "I feel more like myself tonight."

That was a lie, however, for none of her thoughts or feelings were making any sense to her, as she was forcibly repressing the desire to tell Logan to go off somewhere and leave her alone with Darach, as he had done the night before.

Logan raised his cup to tap against hers and she made an effort to appear relaxed and indifferent about the circumstances. If Darach wouldn't talk to her, she could at least engage herself in conversation with Logan.

"Tell me something," she said to him, leaning back against her saddle packs and sipping what was left of her wine. "Darach mentioned that you lost your father. What about your mother? Does she still live?"

Logan regarded her with a devilish spark in his eye, as if he were intrigued by her question. Then he turned his attention to Darach. "Listen to that. The lass wants to know about our family. Should we tell her the whole tragic tale from start to finish, or would that spoil the evening?"

Darach responded testily. "I cannot imagine the lass wants to hear any of it."

"But I do," Larena said, sitting up. "Since we are traveling companions, shouldn't we know at least *something* about each other?"

She was pushing the limits he'd set that morning and she knew it, but she couldn't help herself. Though Logan seemed forthcoming, Darach was the most enigmatic man she'd ever met, and she was frustrated by his disinterest.

But there was more to it than that, she supposed, for whenever he looked at her with those dark, reflective eyes, her heart beat fast and feverishly.

Logan reclined back against his saddle. "My favorite color is blue," he lightly said with a smirk. "What's yours, Larena?"

"I don't have one," she replied, grateful for his facetiousness, for it lightened the mood. "I like them all."

"Cheers to that." Logan raised his cup again to tap against hers, then eyed his brother crossly. He finished what was left in his cup, set it down on the grass beside him and turned his body toward her. "Ignore my brother. He prefers to keep to himself, but that doesn't mean we must be dreary and dull."

She turned to face Logan and tried to hide her disappointment that Darach did not wish to take part in the conversation. "No, it does not."

Logan's gaze roamed over her face. "You asked about our mother. She died giving birth to me, I'm sorry to say."

"And I'm sorry to hear it," Larena replied. "We have that in common, then."

"Aye, because you lost your mother, too."

Larena was intuitively aware of Darach's head turning to look at her. He watched her for a few seconds, then quit sharpening his knife and slid it back into its sheath. Lying down on his bedroll, he stared up at the sky.

"Any brothers or sisters?" Larena asked Logan.

"Two older brothers," he replied. "They fought bravely at the Battle of Sheriffmuir, but died on the field."

"I share your grief in that as well," she replied. "My brothers were killed in the same battle. Though I don't remember them well. I was only six years old at the time." She looked down at the wine in her cup. "Sometimes I wish the Jacobite cause didn't exist at all. So many lives have been lost in the name of the Stuart king."

"We fought for our freedom on that battlefield," Logan argued, "and for that, I have no regrets."

Surprised to hear this, she studied his face in the firelight. "You were there?"

"Aye, lass."

"But it was fifteen years ago," she said. "You couldn't have been more than—"

"I was eleven and Darach was fourteen."

She regarded Darach on the other side of the fire. "You were there, too?"

"I was," he replied, still staring up at the night sky while crickets chirped in the grass. "But I don't see the point in discussing it, especially when your clan was fighting for the English Crown, on the opposite side of the field."

She watched him raise a knee, toss an arm up under his head, and continue to stare up at the stars.

"Did you lose anyone else in that battle?" she asked Logan, choosing to ignore what was in the past and could not be changed. Besides that, her father had recently reversed his political leanings, so she wasn't quite sure what to say about that.

Something dark flickered across Logan's expression. "Darach and I lost *everyone* in that battle, lass, and we were forced to escape the field alone. That's when we were taken in by the great Laird of Kinloch—Angus the Lion's father. He became like a father to us as well, and Angus, like a brother. We've lived at Kinloch ever since."

"So that explains why you are both so loyal to him," she surmised, "and why you agreed to escort me home when I doubt either of you were delighted to be helping a Campbell."

Logan smiled at her. "I can speak for myself at least, lass, when I say that I am happy to do it."

Darach shook his head disapprovingly.

"Thank you for sharing that with me," Larena said to Logan. "You've been very forthcoming, but I should retire now. It's been a long day and tomorrow will be more of the same."

She moved to her bedroll, lay down, and forced herself to close her eyes.

⋘⋇⋙

It took a while for her to fall asleep, and when she finally did, she slept soundly all night—at least until a hand covered her mouth in the pre-dawn hour. Her breath caught in her throat. Suddenly she found herself pinned to the ground, kicking her legs, and blinking up at a ferocious looking Highlander, silhouetted against the faint morning light in the sky.

"*Shhh*...Be quiet, lass," he whispered, applying his solid, massive strength to hold her down while she struggled to make sense of his words. "You must trust me now," he said, "and do what I say, or your father will surely die."

With eyes wide as saucers, Larena frantically nodded her head.

Eleven

Larena waited for Logan to remove his hand from her mouth and explain himself. Swiftly, he surveyed the surrounding area, then slowly sat back on his haunches.

"What do you mean?" she whispered, scrambling to her knees.

"Do not panic." He glanced over his shoulder again and held up a hand. He appeared to be listening to the sounds of the forest, which had gone silent as the grave. "We must leave here now," he said.

"Why?"

"Because my brother doesn't like you very much, lass. As you know, he's held a grudge against the Campbells for a long time, ever since Sheriffmuir when we lost everything, and I fear he might do something impulsive."

"Like what?"

"Like destroy the King's pardon that you carry, or worse, escort you through the castle gates and unleash his vengeance on everyone."

"I don't understand," she said. "What are you saying? This is madness."

"Aye," Logan replied, rising to his feet and gathering up her belongings. "But that's my brother. Mad as a meat ax. You've seen him. You must know…"

No, in fact, she knew nothing...nothing about the dark brother at all.

Logan picked up Rupert's saddle and carried it to where the horses were tethered in the woods.

"But where is he?" she asked, her eyes darting to the empty bedroll on the other side of the fire.

"Do not worry, lass," Logan replied. "He can't catch us. At least not for a while."

"But what happened? Tell me, Logan. I must know."

"We had another disagreement," he explained as he quickly bent to fasten the cinches under Rupert's belly. "This one was worse than the others. I didn't tell you before because I didn't want to worry you, but Darach's been wanting to use you to exact some sort of revenge. I've been trying to talk him out of it, but he lost his patience this morning and stormed off. I didn't know what he might do, so I followed him."

"Where?"

Logan returned to pack up his own bedroll. "Into the woods. It seems a bit idiotic now, but neither of us wanted to wake you."

"I assure you," she replied, "I would have preferred to be awakened so I could at least take part in the discussion. I still don't understand what's happening."

Logan flung a saddle bag over his shoulder, then turned to face her. "I'll explain everything when we're away from here. For now, all you need to know is that I clubbed him over the head and tied him to a tree."

Larena's mouth fell open. "*You did what?* But he's your brother."

"Aye, but he wanted to burn your father's pardon and use you as a pawn. I'm not sure what his plan was after that, but there was some talk about breaking into the armory, setting fire to the munitions, and blowing the whole castle to bits."

"That would be suicide," Larena said, following Logan back to his horse while dozens of ghastly images of destruction flooded her mind. "Even if he managed to escape, he'd never get away with it."

"To be honest, lass, I don't think he cares whether he lives or dies. Now pack up your belongings. We need to leave here and get you home where you'll be safe."

"But do we have the pardon?" she asked in a panic. "He didn't take it, did he?"

Logan crouched down to pick up Larena's saddlebags. He unfastened the larger pouch and dug into it, searching for the document. "It's here. But you need to keep it close to you."

Moving quickly, she stepped forward and seized the pack from his hands. "Believe me, I intend to."

⚜

Darach woke to the peculiar sensation of a large tongue on his eyelids, licking wetly. For a few puzzling seconds he thought he might be dreaming that he was in bed with a randy lass. Then reality came crashing into his brain. His eyes flew open to the sight of his horse, Miller, slobbering all over his face. Miller's huge nostrils flared and he nickered pleasurably. His steamy breath smelled like a barnyard.

"*Ach!*" Darach tossed his head to the side to avoid another giant lick and realized with an explosion of fury that his wrists were tied behind his back and he was bound to a tree.

Pounding agony exploded in his skull and he writhed about violently to free himself.

"Logan!" he roared. *"I'll kill you for this!"*

He sat still for a moment to listen. Was Logan still at the camp? How far away was it? Darach had no idea how far they'd walked in the darkness while arguing the night before. He'd been so bloody distracted by Logan's foolish ideas and ridiculous ambitions. Darach cursed himself for letting his guard down and turning away—back toward the camp where they'd left Larena sleeping alone—but Darach hadn't imagined his own brother was capable of such treachery as this.

God almighty. Had Logan abducted Larena and made off with the King's pardon as well? Just the thought of it inflamed Darach's wrath to an uncontrollable degree, because there was no telling what Logan might do when he reached Leathan Castle.

Darach had always known his brother dreamed of one day taking revenge on Larena's father for what he did to theirs. Logan had been flirting with Larena and gaining her trust since the moment she woke in the prison cell at Kinloch. From the beginning, he'd wanted to use her to get close to Colonel Gregory Chatham, then get his hands on her father. Darach had done his best to talk him out of it because nothing could bring their father back, but obviously he had failed.

An image of Logan attempting to seduce Larena before they even arrived sent a hot flash of rage into Darach's blood, for he couldn't deny his own misplaced desires where the lassie was concerned. And because of that, look at him now? Tied to a tree because he'd been distracted by thoughts of what he'd like to do to her every hour of the day—how he'd like to touch her, hold her, and bury himself in her hot, sweet depths.

Grunting savagely, he struggled and pulled at the bonds.

He never should have accepted this mission, much less allowed Logan to accompany him. He should have flat out refused to allow Logan to come.

Bloody hell. The pain in Darach's head was excruciating. Far worse than the lump he'd taken from Larena in the creek bed. That had been nothing compared to this.

"Logan!" he shouted as he fought in vain against the bonds.

His brother was a rotten little shit for hitting him so hard with that tree branch. Wait till Darach got his hands on him. He was going to thrash him senseless, to within an inch of his life.

⋄⟨⊱⋇⊰⟩⋄

Larena and Logan didn't stop to make camp until the following night when the moon was well on its rise. By that time she was exhausted, starving and feeling more than a little uncertain about the choice she had made that morning at dawn.

She had presumed Logan was her champion, there to rescue her and her clan from his brother's fanatical intentions. But since they'd left Darach behind, something in Logan's demeanor had changed. He had become moody and incommunicative, and despite her protestations about over-exhausting the horses, he had insisted they push on through swollen rivers and thick forests. Clearly he was obsessed with the goal of reaching Leathan Castle before Darach could reach it first.

Logically, of course, this made sense to Larena—for if Darach intended to do harm, it was of the utmost importance that they arrive in time to warn her clan and the officers in charge of the garrison.

Presuming Darach was still alive…

She wasn't entirely sure about that, for Logan said he was unconscious when he'd left him behind. Such a blow to the head could be fatal.

As a result, Larena had begun to question Logan's sense of loyalty. Darach was his own flesh and blood. How could he simply leave his brother for dead? Was Darach truly that much of a villain? Or was there some other rivalry between them that she did not yet understand?

⋇⋇⋇⋇

As soon as a fire was lit near a steep rock face in the woods—and with many questions still poking about in her mind—Larena dug into the packs in search of whatever was left of their provisions, for her belly was growling like a beast.

She found bread and cheese and a small serving of salt pork. On the other side of the fire, Logan uncorked the wine jug and sniffed it. With a finger hooked through the handle, he jiggled it about and rolled his eyes when a small amount sloshed around in the bottom.

"You may have whatever's left," Larena offered. "I'll be happy to take the salt pork in exchange for my share."

"Whatever pleases you, lass," he replied, tipping the jug up to drink thirstily from the spout.

"There's enough bread and cheese for us both," she helpfully proposed.

Logan stood up to circle around the fire and held out his hand. "I'll take some of that, then."

Larena reached out to offer what was left after she claimed her own fair share. Then they sat down across from each other and ate ravenously until everything was gone.

"What will we do tomorrow?" she asked. "Any chance we'll pass through a village where we can replenish our supplies?"

"No chance at all," Logan replied, leaning back against the rock face. "We'll ride as hard as the horses can handle so we don't lose any time."

"Because you're afraid Darach might reach Leathan before us?" she asked, wanting to hear him say it again. She wanted to listen to the tone of his voice and study his eyes when he answered her.

"I'm not afraid of anything," Logan replied with a look of sinister intent that sent a cold shiver down her spine.

She thought it would be best not to arouse his suspicions. "No…of course not."

Logan lay down on his bedroll. "Get some rest, lass."

Eventually Larena lay down as well. For a long while, she stared into the noisy, crackling fire. "Did Darach truly say he would blow Leathan Castle to bits?" she asked out of the blue.

"Aye," Logan replied. "Now go to sleep. Tomorrow will be another long day."

"I'll pray for good weather then." Raising the coverlet up to her ears, Larena feigned sleep, but every few minutes, she opened her eyes to observe Logan through the flames.

⋇⟨⟩⋇

When Larena felt certain that Logan had fallen into a deep slumber, she slid quietly out of her bedroll and opened her saddle pouch. The most important item to retrieve was the King's pardon, which she found inside the pack. Carefully she examined it in the light of the dying fire to make sure it was the actual document she'd started out with.

Ascertaining that all was in order, she slipped it into her cleavage, rose to her feet as quietly as possible, and tiptoed to where Rupert was tethered to a branch next to Logan's horse. Knowing it was too great a risk to try and saddle him, she quietly untied the leather strap and commanded him to kneel so that she might mount.

She was about to hoist herself onto his back and quietly leave the camp when she felt a hand on her shoulder. With a gasp of shock, she whirled around.

"Going somewhere lass?" Logan asked.

Perhaps she should have fought to come up with some believable story about what she was up to, but instead, baser instincts prevailed.

Larena hauled back a fist and socked Logan in the nose. His head snapped back in the darkness, he stumbled over something and fell to the ground. At the same time, Larena doubled over in agony, cupping her knuckles in her hand.

"*Ballocks!*" A fiery burst of adrenaline followed, so she quickly leaped onto Rupert's back and kicked in her heels. "Go, Rupert! Go!"

Confused and disoriented, Rupert nickered as she tried to steer him into the pitch darkness. Logan scrambled to his feet. He grabbed the hem of her skirt and yanked her roughly to the ground. She landed with a heavy thud that shook her ribcage and stole her breath.

Flat on her back, blinking up at the stars, she gulped desperately for air.

Logan gave her no time to recover. He flipped her onto her stomach and wrenched her wrists behind her back, then tied them with a rope.

"I didn't want to have to do this," he said, digging a knee into her back. "But you leave me no choice."

"Then *don't* do it," she grunted with a tightly clenched jaw, her cheek pressed into the dirt.

He leaned down to speak in her ear. "Are you suggesting I trust you to behave yourself and travel with me the rest of the way to Leathan?"

"Yes. I promise!"

He scoffed and sat back to finish tying the knot. "Sorry, but I cannot take your word for it, lass." He tied her ankles together as well and twisted the rope around her legs, all the way up to her thighs. "Especially considering whose daughter you are."

"I don't understand what this is about," she ground out while she struggled against his hold. "Why are you doing this?"

He rolled her onto her back and straddled her. Perched above her on his hands and knees, he peered down at her face. "Now, look at you. All trussed up."

She tried to kick him between the legs but she couldn't bend her knees.

"Stop squirming lass," he said. "You're getting me worked up when you shouldn't be drawing attention to the fact that we're alone and I have a bone to pick with your family."

Larena frowned up at him in bewilderment. "Are you referring to Sheriffmuir? It wasn't our fault that you lost members of your family. We *all* lost people that day."

He scoffed bitterly. "Is that what you think this is about?" He shook his head. "I'm afraid there's a bit more to it than that."

"Then what is it? Why do you hate me so much?"

"It's not *you* I despise," he replied in a low, hostile voice. "It's your father. There are some wrongs that need to be righted."

Her heart raced wildly and her stomach churned with nausea. "What wrongs? My father is a good man and a fair chief."

For a long moment, Logan's disdainful gaze roamed over her face—back and forth slowly from one eye to another, then across her forehead to her cheeks, and down her nose until his eyes settled on her lips.

His chest rose and fell with slow, deep breaths, and all Larena could do was lie still, praying he would back away and leave her alone.

"You know…" he casually said, "I did consider tossing the King's pardon into the fire and being first in line to watch your father lose his head. But I want him to know that it was *me* who brought his daughter home to Leathan."

Logan inclined his head and continued to study her face.

"In case things get dodgy," he continued, "you ought to know that I meant what I said earlier—that I think you're a bonnie lass. I hope you'll forgive me for all this. I think you will when all is said and done."

He wet his lips and slowly bent his head to kiss her, but she squeezed her eyes shut and turned her face away.

"What's the matter, lass?" Logan asked. "I thought we were friends."

"Not anymore," she replied with disdain. Then she spit in his face.

Logan's eyes flared with anger. She braced herself for his retaliation, but the unexpected sound of a pistol cocking caused him to turn his head. Larena looked up to see Darach standing over him.

Thank God. Relief flooded her senses for he was alive and unharmed—and here to stop his brother from beating her, or doing something far worse.

But suddenly her heart sank as she considered that Darach might be here for another dark purpose. What did she ever really know of either of them?

Darach pressed the barrel of his gun firmly against his brother's temple. "If you know what's good for you, Logan, you'll get off the lassie now."

Logan raised his hands over his head and slowly rose to his feet.

"Cut her loose," Darach said with the pistol still cocked and aimed.

"I was just having a bit of fun with her," Logan explained, his hands in the air. "Besides, I had no choice. She just tried to escape with the pardon."

"But she's not our prisoner."

"Says who?" Logan replied. "*You?*"

"Aye. Me and our laird, Angus the Lion."

"He was never our true laird," Logan practically spat. "You know that as well as I do."

Still roped and bound on the ground behind Logan, Larena rolled to her side and quietly struggled to free her wrists, while listening carefully to what the brothers said to each other.

Darach kept the weapon trained on Logan's head as he spoke. "I pledged my oath to Angus, and so did you. He asked us to deliver this woman and the King's pardon to Leathan Castle, and that's what I intend to do."

"What difference does it make if we do what we want when we get there?" Logan asked.

"Angus wants peace," Darach replied.

"Peace?" Logan let out a bitter laugh. "With the English, you mean? Or with the Campbells? After what they did to our father, that's a bloody pipe dream."

"What are you talking about?" Larena asked while she struggled to free herself.

"Quiet lass," Darach said. Then he spoke to Logan again. "I gave Angus my word and I aim to fulfill that oath."

She prayed that would be the case. Perhaps Darach would turn out to be her savior after all...

"But have you forgotten where you come from?" Logan asked with heated intensity. "Have you forgotten who your true family is?"

"Nay, I'll never forget," Darach replied.

Slowly, Logan began to lower his hands. "Then let's do what we are destined to do, Darach. Think of it. What are the odds that we would stumble across Fitzroy Campbell's daughter, unconscious and carrying the pardon to save his life? Surely that was fate. Surely we are meant to return to Leathan and seek justice."

Justice?

"Where is the pardon now?" Darach asked. "What did you do with it?"

"I have it," Larena said, wincing at the burning chafe marks on her wrists.

Logan turned to look down at her, lying at his feet.

"You let her keep it?" Darach asked. "I'm surprised."

He shrugged indifferently. "I figured it would keep her amiable until we reached Leathan."

"And then what did you plan to do with it?" Larena demanded to know. "Steal it from me and destroy it outside the castle gates?"

"Nay, lass," he replied. "I was going to use it to gain entry, to poke around and see what the English are up to."

"I wouldn't have let you," she argued, still fighting with her bonds. "I would have exposed you for what you are. A traitor and a cheat, a man who would assault a woman, strike down his own brother and leave him for dead."

"Darach's not dead," Logan argued, "and I'm not daft. I wasn't going to bring you to the castle with me. I would have done something with you by then. Kept you for assurance somehow—so that I'd have something to negotiate in case things went sour."

"What things?" Larena growled, fighting harder against her bonds and wishing she had her bow so she could shoot Logan straight through the heart.

"You must give me your word," Darach said to him, "that you will let this go. There is no future for us at Leathan. We cannot change the past. Gather up your things now, ride back to Kinloch, and we won't say another word about it."

Logan shook his head. "I cannot let it go."

Darach lowered the pistol to aim it at Logan's knees. "Go now or I will shoot you in the leg."

Larena rolled out of the way.

"You won't do that," Logan said. "I'm your baby brother, the one you saved."

"Aye, but you've lost sight of your honor, Logan. I cannot stand by and let you break your oath to your laird and do as you please. You'll get yourself killed. It's time to gather up your things and leave."

"You dare to speak to me of honor? *You?*" Logan spit on the ground between them.

For a long moment they stared at each other in the gloom of the moonlight while Larena lay absolutely still, praying that Logan would submit.

But even if he did, would she be any safer in Darach's hands? She had no idea what was really going on here. And could Logan be trusted to return to Kinloch? What if he came after them?

Suddenly, in a flash of movement, Logan lunged at Darach. The gun went off in a deafening blast that rang in Larena's ears, but the ball only grazed Logan's leg and embedded itself in a tree.

As soon as the noise faded to silence, Logan threw his whole weight at Darach. They landed in a heap on the forest floor, grunting and shouting like savages. Logan punched Darach in the face, but Darach rolled him onto his back. He struck Logan three times in the jaw until Logan's arms fell listlessly to his sides and his eyes rolled back in his head.

Darach rose to his feet and staggered backwards, wiping his forearm across his bloody mouth. All the while, he kept his eyes on Logan, as if he fully expected him to rise up again and resume the fight.

Larena tugged desperately at her bonds until her wrists were numb from the chafing. At last she freed herself and began to unwrap her legs.

Logan recuperated suddenly. He clambered to his feet, drew his knife, and lunged at Darach.

Darach grabbed hold of his brother's wrist, head-butted him, and pushed him backwards into the steep rock face, where he pounded Logan's hand repeatedly up against the stone. At last the knife fell from Logan's grasp.

In a shrewd maneuver, Darach bent and snapped Logan's arm with a gruesome-sounding *crack*!

Logan bellowed in pain and dropped to his knees, clutching his arm to his abdomen.

"Your fighting arm is broken," Darach informed him, "but you should be able to ride with the other. I'll set the bone in place and you may remain here until morning, but then you must return to Kinloch. Tell Angus you were thrown from your horse and I will put this behind us, Logan. Do otherwise, and I promise you will answer to *him*."

Logan picked up his knife, sheathed it in his boot, and rose unsteadily to his feet. Still cradling his broken arm, he said nothing as he limped past the fire to his horse and awkwardly mounted him bareback.

"Wait," Darach said, following. "Let me set the bone in place first."

"Go to hell," Logan replied and urged his horse into a trot. "I'm done with you."

Larena stepped out of his way, but he stopped in front of her. His horse stomped around skittishly.

"We're not who you think we are, lass," he said. "And you deserve to know the truth."

Darach stepped forward. "Logan, *no*...."

He tossed his head in Darach's direction. "This Highlander who thinks he's full of principle and honor is a bloody liar. His name is Darach Campbell and I am Logan Campbell. We were born at Leathan Castle and our father was Ronald Campbell. Your former chief."

Larena's body stiffened in shock. "You are sons of *Ronald* Campbell?"

Logan nodded.

She shook her head in disbelief. "But you're MacDonalds. You told me you lost your family at Sheriffmuir."

She was overcome by confusion and dismay, for she remembered Ronald Campbell. He had survived the battle at Sheriffmuir, remained chief for more than a decade afterward, but had suffered a tragic death two years ago when he was thrown from his horse during a hunt.

These were his sons? She'd been under the impression all his sons had fallen on that bloody battlefield fifteen years ago and he had no heirs. That is why her father had been chosen to take his place as chief two years ago.

Logan had nothing more to say on the matter. He rode past her and was swallowed up by the darkness of the forest.

Stunned and shaken, Larena stared after him for a long moment. Then she turned to face Darach. Her stomach lurched, for he was glaring at her with intense, murderous eyes. His lip was split open and starting to swell.

He spit blood onto the ground, then thrust Logan's heavy claymore into the dirt and sheathed the knife in his boot.

With menacing purpose, he strode toward Larena. Terror exploded in her belly and she wondered if she should leap onto her horse and bolt as fast as she could in the other direction, for she hadn't the slightest notion who or what she was dealing with.

CHAPTER

ᚾHIRᚾEEN

"Why did you go off with him like that?" Darach asked with seething fury. "I told you not to trust anyone."

"I believed I had no choice," she replied. "He said you planned to destroy the King's pardon and take vengeance on my clan. Based on your behavior since we left Kinloch, I was inclined to believe him over you. Can you blame me?"

Darach stared at her with a frown. "A costly lapse in judgment on your part, because he was lying to you the entire time."

"You were lying to me, too."

He tilted his head back and looked up at the sky for a few tense seconds. "We need to go."

"Why?" Larena asked as he moved quickly to the fire to collect her saddle. "Will Logan return?"

"He's fit to be tied," Darach explained, picking up the saddle. "His arm will slow him down, but there's no guarantee he won't try and finish what he started. He's stubborn that way." Darach carried the saddle to where Rupert was nibbling at some low lying ferns. He quickly set about readying him for the road. "Where is the King's pardon? You should give it to me for safekeeping." Darach bent forward to fasten the cinches.

A spark of uncertainty flared through Larena's blood. She hesitated before answering.

Darach stopped what he was doing and straightened. "What's the matter, lass? You don't trust me?"

Larena stared at him in shock. "After everything that's happened—after you lectured me tirelessly about not trusting anyone—you're asking me *that*?"

His eyes narrowed and he inclined his head at her.

"Oh," she said. "You're having me on."

He continued to study her face for what seemed an eternity, then slowly he approached. Her mouth went bone dry as he closed the distance between them.

"Stop worrying so much," he said in a low voice. "All I want to do is fulfill my duty to my chief. You can keep the pardon if you want. But I see that you've hurt yourself."

He pointed at the abrasions on her wrists. Cautiously, keeping his eyes fixed on hers the entire time, Darach reached down to take hold of her hand and inspect the damage. She wondered briefly if the display of compassion was just a clever distraction to make her forget what was happening here—that he was a Campbell. Son of her former chief. And she had no idea what his intentions were.

"This looks painful," he said, eyes lifting.

"It's nothing."

His touch was gentle as he ran a finger across her open palm. "I'm sorry I didn't reach you sooner. What else did my brother do to you? Nothing worse, I hope."

Feeling as if she were falling into an exhausted trance, Larena shook her head. "He was fine all day long, until I tried to sneak away. Obviously that was a mistake."

"What happened?"

Larena breathed deeply as she recalled her less than brilliant departure plan. "I waited until he was asleep, then I snuck away from the fire. I was just about to ride off when he must have heard me. He tried to stop me, but I punched him in the nose."

Darach seemed unsurprised.

"I managed to mount Rupert," she continued, "but Logan pulled me off and I fell to the ground. Then he tied me up, and that's when you arrived. It's difficult to say what might have occurred otherwise. I might have been disgraced in the worst possible way."

The thought of it caused a sickening knot of dread to form in her belly.

"My brother may be many things," Darach said, "but he's no rapist."

"Am I to trust your word on that as well when you still haven't explained yourself? Why do you pretend to be a MacDonald if you are a Campbell?"

He let go of her hand and backed away. "I'll explain everything as soon as we leave here. Let's get moving."

While she set about gathering up her bedroll, she couldn't help but wonder what was going on in Darach's mind. He'd just broken his brother's arm to protect her and save her father, while he'd openly professed to hate all Campbells—even though he was one himself.

And still the question remained: Why were they raised as MacDonalds? What terrible thing had they done to be expelled from their own clan?

⋘⋙

"I beg of you, lass," Darach said as he strapped the last few packs and blankets onto the back of his horse. "Do not try to sneak away from me, because if I am to fulfill my duty, I must see you safely delivered through the gates of Leathan Castle with the King's pardon in hand."

"I will stay put as long as you don't threaten to tie me up," she replied, "and as long as you promise to tell me what's been going on here."

He tilted his head and spoke with a note of warning. "You're not in a position to make demands."

"And you're not in a position to pass through the gates of Leathan Castle as an imposter. I hope you don't expect me to keep your secret."

"I expect nothing from you, lass. And we'll cross that bridge when we come to it. For now, just get on your horse."

"Fine." She strode with purpose toward Rupert.

A short while later, they were riding at a brisk pace, side by side along a grassy river bank where the water flowed deep and smooth in the silvery moonlight. At that point, she could take it no longer. She had to know the truth.

"Why were you raised as MacDonalds?" she boldly asked, slowing Rupert to a walk. "After Sheriffmuir, your father believed all his sons were dead. What in the world happened? Were you and Logan deserters?"

"Aye, we were," he replied. "We fled like cowards before the battle even began."

Her eyebrows pulled together with dismay. "But everything you just said to Logan about honor…about the importance of keeping your oath to Angus…"

He thought about that for a moment. "I suppose that is the only way I can atone for what I did back then, because it weighs heavily on me."

"But *why* did you do it?" she asked. "You don't strike me as the cowardly type. Not in the slightest."

His broad shoulders rose and fell with a sigh. "I was young. Impulsive. I could see what was coming on that battlefield," he explained. "I saw the Redcoats and I knew we were no match for them—at least not me and my brother, for we were just lads. After we fled, I watched it from a distance and I saw all the killing and carnage. It was exactly as I knew it would be, but when it was over, a Campbell clansman spotted us and promised he would see us hanged for our dishonor, and I believe he would have followed through on that threat if he had survived, but he was run through by a Redcoat moments later. Still, we knew our father would be ashamed of us. We knew we couldn't return home. We thought it would be better if we were presumed dead."

He paused and shook his head with regret.

"I was only fourteen—too young to recognize the enormity of the decision I was making. I couldn't see very far beyond that day."

"What happened next?"

"We waited until it was safe," he continued, "and returned to the outskirts of the battlefield where we found two fallen MacDonald warriors. We removed their tartans and passed ourselves off as members of one of the northern clans. We ended up at Kinloch, vowing to each other that we would never tell anyone the truth about who we really were. Then we just kept digging ourselves in deeper and deeper. There was no way out after that. Not that we could see, because if the laird of Kinloch found out, God knows what he would have done to us. And if we returned home, we would have been disgraced or maybe hanged."

Larena considered the tale he'd spun and grew curious about something. "That doesn't explain why you and Logan hate my father so much. What did Logan mean when he said he wanted justice?"

Darach let out a deep breath. "That's another matter entirely. For years we kept to ourselves at Kinloch where we became absorbed into the MacDonald clan, but always, Logan wanted to return home. He was ashamed of what we'd done, but he still dreamed that one day, he'd be able to prove himself somehow and our father would welcome us back. But two years ago, when we learned he was dead...Logan took it hard."

"I'm sorry," she said. "It's never easy to lose a parent."

Darach eyed her intently. "Especially when there are rumors that it was murder."

"What rumors?" Larena asked with a frown.

"You didn't hear the gossip? That your father murdered ours so that he could take his place as chief?"

"That's ridiculous!"

"Is it? They said your father had a lust for power and the Jacobite cause. Logan and I may have been young when we fled from Leathan, but even then, we knew well enough that our father had always quarreled openly with yours about politics and clan management, women, and everything else under the sun. They were enemies, lass—but you must know that, since you lived there the whole time."

Larena blinked at him with uncertainty, for this was an awkward conversation, deeply personal on so many levels. "Of course I knew it," she admitted. "Everyone knew it. But your father's death was accidental. He fell off his horse during a hunt. The rumors are false."

"You're sure about that?" He slid her a mistrustful look which helped her to understand why he had disliked her so much from the outset.

"Of course I am sure," she firmly replied. "And how can you presume to judge anything when your father's dead and you haven't spoken to him in fifteen years? For that matter, how could you leave your clan and let your family believe you were dead? They would have mourned for you, Darach. Thank God your mother was already in her grave by then, or she would have died of heartbreak regardless, believing she'd lost all her sons on the same day."

With a touch of displeasure, Darach looked away. "I knew I shouldn't have told you."

Feeling a pang of regret for being judgmental, Larena let out a sigh. "I apologize. I shouldn't have said that. You were just a boy—and poor Logan, on the battlefield at the age of eleven."

"Wild horses couldn't have kept him from it," Darach told her. "He's a born warrior. He lives to fight. Our father commanded him to stay behind, but he snuck out and followed."

"And yet he ran away before the battle even began."

Darach's silence sent a shiver down her spine and caused everything to suddenly become clear. She regarded him with understanding.

"Ah. I see now…It was *you*. You must have dragged Logan away. That's why you deserted—to protect *him*. That's why there is tension between you."

"Aye," Darach replied. "He fought me tooth and nail, shouting like a bandit until I knocked him out cold. Bloody well thought I'd killed him. I had to toss him over my shoulder like a sack of grain. The poor lad didn't come to until it was all over, and he's always blamed me for how our lives turned out."

Darach pointed at a bend in the river just ahead. "We'll cross up there where it's shallow and walk the horses in the riverbed for a mile or so to cover our tracks. Beyond that, I know a good place to stop for the rest of the night."

His broad shoulders rose and fell as he inhaled the cool night air. Larena watched his profile in the moon shadows and noted that his brow was creased with concern.

"Are you worried about how Logan is faring?" she asked.

"I think of nothing else." He squinted across the river, always keeping an eye out for something.

"It's obvious that you care for him," Larena said. "Even though you don't agree with his choices, he's still your brother. You want to keep him safe."

The penetrating expression in Darach's eyes answered her question with a clear *yes*, though he never actually spoke the word.

In the seconds that followed, Larena couldn't seem to pull her eyes away from the dark, elusive beauty of his face—the heavy lashes and arched brows, the exquisite sculpted jawline. Now that she knew the whole story about this rugged and reticent Highlander, she couldn't deny that he stirred all the quiet places in her soul. The truth, at last, had aroused a feeling of compassion in her, mixed with fascination and admiration.

"You're observant," he said.

The silky timbre of his voice sent a small shudder across her flesh. "It was obvious to me before," she replied, "when you told Logan to return to Kinloch. You promised to keep what happened a secret. You *still* want to protect him."

Darach glanced away. "Maybe he no longer needs my protection. He's a man now—quick-witted, a master swordsman. I've no doubt he can take care of himself, but the fact remains, he'll always be my baby brother, and he has a foolish temper sometimes. I don't know what he thinks he can accomplish by returning to Leathan Castle now. He can never bring our father back. He can't win back his approval, no matter what he does to yours. Our father is gone now and we left the clan a lifetime ago. If it's vengeance he wants, it's coming from a dark place in his soul, and I wish he could let go of it."

"And you feel badly because you broke his arm," she said.

Darach looked down at the pommel. "Even that, I did for his protection—so he wouldn't go raging about the Highlands stirring up trouble. I want him to survive."

"And you believe he will die if he carries out this plan, whatever it may be."

"I do." Darach clicked his tongue and urged his horse into a trot.

Larena followed him down onto the riverbed where the horses' hooves splashed through the shallow water. She felt slightly beguiled, riding beside Darach.

"Thank you," she said after a time, "for pursuing Logan and me, and for coming to my rescue. Where would I be now if you hadn't come?"

"Don't thank me until we reach Leathan and deliver the King's pardon," he said. " Until then, nothing is certain." He nodded his head at another bend in the river. "We'll make camp just ahead."

They broke into a gallop and climbed the riverbank toward a clearing.

CHAPTER

FOURTEEN

It was going to be a long night, Darach thought irritably as he lay down on the bedroll across the fire from Larena. She was a bonnie lass to be sure and he couldn't believe he'd just told her everything about his past when he had never confessed his true identity to anyone. Not once, in fifteen years.

He was taken with her, plain and simple, enough to cause physical harm to the brother he'd always sought to protect. But when Darach found Logan on top of Larena in the moonlit glade, a violent madness had flooded his brain. It was so intense, his hand had trembled as he'd aimed the pistol. It was a miracle he hadn't accidentally pulled the trigger and blown his brother's brains out.

Nevertheless, Darach could not allow himself to forget that Larena was not for him. He had no claim on her and in a few days, he would escort her through the gates of the Campbell stronghold—ground he'd not set foot upon since adolescence, before his fateful disgrace. More importantly, it was his duty to hand her over to her betrothed, a half-English, half-Scottish colonel who would take his place not only as her husband, but as chief of the Campbells.

Perhaps that's what was keeping Darach awake. Her marriage was too much to stomach after finding her on her back in the woods, struggling against his brother's misguided attentions. He didn't want to think about Chatham putting his hands on her, touching her, claiming her in his bed on their wedding night.

Larena said she barely knew Chatham but she remembered him as a kind and gentle boy.

Regrettably, Darach remembered that, too.

Opening his eyes, Darach peered through the flames. He was surprised to discover Larena awake also, her boundless blue eyes blinking slowly in the firelight as she stared at him.

Darach shifted on the bedroll and felt terribly exposed, as if she'd heard every word of his blaring thoughts just now.

She hadn't, of course. It was pure idiocy to think so. But he was unsettled by it, nonetheless.

Perhaps he should have said something to her, made some effort at polite conversation as Logan would have done, but Darach couldn't seem to form coherent thoughts in his brain. All he could do was gaze at her through the dancing firelight and imagine his hands roving over her soft naked flesh, his mouth tasting the sweetness of her nipples while she sighed with pleasure and longing and begged him to make love to her.

She, too, lay in silence, her hand tucked up under her cheek, her tongue sliding out to wet her lips in a slow, erotic gesture that left him stiff as a brick and aching with need.

After a while, her eyes fell closed, which left Darach feeling shaken and irritated. He shouldn't be torturing himself with such thoughts and imaginings. She was not for him and nothing good could come of them.

⊰⊱

The following day, it rained again. The foul weather arrived with high winds and another unseasonable chill from the north.

They rode as far as they could in the morning, but by noon, Larena was growing increasingly weary and began to shiver so badly that Darach insisted they stop at the nearest village to take shelter at the alehouse.

"You're not worried Logan will look for us here?" Larena asked as they walked into the crowded pub.

Darach escorted her to a small table for two near the giant hearth at the back. "I've been keeping an eye out," he replied, "but there's scarce chance he's even fit to travel."

"Was it that bad of a break?" she asked as she sat down, feeling more than ready to bathe herself in the warmth of the fire.

Darach nodded. "He should have let me set the bone in place before he rode off. I told you, he's stubborn and full of foolish pride."

The tavern maid approached and offered them a choice of either beef stew or roast lamb with fresh field greens. They selected the lamb and ordered two tankards of ale.

Outside, the rain battered the small leaded windows and ran down the glass in fast, undulating rivulets, while inside, the tavern hummed with the noisy conversation and laughter of men.

"Your teeth are chattering," Darach said with a frown. "We'll stay here until you're dried out."

"That may take a while," she replied, holding her hands out to warm them at the fire. "I'm drenched to the bone."

He watched her for a moment or two. "You've been on the road for many days, lass. You've been shot and you tumbled into a ravine. Are you sure you're feeling all right?"

"I'm fine," she assured him, though she couldn't seem to stop shivering.

Darach reached across the table and touched her forehead. "Holy crow, lass. You're burning up. And you look like death warmed over." He glanced around the tavern, pushed his chair back and stood. "Stay here."

Larena remained at the table while he went to speak to the ruddy-faced, red-bearded Scot behind the bar. Darach turned and pointed a finger at her. The barman studied her carefully for a moment, then nodded and disappeared into a back room.

A moment later he returned and handed Darach a key. Darach dug into his sporran and paid him a few coins.

"What's going on?" Larena asked when he returned and sat down.

"I got us a room upstairs so you can rest and dry out."

"I don't need to rest," she replied. "I need to get home. We've lost enough time already."

"You won't be going anywhere, lass. If you don't rest and recover, you'll end up as a corpse."

She closed her eyes and tried to breathe slowly. All her muscles ached and she was sweating profusely. "I admit, I'm not at my best, but I want to continue. I just need a hot meal, then I'll be fine. Just get me back in the saddle."

"No, lass. You'll pass out and land on your head."

Larena leaned forward to rest her cheek on the table, suddenly too tired to even argue about it. All she wanted to do was lie down and curl up under a thick, heavy blanket.

"Maybe just for a few hours," she said wearily, "until my clothes dry out."

"Now you're making some sense." He stood and offered his hand. "Come. Jean will bring our supper upstairs."

She took his hand and went with him.

FIFTEEN

Though Larena made no complaint and did not admit to any discomfort, Darach knew she was in far worse condition than she let on. Her complexion was pasty gray and when they were halfway up the creaky stairs, she had to pause, take a few breaths, and summon enough strength to continue the rest of the way.

Darach found the room at the end of the hall and inserted the key into the lock. "This is it." He pushed the door open. "Can I do anything for you?"

"I just need to lie down for a while."

"Then come inside." He led her into the small, tidy room which contained a brass bed big enough for two beneath a steep, slanted roof, and a small round table with two wooden chairs tucked snugly into the corner. A bucket of kindling had been provided for them, set out next to the stone hearth.

Darach set the saddle packs on the floor. "I'll light a fire, but first you must get out of those wet clothes."

Larena sank onto the mattress and looked up at him suspiciously. "You are constantly telling me not to trust you, and now you're suggesting I take off my dress. Was I imprudent to follow you up here?"

"You're not well, lass. Admit it and tell me what I can do for you. I can leave you alone if you like."

She considered that for a moment and glanced longingly at the unlit fire. "Could you light that first, then leave me until the food arrives?"

A knock sounded at the door just then. It was Jean, the tavern keeper's wife, carrying a large supper tray. Darach invited her in.

She set the tray on the table and glanced around the room. "Look at you both—like a couple of drowned rats. You need to get that fire going, sir. May I light it for you?"

"Thank you, Jean." Darach stepped out of her way as she moved to the hearth.

A few minutes later, after the fire was lit and she was gone from the room, he turned back around to find Larena sound asleep on the bed.

Not wanting to wake her, Darach devoured his own supper, then leaned back in his chair and rested his eyes for a moment. He must have dozed off for a short while, for when he woke, the fire had nearly gone out. Rising from the chair, he added a log to the grate, pushed it around with the poker until it accepted the flame, then he turned to check on Larena.

Laying his hand on her forehead, he discovered she was hot as a firebrand and perspiring heavily.

He pulled the blanket off her. "Wake up, Larena," he said. "You're feverish and you're still soaking wet."

She offered no response, so he began to unlace her bodice with a goal of drying her out and cooling her off. He stripped her down to her shift and draped the wet garments in front of the fire to dry, then sat on the edge of the bed and took hold of her hand. He patted it a few times and lightly tapped her cheek.

At last her eyes fluttered open and she gazed up at him with a glassy, vacant expression.

"Are we home?" she asked.

"Not yet," he replied. "You're sick, darling. We need to rest awhile."

"I'm not sick. I'm just tired. We'll go soon."

He touched the back of his hand to her forehead and frowned. "How about some supper?" he asked. "Can you eat something? You need to keep your strength up." He reached for the fork to offer her some meat.

She shook her head and turned her face away. "Later."

As Darach set the fork down, she rolled onto her side to face the wall.

She must be sick indeed, Darach thought, if she'd failed to notice that he'd undressed her.

⊰❈⊱

By nightfall, Larena's symptoms had worsened and Darach was pacing the room, praying for the doctor to arrive. Jean had sent for the man hours earlier, but they were told he'd traveled to the next village for some potions and medicines. On account of the weather, he was not expected to return until the following day.

As a result, Darach was powerless to help Larena. All he knew how to do was press a cool, damp cloth to her forehead when she moaned in her sleep, or encourage her to sip some warm broth when she was lucid enough to understand what he was saying.

He sat on the edge of the bed and rinsed the cloth in the water basin, dabbed at her forehead, her cheeks, and down the slender length of her neck to the delicate ridge of her collarbone where her skin glistened with moisture.

She did not wake, as he was gentle in the way he touched her, his movements quiet in the flickering candlelight.

Larena stirred in that moment, inhaled deeply, then rolled to her side again. She curled her body up in a ball and laid her cheek on Darach's thigh, as if his leg were a pillow.

At first, Darach made no move to wake her. He simply stroked her damp hair away from her forehead until she reached a hand up and squeezed at the fabric of his kilt, tugging it upward slightly and nuzzling her lips and nose into the firm bands of muscle above his knee. Very briefly, he allowed himself to enjoy the sensations, but then he took a few shaky breaths, waited for her to drift off again, and carefully slid out from under her.

His pulse beating rapidly, his body on fire with desire, he rose to his feet and stood for a moment, wanting nothing more than to lie with her on the bed and hold her against him. He began to imagine all the ways he would touch her if she were his for the taking, but he'd been through this the night before. It had been a cruel and pointless punishment, so he forced himself to back away and sit down in the chair on the opposite side of the room and think of all the reasons why he needed to deliver her home, bid her farewell, and return to his chief as quickly as possible.

⟨₹⟩⟨₹⟩

All night long, the fever held Larena tightly in its grip and caused her to speak nonsense in her sleep. Sporadically, Darach rose to check her temperature and wipe the perspiration from her body, but she remained in a disturbing state of oblivion, unaware of his presence in the room or the importance of their journey to Leathan.

He glanced at the saddlebags on the floor and wondered if he should depart on his own at sunrise and ride to Leathan to deliver the pardon. Was it not his mission to save Fitzroy Campbell from the gallows? There had already been far too many delays and time was getting short. If they did not leave in the morning, there was little chance they would make it in time.

But as he sat in the dim candlelight, watching over Larena with an escalating desire that worried him—and a fear that her condition might worsen—he knew that duty or no duty, he could not leave her.

SIXTEEN

Larena wasn't sure if it was the sound of the birds chirping outside the window or the soothing sensation of a hand brushing lightly across her cheek that raised her out of the darkness.

Before she was able to open her eyes or make sense of where she was, a voice beckoned. It was husky and low…intimately familiar and both calming and exhilarating to her senses. She wanted nothing more than to see the face of the man who spoke to her, but then she wondered if this was not life but death, and his was a voice from heaven.

As memories and consciousness took form, she slowly began to realize that she was still among the living and the voice was no spirit. It belonged to the Highland scout who had found her in the woods.

Darach…

"That's it, lass," he whispered. "Wake up now. The fever's broken."

Her heavy eyelids fluttered open to the sight of his face—that beautiful face that pained her, for he was an outcast…an imposter, and she was pledged to another.

Oh, God, her father…

Larena's heart raced suddenly with fear that it was too late, that she had missed the deadline to save him.

A hot rush of panic invaded her belly as she recalled the past week's ordeals: the invasion at Leathan…her father beaten and dragged away in front of her clan, sentenced to death. Then the ambush on the forest road and the deaths of her British escorts, and that excruciating moment when her horse galloped off with the King's pardon.

"What day is it?" she asked, straining to sit up. "Where is Rupert?"

"Do not worry, lass," Darach said. "Your saddle bags are here, safe and tucked away beside me. There is still time to reach Leathan, but you're weak and you've been ill. You cannot travel yet."

She glanced around the room. "How long have I been asleep?"

"Since yesterday afternoon," he told her. "It's just as well. We couldn't have gotten far in that storm."

She squinted toward a chair in front of the hearth where her skirt and bodice and stockings were hung up to dry. Then she peered down at herself under the covers. She wore only her loose white shift.

"Did you undress me?" she asked.

"Aye, lass. You were burning up and I had to do something to cool you down."

She couldn't help but wonder how that had played out while she was unconscious—had she been aware of his hands on her body?—but under the circumstances, she couldn't afford to concern herself with unimportant rules of propriety. She had to get home. That was all that mattered.

It took significant effort, but she managed to rise up on her elbows. "Thank you for bringing me here and caring for me."

"It was no trouble."

Something unexpected possessed her in that moment and she reached for his hand. "You look tired, Darach. Did you get any sleep?"

"Not much," he replied, keeping his gaze lowered.

She stared at him for a few seconds, then let go of his hand and sat up straighter on the bed. "We need to go."

"Aye."

Darach stood and she tossed the covers aside, swung her legs to the floor...But a wave of nausea slowed her progress. The room began to spin.

"You all right, lass?" Darach asked.

"I sat up too fast," she replied, lying back down again. "I feel a bit woozy."

Darach covered her with the blanket and moved to the door. "You haven't eaten since yesterday. I'll fetch you some bread and tea."

"But we need to go," she insisted as he opened the door.

"Not until you're able."

He walked out and closed the door behind him, leaving her feeling weak and powerless and completely at his mercy.

⋘⋙

"I can ride," she swore an hour later as she fastened the ties on her bodice. "I feel much better now. Honestly."

"I don't think you're well enough," Darach replied from where he stood on the small braided carpet by the door. "You're still weak and you hardly ate a thing."

"My appetite will return soon enough, and I'm not suggesting we gallop at a breakneck pace. If we walk the horses, I'll be fine. But I cannot stay here another day, Darach. Not when my father's life is at stake."

He stared at her reluctantly, then bowed his head, shook it, and let out a breath of defeat. "Fine." He reached for his weapons and donned his sword belt. "I'll prepare the horses and gather some provisions. I'll be back to fetch you in a bit. Sit down and rest until I return. Do not leave this room."

On his way out, he stopped in front of her—so close she could feel the heat of his breath on her cheeks. Her pulse fluttered alarmingly in her veins and she felt utterly overcome.

He remained there, looming over her like a mountain, his gaze raking over her body with scrutiny. Then he strode to the door. "Only one more day of this, lass. Then tomorrow we'll be free of each other."

As soon as he was gone, she sank, boneless, onto the bed, wondering uneasily about the meaning behind his words. Did he loath her that much? Or did he feel the same forbidden desire she did?

She supposed it would be best if she never learned the answer to those questions. What mattered was finding a way to survive one more day in his company without losing total control of her heart.

⋄⟨⟩⋄

Larena made it as far as the staircase before she had to pause to gather enough strength to descend, for all she wanted to do was lie down again, right there on the landing.

She felt Darach's hand on the small of her back and turned to find him peering down at her with concern.

"If I had my druthers," he said, "you'd still be in bed. But since we have places to go and people to see..." He moved to stand before her. "Put your hands around my neck."

Without waiting for her to protest, he swept her up into his big strong, capable arms and she felt a flurry of excitement in her blood.

She held tight to his massive shoulders as he descended the stairs. His face was so close, she was half-tempted to brush her nose and lips across his unshaven jaw, to breathe in the scent of his wavy hair, to run her fingers down his muscular chest. None of this was sensible, of course, but she couldn't help any of it.

Just get me home, she pleaded surreptitiously to the heavens. *And the sooner the better.*

When they reached the ground floor, Darach continued through the taproom without setting her down. A raucous group of Highlanders cheered for him and broke into an enthusiastic round of applause.

"I'm sure I can walk now," she suggested as they arrived at the front door, for she knew she was at risk—at risk of enjoying the feel of his body far more than she should.

He paused on the stoop to consider it. "No point in stopping now. The mud's slicker than butter. Wouldn't want you to land on your bum and soil your skirts."

"I won't fall," she argued. "Besides, my skirts are already soiled beyond repair." She worked hard to sound casual when her heart was beating raggedly in her chest and she was short of breath.

"Still," he said, "I must get my jollies where I can."

Fighting to ignore the fact that she was secretly thrilled by his remark, she held tighter still as he hopped over a puddle.

They entered the stable yard and Darach paused to study the geography of the terrain, his eyes searching for a clear route to the horses on the other side.

"I think I was wrong about you," Larena said, watching his profile in the morning light.

"In what way, lass?" he asked, distracted.

"I thought you were a bully that first day, but now I see that you are very chivalrous."

He stepped over a puddle onto a wide wooden plank that had been laid across the boggy yard. "You shouldn't say things like that."

"Why not?"

"Just because."

That was the moment she knew that he *was* aware of the attraction between them—at least on her part. Whether or not he felt a similar desire, she knew not.

At last he reached the dry floor of the stable and set her down. "It's time to get on the road, lass. If we do well today, we'll make it to Leathan by sunset tomorrow. Up you go now."

He led her to Rupert and encouraged no more conversation as he helped her mount—and though she was eager to see her father again and tell him the good news about the King's pardon, she was growing increasingly unsettled by her feelings toward Darach. She dreaded saying good-bye to him, and she was further troubled by thoughts of meeting her betrothed.

What would she and Gregory say to each other after all these years? Would he be chivalrous as well? Would she find him as handsome and physically appealing as Darach?

She had to admit, she hadn't given much thought to the reality of her forthcoming marriage until this very moment when she watched Darach mount his horse. Once he was in the saddle, her gazed dipped to his muscular thigh and long leg, then upward to his thick forearms and big hands as he gathered up the reins. Something about the way he turned his body and shoulders and thrust his hips to steer his horse out of the stable struck her as virile and raw. A powerful sexual yearning coursed through her blood, and all she wanted was *more*. More of that scorching hot feeling.

More of *him*. And that was, undoubtedly, a dangerous thing.

SEVENTEEN

Though the weather improved considerably over the previous day's rainstorm, and the noonday sun was blessedly warm on Larena's shoulders, by nightfall a thick fog had descended from the mountain peaks. With it came a shockingly damp chill, like a ghostly vapor, floating onto the moors.

Recognizing Larena's fatigue—which she rebuffed and denied at every turn—Darach insisted they stop near a cluster of granite boulders among the rolling hills, which would provide some shelter from the mist.

After a few unsuccessful attempts at lighting a fire, Darach finally managed to get a robust blaze going, and they settled in for a meal of salt beef and hearty bread with cheese and wine.

"Did we fall behind today?" Larena asked as she finished and set her pewter plate aside. She gathered her woolen shawl more tightly about her shoulders. "There were times I wished we could gallop, but I honestly couldn't muster the strength. If I continue to slow us down tomorrow, I must insist that you ride on without me."

"I won't leave you, lass."

"I certainly don't want you to," she said with a pang of regret, "but my father's execution is set for the day after tomorrow. We cannot take any chances."

Darach nodded and raised his leather flask to his lips. His dark eyes were sensually hooded, his long booted legs stretched out lazily before him. Heaven help her, this sexual longing she felt was growing stronger with every hour she spent in his company. It was compounding at an alarming rate that was beginning to frighten her for all that it implied and how it might affect her future.

"I must confess," she said uneasily, "that when we first set out on this journey, I didn't think I needed protection, but I don't know where I would be right now if it weren't for you. I owe you my life, Darach, and my father will owe you his as well."

She shivered in the evening chill and again gathered her shawl more snugly about her shoulders.

"Are you cold, lass?" Darach asked, setting his flask aside, not waiting for her to answer before he rose to his feet and circled around the fire.

His relaxed approach filled her with unbidden heat. As he squatted beside her and cupped the top of her head in both his big hands, pressed his palm to her forehead, her eyes fell closed and she melted under his touch. There must be some sort of magic in his hands, she thought, for they lulled her into a state of pure rapture.

"There's no fever," he said in that soft, husky voice. "It's this northern fog. Makes the air feel cold as a tomb, even by the fire." He moved to fetch his bedroll, brought it closer and stood over her. "Lie down," he said commandingly. "You've been ill, lass. You need to stay warm."

A flock of excited butterflies took flight in her belly. "Do you mean to lie with me?"

"Aye, with your permission."

She stared at him with wide eyes.

"If you're worried I'll be hankering to take advantage of you," he added, "I can't promise I won't be tempted, because you're a bonnie lass and Lord knows it's been a long journey. But if I wanted to have you against your will, I would have done that back at the inn where the bed was soft and you were mumbling nonsense."

"But you *didn't* take advantage," she replied, needing further clarification because she remembered nothing.

Though she wished she did. She wished she could relive every moment in that room with him—while conscious, of course.

"I slept on the floor, lass, and in the chair. Now push over so we can get some rest."

Sidling toward her bedroll, she watched Darach spread his on the ground beside hers and lie down on it.

"Come closer, lass," he said. "You need to stop shivering before you set the whole world to quaking."

As she lay down on her side, he inched closer and tucked his knees into the backs of hers. The heat of his body pressing cozily against hers took her breath away.

Draping his arm over her hip, Darach covered both her hands with his to warm them. "Is that better?"

"Much better," she replied. "Thank you."

"It's my pleasure, lass," he cheerfully said. "Truly."

Maybe it was her nerves that got the better of her, for she couldn't help but laugh quietly to herself.

Darach lifted his head. "Is something funny?"

She tried to stop herself, but couldn't. "Is it really your pleasure, Darach? Or are you being facetious?"

He chuckled as well. "If you must know, it's more torture than pleasure, because I promised I'd behave myself, so as much as I'd love to tempt you into a lively shag this evening, I'll do my best to keep my hands to myself."

She laughed a little longer and hugged his hands close to her belly. When the moment passed, they continued to lay quietly, motionless in the darkness. The mist rolled like a phantom across the moor and Larena tried with all her might to fall asleep, but with Darach's muscular form pressed so tightly against hers, and with the thrill of his lips at the back of her neck, her insides ignited with excitement. All her senses purred and hummed, and eventually a slow ache began between her thighs.

She could do nothing to control it. Quite involuntarily, she wiggled in the smallest degree, but it was enough to arouse a matched response in Darach, who swiveled his pelvis as if he were moving to achieve a more comfortable position, but she knew that was a ruse. Their mutual arousal was undeniable. He was rubbing up against her, and it sent a flood of erotic heat into the pit of her belly.

Intellectually, she knew she should put a stop to this immediately and think of her pledge to another—a man she would meet the next day—but nothing outside of this moment seemed to exist. All that mattered was the delicious allure of Darach's touch, her awareness of his arousal pressing against her backside, and the rising tide of her own pulsing, aching desires.

And the fact that this was their last night together.

"Are you trying to start trouble, lass?" he whispered in her ear, then nuzzled her hair and sent tantalizing ripples of delight across her flesh.

"I can't help it," she breathlessly replied.

He gently thrust his hips in tiny, irresistible circles that made it difficult to remember her own name.

"But I just promised I'd keep my hands to myself," he said.

"What if I didn't want you to? What if I asked you to kiss me?"

This was dangerous territory and she knew it, but wicked, enticing sensations were quickly overtaking reason.

Darach spoke softly in her ear. "Then you'd be putting me in a difficult position, because it's my duty to deliver you to your betrothed tomorrow. When the sun rises, I must take you home, whether I want to or not."

Her betrothed. She didn't want to think about that. Maybe it was simply cold feet because of the unknown—the sort of fear every future bride must feel. Maybe that's why she was fighting such a powerful attraction to Darach. It was a way to escape her fate for a brief moment in time. One last chance to be free, to choose what her heart and body wanted before committing to a lifetime of duty and fidelity to the unknown.

"I must save my father," she whispered defensively, still wiggling her hips, arching her back, and pressing her behind up against Darach's rock hard arousal. "I cannot change my future, but I do not know Colonel Chatham. We were children the last time we saw each other. I don't love him, Darach. All I know now is what I feel for you."

"And what is that, lass?"

Heart thumping wildly, she paused to consider the question, but she wasn't sure of the answer. "All I know is that I want to touch you and feel your hands on me. But of course that's wrong, and I don't understand why this is happening. It wasn't part of the plan."

He eased her onto her back and slid on top of her. Her legs instinctively parted for him.

"I've been wanting you since the first moment I laid eyes on you in the woods." He looked into her eyes and stroked his hand down her hip and under her bottom.

"But you despised me that day."

"Aye. I despised you for being Fitzroy's daughter, and for making me remember where I come from and what I'd done. I also despised you for making me want you. Maybe part of me still does, but I'm still going to kiss you."

At last, his lips found hers in the darkness. All her shivering ceased as her body melted into his...sizzling beneath the sweltering glide of his open mouth and probing tongue. It all felt terribly sinful, but she wanted to drown herself in it, to open herself fully to the pressures of his driving hips.

His silky hair fell across her face. *Take me*, she wanted to say, but she resisted the urge to speak those words, for she knew, deep down, that it was wrong.

But she wanted it, regardless.

The kissing went on for many moments, lifting her up into a divine world of pleasure and sensation. Darach's mouth was hungry, possessive, and sexual. When he came away, she felt stunned and branded, desperate for more.

He rose up to brace himself on both arms above her while his hips continued to thrust in exotic circles. "I need to ask you something."

"*Now?*" She wasn't sure her brain could make sense of any sort of verbal enquiry. She felt rather thickheaded.

"Are you a virgin, lass?"

She blinked up at him for several heart-stopping seconds. On some level she knew why he needed to know, but her answer was the simple honest truth, without strategy or consideration for the future. "Yes."

He bowed his head and looked down to where they were intimately connected, with only his kilt and her skirt as barriers to lovemaking.

He seemed to be working hard to control his movements down below.

"Why do you want to know that?" she asked.

His eyes lifted. They were on fire with lust. "If you were not a virgin, it wouldn't matter so much what we did tonight. No one would be able to prove anything, but seeing as you are innocent, I must be careful."

"You mean that if I had been with a man before, you would be willing to make love to me tonight, even though I was pledged to another?"

"If you asked me to...Aye. How is that for honor, lass? Clearly I have none."

She shook her head frantically. "That's not true. If you had no honor, you would deflower me now, without ever asking. I am under your spell, Darach, but Gregory Chatham will expect me to be untouched on our wedding night. I must remain so, for I cannot take chances with my father's life."

Darach squeezed his eyes shut. "It kills me to hear you speak of your wedding night."

He thrust his hips more firmly in angry circles.

"Please, Darach.... Maybe we should stop."

His movements stilled. Then he opened his eyes and gazed down at her. "You don't need to be afraid of me."

"But won't this make it more difficult? Especially when we arrive at the castle?" She took a breath and swallowed uncomfortably. "I don't know what's happening here. I've never done anything like this before. We barely know each other."

"I know everything I need to know about you, lass."

"But after tonight, we must forget each other. You mustn't tell anyone about this."

A blinding fury in his eyes reflected the dancing flames of the fire.

"I won't forget you," he firmly said. "I will remember every last detail of your face and every word you've ever spoken to me. I'll remember the flavor of your lips and the scent of your skin. I want you to remember me, too, lass."

Her passions rose up suddenly and she lifted her head off the bedroll to kiss him deeply on the mouth. He crushed his full weight upon her, his lips hot and silky, his big hand roving down over the curve of her hip to the top of her thigh.

Wanting him urgently, she dug her fingers into the rippling muscles of his back, clutched at the fabric of his shirt, tugged at his tartan.

He gathered her skirt in his fist and drew it up until he could cup her bare knee and slide his hand up the inside of her thigh.

"Oh, Darach," she whispered, "it feels so good when you touch me."

"I want to make love to you," he said. "Drive myself into you, take you as my own."

Oh, how she wanted to give herself over to this incredible passion, this wanton desire that was quickly taking possession of her body. His hands, his mouth…. Heaven help her, she wanted all of him.

Hungry for more, she leaned up and tasted his neck, licking the salty skin just above the collar of his shirt. Then she greedily began to tug his shirt up until he sat back on his haunches and tore it off over his head. Smoothly, he lay back down, covering her with his hot skin. She ran her hands up and down his back, squeezing at the hard muscles, then slid them down lower over his kilt to his firm buttocks. He continued to thrust his hips and rub his manhood against the tender throbbing flesh between her open thighs.

But still...the fabric of her skirts and his kilt were barriers against penetration, and though it was a wise thing not to sweep the garments out of the way, it took immense power of will to resist it.

"I want to take this off you," he ground out while laying wet, sucking kisses down the side of her neck and licking the tops of her breasts, just above the neckline of her shift and bodice. "I want to touch you and pleasure you. We're safe above the waist. I could unlace you, lass. Touch you up here and not take your virginity. Please...let me have you up here."

Breathless and dizzy, she nodded her head. He began at once, with fast roving fingers, to untie her laces and remove her bodice. He then used his teeth to pick at the knotted ribbon of her shift, opening it down to her belly and baring her breasts to the cool night air.

Her nipples tightened into firm peaks as he promptly took one into his mouth. Larena gasped in shock at the astonishing pleasure, for she'd never imagined a man could deliver such staggering delight by licking and suckling at a woman's breasts. He groaned with hungry lust and tended to one breast devotedly before moving to the other. All she could do was throw her head back and cup his head in her hands, rake her fingers through his hair, and sigh with bliss.

"What are you doing to me?" she begged to know as his hand slid up under her skirt to the damp nest between her legs. Gently he used the heel of his palm to massage her, and the dual sensations from his tongue at her breast and his hand between her legs sent her into a frenzy of passion.

She was drowning in sensation, trapped between intolerable mounting pleasure and the desperate need for release. Her body tightened and her breathing grew rough and labored until a rush of heat shot outward from her core and all her muscles tensed and quivered. Her body became lost in spasms as she cried out, fisting thick wavy locks of Darach's hair and grinding her hips forward.

He crushed her mouth with his own, silencing her cries with a kiss that prolonged the agony of his pulsing hand down below, bringing her to the very edges of sanity. Out of control with wanting, she wrapped her legs around his hips and locked her ankles together, while pulling him close, clutching at his broad shoulders, burying her face in his neck.

He groaned with need. "Ah lass, what I wouldn't give to be inside you right now."

"We can't," she replied, which was the wrong thing to say. She wasn't sure what the *right* thing would have been, but clearly this was not it, for he lifted his head and stared down at her with frustration.

A single heartbeat later, he rolled off her and rose to his feet, raked his hand through his hair and strode away from their tiny sanctuary in the rocks. The fog on the moor was thick as soup. As soon as he was away from the fire, he was completely gone from sight—as if he'd vanished into the mist. Only the crackling of the fire broke the interminable silence.

Larena sat up and tied the ribbons of her shift to close it over her breasts, then shrugged back into her bodice, and stood.

"Darach?" She looked all around. "Where are you?"

He offered no reply, and she had no idea how far he had walked or how long he would stay away.

Strolling to one of the big boulders and laying her hand on the rough stone, she strained to peer through the darkness. "Darach?" she called out again.

Eventually, the sound of footsteps stalking across the tangled bracken caused her to perk up, and she prayed it would be Darach and not some other uninvited guest.

Logan came to mind.

Like an apparition out of the fog, Darach appeared before her.

"I know I am supposed to hand you over tomorrow," he said. "I gave you my word that's what I would do, but the thought of it makes me sick, lass. It makes me want to strangle someone."

"Not me, I hope."

"Nay, not you. *Him.*"

She trembled with apprehension. "You don't even know him."

"Neither do you," he practically spat. Then he brushed past her and returned to the fire. "It does not matter anyway. You've agreed to it, you've pledged a vow, so you'll be giving yourself to him on your wedding night. But every time I imagine him touching you, undressing you, putting his hands on your body, my blood boils and my guts turns to acid."

"I feel the same way," she said, following him. "I'm sorry. I didn't expect this to happen. Everything seemed so simple a week ago."

Darach eyes lifted with a look of savage fury. "I know I have no right to you, lass, but the fact is…I'm in a jealous rage at the moment and I don't know how I'm going to fulfill my duty to my chief tomorrow—or to you, for I know this is what you want. I know I cannot make you change your mind."

She wanted to reach out to him but was afraid of pushing things further. Whenever they touched, her body came alive and the world sparked into a blazing inferno. "I'm not sure what to say, except that I'd be jealous, too, if you were betrothed to another. I didn't know I could feel this way, but it happened. And if you must know, I'm beside myself with dread at the idea of another man touching me, especially after tonight."

Darach turned away from her again and strode to the edge of the camp where he stared out at the darkness. "I don't know if I can do this, lass."

She felt a stab of fear and desperation. "But you must. My father will die if I break my vow to Lord Rutherford."

Darach continued to stand with his back to her for the longest while. Then he faced her. "In that case, we both need to accept that this is all there will ever be for us, lass. Tomorrow we will rise and I will take you home to Leathan, and you will do what you must to save your father from the gallows." Slowly, he strode closer. "But if you change your mind, or if you ever require protection, you know where to find me."

"At Kinloch," she said.

"Aye."

"But you're a Campbell, Darach. Is there no chance you might wish to stay?"

He shook his head. "Nay. I am a MacDonald now. As far as the Campbell clan is concerned, I am dead to them. I do not belong here. I never will."

She looked down at the ground. "But I don't want to say good-bye."

He cradled her chin in his hand and gently lifted her face. "Look at me, lass. I don't want to say it either, but if I stayed at Leathan, you know I'd cause trouble. You'd never make it down the aisle."

A terrible pain squeezed at Larena's heart, while her body continued to burn with desire for this extraordinary man who had awakened her passions and her soul. "What about tonight?" she asked. "We still have until dawn."

He inclined his head with a look of apology. "I'll hold you in my arms to keep you warm," he answered, "but we can do no more than that. If I make love to you, it will change everything."

Her heart ached with sorrow and hot tears filled her eyes. "Will you at least kiss me again, just one more time? And again tomorrow when we say good-bye?"

He stroked her cheek with his thumb, then bent his head and pressed his lips to hers.

Leathan Castle

The sun was just setting when Larena and Darach reined in their mounts a mile from the castle gate. They stopped on a high rocky cliff overlooking the loch below.

"There it is," Larena said, pointing to her beloved home—a monstrous fifteenth century stone bastion further along the cliff that jutted out over the water. Her heart raced with pride at its magnificence in the fiery glow of the setting sun. With striking baronial style corner turrets adorning an impressive tower house, it was a threatening spectacle indeed—a powerful and intimidating Scottish fortress that had always made her feel safe and protected.

Though it had not been powerful enough a fortnight ago to defend against the English invasion….

"Do you see the Redcoats patrolling the battlements?" she asked, turning toward Darach who sat in his saddle, frowning at the castle.

What must he be feeling? she wondered suddenly. He'd probably imagined he'd never lay eyes on this place again. Was he happy to see his old home? Or was this torture for him?

"Does it trouble you to see it?" she gently asked.

He started slightly as if she'd just yanked him out of a trance. "Nay, lass, it matters not. But are you sure about this? Are you positive you can trust Rutherford to let your father live?"

"I have the pardon right here in my bag, with his signature on it," she replied.

"What about Chatham?" he asked. "Are you sure he'll be a fair chief? He's half English and he's an officer in the King's army. Look what you'll be living with." He tossed his head to gesture toward the guards on the rooftop.

"Chatham is also half Scottish," she reminded him, "and he wishes to remain here as such—as leader of our clan. He does not intend for Leathan to remain an English garrison forever. At least, that is what Lord Rutherford implied."

Darach regarded her steadily in the brilliance of the setting sun. "I hope you're right about that. Either way, nothing will be the same as it was."

She turned her eyes back to the castle and felt a sinking sensation where her heart was located. "No, it won't, but we've had this conversation before, Darach. I cannot simply let my father die."

Darach hesitated briefly, then without responding to that, he clicked his tongue to urge his horse into a slow walk along the top of the mountain.

"Wait," she said, following him. "What will we do when we arrive at the gate? Will you come inside with me? I know you don't wish to be recognized, but I can't let you leave without at least offering you a hot meal. I must thank you for all that you've done."

He did not look back as he rode ahead of her. "I'll see you through the castle gates, lass, just to make sure you're safe and sound and everything is as it should be, but then I will go."

Her body shuddered at the notion of never seeing him again. "But you promised me one last kiss," she quietly mentioned, knowing it was wrong to remind him of such a thing when she was about to meet her betrothed.

Before he had a chance to reply, his horse suddenly reared up on the path and he was thrown to the ground with a heavy thud. Miller galloped off, back in the direction from where they had come.

Larena fought to keep Rupert under control as he too spooked and reared up. With only a few seconds to comprehend what was happening, she found herself staring down the barrel of a pistol—held in the tight grip of an English Redcoat.

There were three soldiers who had risen up from behind large boulders on either side of the path. Two were now standing over Darach with weapons aimed at his face while the third was grabbing hold of Rupert's bridle.

Lying on his back, Darach slowly raised his hands in surrender. "Don't everyone panic at once," he said in a casual tone, gazing up at them. "We're here with a message from the King."

"Are you Larena Campbell?" one of them asked her. "Daughter of Fitzroy?"

"Yes," she quickly answered. "I am she."

The soldier nearest to her holstered his weapon. "Well then…." He relaxed his stance. "Welcome home, Mistress Campbell. We've been expecting you."

All the breath sailed out of her lungs and she felt the tension drain from her shoulders. "You knew I was coming?"

"We didn't know for sure, but we were told to keep an eye out for you when we learned about the ambush."

"How did you hear of it?" she asked.

"One of our lieutenants rode in two days ago," the soldier replied. "He was with you during the attack but managed to escape. He said he searched everywhere for you afterward but he couldn't find you or your horse. He assumed you'd escaped and would make your own way back here with the King's pardon."

"So you know about the pardon on my father's life?" she asked, desperate to be sure of it.

"Yes, ma'am. Colonel Chatham called off the execution as soon as he learned of it."

Larena could have collapsed with relief. "How grateful I am. Thank you, sir. You have no idea how happy you've made me."

Suddenly aware of Darach, still lying on the ground with two weapons aimed at his head, she spoke firmly to the other two soldiers. "Please, gentlemen. Lower your weapons. This man is no threat. He saved my life after the ambush and guided me home."

"But he's a MacDonald," one of them said. "We were told you were passing through MacDonald lands when you were attacked."

"Aye," she replied, "but the attackers were rebels from another clan. This man is from Kinloch Castle and I assure you, he has been an invaluable aid to me."

The soldier standing beside her horse nodded at them to lower their guns and allow Darach to stand.

"Relieve him of his weapons and put him in irons," the leader said.

"That's not necessary," Larena argued.

"It's fine," Darach assured her, though his eyes glimmered with angry doggedness as the soldiers confiscated his sword, pistol, and knife, then clamped irons around his wrists.

"Come along then, miss," the soldier said to her as he began to lead Rupert along the path while Darach and the others walked ahead of them. "Colonel Chatham will wish to see you and find out everything that happened to you. And I reckon he'll be eager to catch those rebels who attacked you. He'll want to bring them to justice."

"I believe most of them are dead," she told him. "And from what I understand, they were just a bunch of young ruffians setting out to imitate the Butcher of the Highlands."

He seemed to carefully consider that. "You're sure they weren't MacDonalds?"

"They were MacDuffs," Darach offered, speaking over his shoulder.

"And what were MacDuffs doing on MacDonald lands?" the leader asked suspiciously.

"I have no answer to that. I was out on a routine scouting mission when I heard the musketfire. It was over by the time I arrived."

Larena noticed he did not say "we."

"A scouting mission, eh?" the soldier replied. "Do you serve Angus the Lion?"

"Aye."

"And did he send you here to discuss politics with Colonel Chatham?"

"Nay," Darach replied. "I'm just here to deliver the lady and the pardon. Nothing more."

"Well, we'll see about that," one of them said, poking Darach in the ribs with the barrel of his gun. "Move faster, Highlander. We want to reach the gates before nightfall. No doubt the colonel will have plenty of questions for you."

"But why?" Larena asked as a shiver of dread moved up her spine. "He already told you that he's just here as my escort. He only wants to be on his way home again." She glanced all around the mountainside. "And his horse must be recovered."

The leader looked up at her with menace. "Angus the Lion has a distinguished reputation when it comes to warfare, Miss Campbell. He's known to have Jacobite sympathies like his father before him. Surely you know that."

She raised her chin defiantly. "I have heard stories…yes. But I had the pleasure of meeting Angus MacDonald after the attack and he assured me that he desires peace. It was he who assigned this man to escort me here safely and deliver the King's document."

The soldier leading Rupert regarded her with suspicion for a few heated seconds, then one of them poked Darach with his musket again. He stumbled forward a few steps.

"You can tell all that to the colonel," the soldier said.

"I will, but you must give me your word that this man will not be harmed or detained." With that she allowed the soldier to lead Rupert along the mountain path, while Darach walked ahead of her.

There was a flurry of activity in the bailey as the giant iron portcullis lifted and they passed beneath it. As soon as they entered, the chains rattled noisily and it was lowered back down.

The soldier leading Rupert snapped his fingers and shouted at a groom who was carrying empty buckets across the bailey. She recognized him as one of her fellow clansmen. There were not many around. Most had fled after her father was taken into custody.

"You there!" the soldier said. "Come here at once and do your duty!"

The clansman dropped the buckets and hurried over. "Miss Campbell!" His eyebrows lifted at the sight of her. "Welcome home. No one knew what became of you."

"I'm quite fine, Alastair. Thank you."

He glanced uneasily at Darach who was still in irons. Alastair's eyes focused on the MacDonald tartan and clan badge.

"This man came to my aid and brought me home," she explained in an effort to ensure there were no misunderstandings. "I owe him my life."

"Get a move on, Highlander," one of the soldiers said, jabbing Darach in the ribs again.

"Where are you taking him?" Larena demanded.

"No need to concern yourself with that, miss. We'll just hold him until the colonel's ready to question him. Then I'm sure we'll send him on his way."

As Alistair helped her dismount and took hold of Rupert, dread and agitation gripped her, for this could be the last time she would ever see Darach. Perhaps they would question him immediately and he would be gone within the hour, without ever saying good-bye, or perhaps they would not be so gracious in allowing him to leave.

Her heart pounded with apprehension as she watched the soldiers lead Darach away. In the final few seconds before he entered the stone keep, he glanced back over his shoulder and held her immobilized in the intensity of his gaze. It was enough to wrench painfully at her core and pull a small prayer from her lips.

Keep him safe. Let this not be the final good-bye.

⊰⊱

With his wrists still in irons, Darach followed the British soldier through the stone corridors of the keep while a flood of memories—both good and bad—inundated his brain.

Though it had been fifteen years, he still knew these passageways like the back of his hand. How clearly he recalled dashing through them as a young lad, playing hide and seek with his brothers, getting into fist fights with other lads and causing all sorts of trouble with the lassies who didn't enjoy getting their hair pulled.

Later, the games had changed where lassies were concerned. He'd stolen his first kiss in the stable one night after a feast and had fancied himself in love for a few days. He remembered the lassie well. She was a cheeky little redhead named Tavia who went on to kiss every other lad at Leathan.

Though his family was all gone now, Darach wondered if anyone from his past might recognize him. It was not something he had a hankering for, so he would simply have to do his best to stay out of sight and keep his head down.

Unfortunately there wasn't much he could do about Gregory Chatham.

Darach was not surprised when the soldiers led him toward the prison stairs. He'd suspected this was where they would take him.

They descended quickly, without explanation.

In short order, he was shoved into a cell. At least the guards had the decency to remove the irons from his wrists before they slammed the heavy oak door shut in his face.

With a sigh of resignation, Darach sat down on the cot and wondered how long he would have to remain there, waiting for something to happen.

And what, in the meantime, was happening to Larena?

❧❀❧

"Apologies, Miss Campbell," the cook said as she walked Larena through the torch-lit stone corridors and up the tower stairs to her bedchamber. "One of the officers took your room as his own, but as soon as the colonel learned you might be on your way, he cleared that man right out of there and asked me to freshen everything for your return. He was very hopeful, you see."

Larena followed Mrs. Henderson through the chamber door and let out a sigh of relief when she found everything as it had been—her own comfortable bed and floral coverings, the thick fur rug on the floor in front of the fireplace, the tapestry on the wall, and her collection of books. They stood just as she had left them, in a tall, leaning pile on the bench beneath the window.

"It's so good to be home," she said, feeling briefly as if nothing had changed, though she knew that was not the case at all if an English officer had been sleeping here for the past fortnight.

"I'll have one of the girls light a fire for you right away." Mrs. Henderson moved to fluff the pillows on the bed.

"How many of you remained after the attack?" Larena asked.

"There are only a few of us working in the kitchen. They're paying us handsomely to cook for the men." Clearing her throat, she continued to fluff the pillows. "A tub is on its way. You'll have a chance to bathe and rest awhile before you meet the colonel."

Larena swallowed uneasily. "Have you met him yourself, Mrs. Henderson? How is he? What do you think of him?"

Mrs. Henderson set the pillow back down and slowly turned to face Larena. She seemed to struggle with how best to answer the question. "He's grown into a handsome man," she said at last. "There can be no argument there. But we're all a bit confused, if you must know. We understand why you agreed to marry the colonel—to save your father from the executioner—but we're not sure what this will mean for the clan. Colonel Chatham still wears the uniform of the English, yet he is to be our laird?"

"That is correct," Larena confirmed. "And I wish I could tell you what to expect, but I'm not even sure myself. I haven't spoken to Gregory Chatham since I was eleven years old, but if it helps you to know, when I discussed the terms of our marriage with Lord Rutherford at Fort William, he told me that his son has always considered Scotland to be his true home and that he maintains a genuine affection for our clan. Rutherford also suggested that as soon as the threat of a Jacobite uprising is eradicated, the soldiers will leave and Colonel Chatham will resign his commission with the army."

Mrs. Henderson's ample bosom rose and fell with noticeable relief. "That sounds promising. I hope that will be the case, miss, and if so, the clan thanks you for your courage in traveling to Fort William, and your sacrifice in agreeing to the marriage. Perhaps, with a good woman like you at his side, the colonel will turn out to be a fair-minded laird in the end."

"That is my hope," Larena replied. "I will certainly speak to Colonel Chatham about all of this as soon as I meet with him. But first, I must see my father. Can you take me to him?"

"Ooh, I don't know about that, lass. He's locked up in the prison. I reckon you'll have to ask the colonel."

She felt a prickle of unease at the thought. "When will I see him?"

The empty tub arrived just then, bumping through the door in the arms of two maids she recognized—Eileen and Edina.

Mrs. Henderson waved them in and directed them to the area in front of the hearth. "He's arranged for you to join him for dinner in his private apartments at nine."

Larena watched the women set the tub down. "His private apartments…. I suppose you mean my father's chambers?"

She faced Larena again. "Your father's *former* chambers, miss. Now let's get you cleaned up, shall we? It's not every day a lassie meets her future husband."

While a brigade of buckets arrived through the door, containing hot water, Larena couldn't help but imagine a very different future husband for herself—a dark-haired Highlander who was presently clamped in irons somewhere in the castle.

Sadly, as Mrs. Henderson began to unlace her, she knew such thoughts were unwise and unrealistic, and it would be best to sweep them from her mind completely.

⊰❈⊱

Darach must have drifted off, but for how long he had no notion, for there were no windows in the cell to indicate the time of day.

The cell door opened with a heavy clank. Darach rose instantly to his feet.

Two soldiers walked in. They carried another pair of irons and moved in to close them around Darach's wrists.

"Is this necessary?" he asked. "You've already seized my weapons and clearly I'm outnumbered."

"The colonel doesn't want to take any chances," one of them replied. "He knows there's no love lost between the Campbells and MacDonalds."

With no interest in debating the issue, Darach followed them out the door and back up the stone staircase.

"Where are we going?" he asked, keeping his eyes peeled for Larena as they emerged onto the open bailey again. It was full dark by now. A dense cloud cover blotted out any light from the moon and the area was illuminated by torches. The flames danced wildly in the wind.

"To see the colonel of course."

"I can't imagine why."

"You'll find out soon enough."

Darach inhaled deeply with a sense of foreboding, for Chatham was one of the last people he wanted to see here at

Leathan—though he was curious about the sort of husband he would make for Larena. It wouldn't hurt for Darach to assure himself that the man was honorable.

The soldiers shoved Darach through the East Tower doorway and pushed him up the curved staircase.

"All the way to the top," one of them said.

These stairs were all too familiar to him as well, for they led to his late father's former chambers where Darach had been summoned more often than he cared to recall—usually to receive some form of punishment for one thing or another.

How ironic that Gregory Chatham now inhabited these rooms and had risen to a position where he could be the one to summon Darach up these stairs. He supposed that proved it then: *No bad deed goes unpunished. We reap what we sow.*

They reached the door and one of the soldiers knocked.

"Enter!" shouted a voice of command from within.

They pushed the door open and nudged Darach over the threshold. "We brought the MacDonald."

And there, at last, behind the desk, was Gregory Chatham—the man who would become Larena's husband.

Darach felt a muscle clench at his jaw as he beheld the finely dressed English officer, seated with his back to the dark window. Chatham's eyes lifted at the sound of Darach's approach. Setting down his quill pen, he slowly rose to his feet and took in Darach's appearance from head to foot.

Darach regarded him warily, for there could be no doubt in his mind that this was the lad he remembered from his youth—the lad he and his brothers bullied and taunted mercilessly, at least for a time. Darach braced himself, wondering how long it would take for the man to recognize him.

Twenty

"They tell me you're the Highlander who rescued my future bride from certain peril," Chatham said as he moved around the desk to stand before Darach. With one hand resting on the gleaming hilt of his dress saber, he now matched Darach in both height and stature. Chatham relaxed his stance and stared into Darach's eyes for what seemed an eternity. "Thank you for bringing her home to me."

"You're welcome," Darach replied. Then he raised his wrists up high, in front of Chatham's face. "Can you have your men remove these now?"

Something flickered in Chatham's eyes—a flash of annoyance perhaps—but he nevertheless signaled to the guard inside the door. "Release him."

While the guard slipped the key into the lock and freed Darach, Chatham returned to the opposite side of the desk. Before he sat down, he gestured to the empty wooden chair behind Darach.

"Take a seat. We have much to discuss."

Darach hesitated briefly, then sat down. The guard quietly left the room and closed the door behind him.

Chatham folded his hands on top of a pile of papers. "Darach MacDonald. They tell me you are a scout for Angus the Lion of Kinloch Castle."

"Aye."

"And what can you tell me about his politics?" Chatham asked, leaning casually back in his chair and regarding Darach with interest.

"Not much. I'm just a scout."

"But surely you know the leanings of your laird and fellow clansmen. Even I know that your people fought against us at the Battle of Sheriffmuir in support of the Stuart pretender."

"That was a long time ago," Darach replied, "and it was Angus's father who led the charge, not Angus. His father is dead now."

Chatham's eyes narrowed with cynicism. "So you are telling me that his son, who also fought in that same battle, supports the House of Hanover now?"

"I'm telling you no such thing," Darach replied. "All I know is that he wants peace at Kinloch."

"So you *do* know something of his political leanings," Chatham replied, crossing one leg over the other and carefully scrutinizing Darach's face.

Darach looked away. "No one at Kinloch wants another war."

"But wasn't there some upheaval a few years back?" Chatham asked. "The castle was seized from the MacDonalds who were considered Jacobite traitors and awarded to the MacEwens for their service to the Crown. Angus took it back by force and claimed a MacEwan for a wife...if memory serves me correctly?"

"Aye," Darach replied, "but that had nothing to do with kings and crowns. Angus only wanted his home back, and after he reclaimed it, he discovered a Jacobite rebel amongst the MacEwans and turned that man in to Colonel Worthington at Fort William. From what I've heard, the colonel holds Angus in high regard. He sends him a bottle of Moncrieffe Whisky every year at yuletide."

"For a scout who knows nothing," Chatham said with a suspicious tone, "you seem to know a great deal."

Darach exhaled sharply. "Are we done here, colonel? I am expected back at Kinloch."

"No," Chatham firmly replied. "We are not done." His eyes practically burned into Darach's. "I have not yet thanked you properly for your service to the Crown, and to me personally. You must share a drink with me. We will raise our glasses in honor of my future nuptials."

Without waiting for Darach to respond, he rose from his chair, moved to the sideboard, uncorked a crystal decanter, and poured two glasses of whisky. He handed one to Darach.

Darach did not make eye contact as he accepted it.

In a leisurely manner, Chatham moved behind the desk again and held up his glass. "To my beautiful bride, Larena Campbell."

Rising to his feet, Darach raised his glass as well. "To the bride." He downed the entire contents in one gulp and set the glass down on the desk.

They both remained on their feet, staring at each other intensely.

Within seconds, a burning sensation erupted in Darach's gut as he imagined this man at the altar with Larena, taking her into his arms, pressing his mouth to hers. He had to bite back the urge to release a bellowing war cry and leap over the desk to strangle Larena's fiancé until he was dead.

"There's something familiar about you," Chatham casually mentioned. "Have we met before?"

Damn...

"Have you ever visited Kinloch?" Darach replied.

"I cannot say that I have had the pleasure."

Chatham's polite English manners made Darach want to spit. He shook his head. "Then we haven't met."

The silence in the room grew dangerously conspicuous until the sound of the clock ticking on the mantle drew Darach's attention.

It was the same clock his father had owned. Darach would know the sound of it anywhere, for it represented every moment of dread he'd ever felt as a lad while awaiting his father's discipline. Always in this room.

A knock sounded at the door just then and wrenched him from thoughts of the past.

"Come in," Chatham answered.

The door opened and Chatham's expression softened. He blinked a few times and his cheeks flushed red. "Larena..."

At the sound of her name, Darach turned and was instantly struck by the sight of her unfathomable beauty. Since they'd parted in the bailey earlier, she had bathed, swept her golden hair into a tidy braided knot, and donned a blue silk dinner gown with jewels. He couldn't seem to think or breathe, and bloody hell...he wanted her. He wanted to take her away from here, unlace that gown, toss it to the ground, and sink himself into her depths.

Chatham practically stumbled out from behind the desk to greet her, while Darach could do nothing but stand and watch their reunion play out.

Chatham shouldered his way by. "My dear, how long has it been? Seeing you again after all these years leaves me speechless. You are ten times more beautiful than I remember." He reached for her hand and kissed the back of it.

Darach fought to keep his breathing in check when what he really wanted to do was grab Chatham by the throat and squeeze with all his might.

"It's been a long time," Larena replied. "Ten years, I believe."

Chatham smiled at her. "Indeed. I was sixteen when I left Leatham. I am six-and-twenty now. You must be...?"

"One-and-twenty," she replied, sliding her hand from his and letting it fall to her side. "I was eleven when you left."

"Ah yes," Chatham said, stepping back and laying a hand over his heart. "It does me good to see you. I cannot tell you how pleased I was to hear that we could come to this arrangement. It was fate, I believe. Perhaps it was even written in the stars."

Darach wanted to puke.

Meanwhile, Larena looked down at the floor.

An awkward silence ensued.

Chatham glanced at the clock. "But you've come early my dear," he said. "I wasn't expecting you until nine. I apologize..." He gestured toward Darach, as if he were a stain on the room that had not yet been scrubbed clean.

"I was impatient to see you," Larena replied.

Impatient to meet her betrothed? Darach's stomach clenched tight with jealous fury. *God's blood, this was hell.*

"I haven't seen my father yet," Larena quickly added. "I was hoping there would be an opportunity for me to visit him before dinner."

Ah. She wanted to see her father. Of course she did.

Darach glanced at Chatham to observe his reaction.

"Oh, my dearest one," Chatham replied. "How thoughtless of me. I will see to it immediately and have you escorted to his cell. Dinner can wait."

"Thank you." She turned to Darach. "Hello, Darach. I hope you are being treated well. I owe you a great debt, after all."

He decided to be blunt. "I can't say I've been enjoying my incarceration. The dungeon here stinks of rats, but at least I was offered a drink just now."

Larena's lips tightened into a hard line. "I'm sure Colonel Chatham will do his best to make it up to you, since I would not be here if it weren't for you."

"That goes without saying," Chatham gallantly offered. "I will see to it personally that this man is given a hot meal and a place to sleep in the barracks if he wishes to remain until morning."

"I'd prefer to be on my way tonight," Darach replied.

"Tonight?" Larena said too quickly. Then she cleared her throat and calmed her voice. "What about your weapons and your horse?"

"His horse was recovered about an hour ago and was taken to the stables," Chatham informed her. "I don't know about the weapons. I will speak to Lieutenant Johnson about that."

Larena kept her eyes fixed on Darach's. Another awkward moment of silence ensued until Chatham strode to the door and spoke to the soldiers outside. "You there. Take Miss Campbell to the prison to see her father. Remain there until she is ready to return here for supper. And you, take the Highlander to the stables and make sure he has everything he needs so that he can leave here tonight."

"Yes, sir," they both responded at the same time.

"Thank you, Gregory," Larena said. She made a move to leave the room, but stopped and returned to where Darach stood in front of the desk. She held out her hand. "Good-bye and good luck to you, sir."

With a mix of desire and fury, he took hold of her hand, raised it to his lips and kissed it. "Good luck to you, too, Miss Campbell."

She quickly turned and walked out.

Two seconds later, a soldier grabbed Darach roughly by the arm and shoved him out the door in the opposite direction.

⚜

As soon as the heavy cell door swung open, Larena dashed into her father's arms and buried her face in his bushy red beard. He immediately picked her up, swung her around, and squeezed her tightly as she wept tears of joy.

"Oh, Father." She stepped back to look up at him, barely noticing when the door swung shut behind her. "I'm so happy to see you. I was afraid I wouldn't make it home in time."

But, dear Lord, he looked so thin. It had been only just over a week. Were they starving him?

"To save me from the executioner?" he asked. "*Bah!* You shouldn't be concerning yourself with such things, my sweet lassie. You know me. I never go down without a fight."

She laughed tearfully at his words, for it was a phrase he'd often thrown about during her childhood. Whenever they played any sort of game and he let her win, that is exactly what he would say to her.

"I was worried about you, lass," he said in his deep, boisterous timbre. "They told me you disappeared after I was taken away. No one knew where you went. I imagined the worst."

"I'm so sorry I couldn't tell you, but I was afraid they would lock me up if they found me, just for being your daughter. I rode out as soon as they announced your sentence."

"They tell me you made a deal with Lord Rutherford at Fort William," he replied. "That you agreed to marry Colonel Chatham to save my life. I didn't believe it at first, but they assure me it's true. Is it?"

"Aye," she replied. "It was the only way I could save you—the only way I knew how. There was so little time. All I could do was say yes when Rutherford suggested it. It seemed like a good idea at the time."

Her father laid a hand on her cheek. "But my darling girl, it's a price you will pay for the rest of your life. Are you sure it's what you want? Because I would not hold you to it if Chatham is not the sort of man who could make you happy. I would give my own life and hand this castle over to the English before I would see you miserable forever."

"But what about the clan?" she asked. "You're their chief."

"*Ach*, they'd find another chief to replace me in a heartbeat. The Campbells aren't a dying breed."

Larena's heart sank at the possibility that there might have been other options—for a marriage to Gregory Chatham had suddenly become a far higher price to pay than she'd initially imagined.

But still, if it meant that her father could live....

"I gave him my word," she said, "and because of that, you will not be taken away from me. I cannot change my mind now. I won't, not if it means I will lose you."

He regarded her with sympathy. "I'm not afraid of death, lass."

"Perhaps *you're* not," she argued, "but I am terrified of losing you. I couldn't possibly live without you."

He pulled her into his arms again. "One day, you will have to, lass. It's the way of the world. All children must eventually let go of their parents and live their own lives."

She buried her face in his chest and squeezed her eyes shut. "Not yet. I'm not ready."

He held her a moment longer, then stepped back. "Wipe away your tears now. You must be strong for yourself and for the good of the clan. If you do not wish to marry the colonel, you must tell him so. I won't be angry if you break your vow to him and destroy the King's pardon, for I knew what I was risking when I took up the sword for the Jacobite cause. You should not have to pay for my choices."

"But why, Father?" she asked at last. It was a question that had been burning in her mind ever since the English army broke through the gates. "Our clan has always sided with the Hanovers. What changed your mind? What made you turn your allegiance toward the Stuarts?"

"Nothing changed my mind, lass. I've *always* believed in the true Scottish king. I just never revealed my opinions to anyone. But when I became chief and had the power to change people's minds, I did what I could."

"So you truly are guilty then," she said. "Guilty of being a Jacobite?"

"Aye, and I have confessed it."

She turned away and strode to the opposite wall. "Then I must marry Chatham. If it means they will spare your life." She faced him again. "It won't be so bad. I met him tonight and he is handsome, at least. And I remember him from my childhood. He taught me to read and gave me books—books that I still own. You mustn't fret, Father. He is half Campbell by blood and I have every reason to believe the marriage will be a success and the saving grace for our clan."

"Only if you're certain, lass."

"Of course I am certain." She stepped forward to wrap her arms around his waist. Larena squeezed her eyes shut, for it was the first time she'd ever lied to her father.

She tried to focus on the fact that Darach would be gone that night and she would never see him again. She would do what she must to push him from her mind completely and accept her future as it was.

But when the guard escorted her out of the cell and locked her father in…. When it was time to return up the tower stairs to meet Chatham for dinner….

Oh God, Larena felt as if a hand were closing around her throat. Her heart began to race uncontrollably and she felt sick to her stomach.

Darach would leave tonight. He had told her so. She had said good-bye to him in the tower and he had kissed her hand and wished her luck.

But she had not said good-bye to him the way she'd wanted to, one last time. Could she live with that? Or would it haunt her forever?

When they reached the top of the stairs, Larena stopped and faced the soldier. "Please tell Colonel Chatham that I will dine with him shortly."

"Where are you off to, Miss Campbell?" he asked with a slight frown.

"I must return to my chamber. I need to…." She paused. "I must take care of a personal matter."

"I will escort you," he helpfully replied, starting off toward the door to the southern tower where her rooms were located.

Rather than argue, she allowed him to walk with her, while gazing surreptitiously toward the stables where Darach must surely be, preparing to leave the castle.

Do not be foolish, Larena. You must be strong and let him go. Your father's life depends on it.

But as she entered the South Tower and became lost in the memory of Darach's hands on her body, his lips touching hers, and the intoxicating sounds of his voice in her ear, she was overcome by a mad desire that threatened to destroy any shred of discipline that remained in her heart.

It wasn't over. It couldn't be. She wasn't ready.

Larena spoke firmly to the soldier as she entered her room and paused at the door. "There is no need for you to wait for me. I might be a while. I've decided I want to change my gown and probably my hair as well." She looked down at herself. "This is all wrong. I don't feel right in this rag. I may want to change my jewels, too," she added for good measure.

"But miss…" he said with dismay, "I think you look lovely just as you are. Prettier than a picture."

"Thank you." She pasted on a smile. "But truly…you mustn't let me hold you up. Go and join your friends in the feasting hall. I assure you I can find my way to the colonel's chambers at nine without any trouble at all. I know my way around this castle better than you do. Every nook and cranny."

"I'd prefer to wait here," he said uneasily. "This castle is a garrison now, miss, and you don't know what soldiers can be like after a few cups of rum in their bellies. And I have my orders from the colonel. No need to hurry. I've got nothing better to do this evening than make sure you're delivered safely to dinner and back to your chambers again afterward."

Larena sighed irritably, for this was taking far too long.

"Fine." Without another word, she shut the door, locked it and rushed to the window to look out onto the bailey below, hoping to catch a glimpse of Darach on his way to or from the stables. If she saw him, she would simply tell Lieutenant

Roberts the truth—that she needed to say good-bye to Darach one last time.

For a long, anxiety-ridden moment, she watched the activity outside her window. It was fairly quiet. There were only a few soldiers milling about in the darkness, chatting idly with each other, sitting about in small groups sipping ale in the torchlight. She cupped her hands to the glass, hoping to see inside the stable, but it was no use. The stable doors were closed.

"What are you searching for, lass?" a deep voice whispered in her ear. She whirled about in surprise.

"Darach!"

There he was, like a mysterious archangel warrior in the candlelight, standing before her, his hands sliding onto the curve of her hips, his mouth brushing over hers in a soft feather-like caress. *Was she dreaming?* She was afraid to believe this was real. Then her body thrilled at his touch and she knew in that moment that he was truly standing before her, embracing her.

"What are you doing here?" she asked, keeping her voice low, leaning to peer around him and ensure the door was closed.

It was closed, but was it locked?

Yes…yes it was.

"I couldn't leave without keeping my promise to you," he whispered in reply. "I wanted to, but I couldn't."

"What promise?"

"Surely you know…."

"One last kiss?"

"Aye."

With that, he bent his head and pressed his mouth to hers in a soul-reaching kiss that aroused her fiery passions. It caused her to overlook the fact that everything in her life was imperfect compared to this single scorching kiss. She felt as if she were floating in another time and place where everything was as she wished it to be. That her father was safe and warm in his bed, and Darach was the only man who could ever claim her as his own. How she wished it were so.

He bent at the knees and thrust his massive body up against hers, stepping forward to drag her sideways and crowd her up against the wall beside the window, out of sight of any onlookers from the bailey below.

Her whole body melted as his tongue swept into her mouth and he nipped at her lower lip, sucked at the sensitive flesh and ate at her mouth like a starving man.

She opened to him willingly, wanting him with every measure of her being, clutching at his broad, muscular shoulders, and tugging at the tartan draped across his back.

His hand cupped the side of her head and his thumb toyed with the delicate flesh at her ear. Tingles of pleasure coursed down the length of her body as she devoured him at the mouth, but it was not enough. Not nearly enough. She wanted so much more.

Pressing his forehead against hers and breaking the kiss, he laced his fingers through hers at their sides. "I don't want to leave you," he said. "I cannot bear the thought of another man's hands on you when you belong to me, lass. I must have you."

"I cannot bear it either," she replied, kissing him again, lifting her hands up to run her fingers through his wavy, dark hair. She gazed into his eyes with pleading. "I can't stop thinking about you and wanting you. It's like some kind of fever that won't break. Seeing you in the tower room was torture. I thought I would die when I had to pretend as if you were nothing to me, because you are everything."

"Ah, lassie…." His hips ground against hers and he laid hungry, wet kisses across her cheek, down the sensitive length of her neck, and the top of her shoulder. He sucked fiercely at her flesh and drove her mad with hot waves of yearning.

Closing her eyes, she threw her head back as he dropped to his knees before her and slid his hands up under her skirts.

"You're the most beautiful woman I've ever known," he said. "I want to touch you and kiss you everywhere."

Heaven help her. Her body was on fire with lust and a complete inability to resist what he offered. His hands were surely enchanted, for she was falling into a deep whirlwind of surrender.

He pressed firm kisses to her breasts and belly, over the surface of her silk and brocade gown, down low, and across her hip bone. All the while, his hands slid expertly up her legs, thumbing her knees and stroking her tender, trembling inner thighs.

Larena couldn't think. All she could do was focus on sensation as he lifted her heavy skirts higher and higher, then whispered huskily, "So beautiful...."

Then he pressed his mouth to the sensitive flesh at her core, where all her desires were centered and burning for his touch.

She felt a tremor of response in every part of her body, inside and out, as the lush heat of his mouth invaded her being and drove her into a wild frenzy of need.

"What are you doing to me?" she asked, fisting bunches of the draperies in her hands to keep from collapsing in a faint—for she wanted to enjoy every minute of this unbelievable ecstasy.

"I promised you one last kiss," he replied in a gruff, ravenous voice. The heat of his breath against her damp curls sent a fresh shiver of lust to her brain and weakened her knees.

"I didn't know kisses like this were possible," she whispered on a sigh of pleasure and disbelief.

He continued to make love to her with his mouth, stroking and probing with his tongue until a sizzle of rapture exploded below and she fought against the urge to cry out. Her stomach muscles clenched and the whole world shook as she fought to control her body's wild carnal response, but it was no use to fight it. She shuddered violently up against the wall.

When the agonizing wave of ecstasy subsided, Darach rose to his full height before her and pulled her into his arms, kissing her deeply on the mouth, spinning her around toward the bed. He walked her there, then eased her down upon it while cupping the back of her head with his big hand, laying her gently onto the pillows. He never took his eyes off hers as he set his weapons aside and climbed over her on all fours.

"I won't leave you," he said. "I don't know what you did to me on the road, lass, but I'm under your spell. I cannot go. Not without you."

"That's not possible," she said, still reeling with pleasure as he lowered his body to hers. "I promised Lord Rutherford. Chatham is expecting me for dinner. There is a guard outside the door."

Darach glanced back at it. "He won't come in. I heard you tell him you were changing your gown."

"You were listening?" she asked breathlessly as he returned his attention to her body and laid tantalizing kisses down the side of her neck.

"Aye—from under the bed."

"But how did you know this was my chamber?" she asked, though it hardly mattered. Nothing mattered but the exquisite sensation of his lips and tongue roving across her flesh.

He was here. There was nothing else she needed to know.

"This room belonged to my brothers once," he explained, lifting his head to look down at her. "The laird's children have always lived in this tower. When I found the books on the bench under the window, I knew this was where you must lay your head at night."

He kissed her again and she pulled him close, wrapped her legs around his hips, and fought hard against all the unwelcome thoughts of her future without him. All she wanted was to be held in Darach's arms forever and pretend this was all there was, all there would ever be.

But it wasn't all, and she knew she had to keep her head.

"Darach," she whispered, pressing her palms against his broad chest and pushing him back slightly. "You know I can't leave with you."

He gazed down at her, then bowed his head.

"If I did that," she continued, "I don't know what Chatham would do. Surely he wouldn't see any point in letting my father live."

Darach's eyes lifted. "I could abduct you so it wouldn't appear to be your fault. I could steal you away tonight. Maybe then they'd keep their promise."

"They'd come after us. Besides, I can't gamble on maybes—not when my father's life is at stake."

Darach rolled off her onto his back, tossed his arm up under his head and stared at the ceiling. "So, you plan to go through with it then. You'll marry Chatham?"

"It's what I agreed to," she explained. "You knew that was my fate—and my choice—all along. It's why you brought me here. I cannot break that oath."

He rose to his feet, stalked across the room, and sat down in the chair before the dying fire. "I agreed to bring you here before I knew what sort of woman you were."

"And what sort is that?" she asked, rising onto her elbows, hoping he would not accuse her of being shallow and loose with her affections.

"The kind of woman that a man like me cannot live without," he replied. "I am in love with you, Larena Campbell. I must take you home with me."

Her eyebrows lifted, for she was flattered that he wanted her so badly. She couldn't deny the joy that engulfed her at the sound of those words on his lips. He was truly in love with her?

But was she in love with him? Or was this only lust? How could she be sure? She desired him. That was obvious. But what did she know of love?

"We barely know each other," she argued. "How can you say something like that after only a week?"

"I've been asking myself that, lass," he replied. "Maybe I'm mad." He pushed himself out of the chair and paced around the room, raking his fingers through his hair. "I must be losing my mind. I shouldn't have come." He glanced toward the door and window as if he were desperate for some means of escape.

Larena swung her legs to the floor and hurried to his side. "No, I am glad that you did. If you hadn't come, I would be searching for you now in the stables or hunting all around the castle until I found you. I had to see you one last time, and you must believe me when I say that I am in hell right now. I don't *want* you to leave. If I could have what I want, I would tell the English army to leave here immediately and never come back.

I would free my father from prison. Then I would do whatever I pleased."

"And what would that be?"

She felt completely lost in the depths of his dark, stormy eyes. "Right now, all I want to do is lie with you here on my bed, feel your arms around me, hold you close, and never let you go." She backed away as a painful shiver coursed through her. "But a guard is standing outside that door and my father might still be executed if I do not keep my oath to Lord Rutherford. If I don't go to Chatham tonight, I might as well sign my father's death warrant. What would you have me do, Darach?"

He regarded her with fierce intensity. "Come away with me."

She angrily shook her head. "How can you suggest that? You are asking me to choose between you and my father."

"Aye," he replied.

Growing angrier still, she turned away and strode to the opposite side of the room. "Maybe it's easier for you. Your father is already dead and you have no family of your own, except for Logan. You abandoned your clan years ago, but I am not built like that. I am loyal to those I love."

"Do not insult me, lass. I am loyal, too," he said, his footfalls slow across the floor as he approached. "And *you* would be my family. I would be loyal to *you*."

She whirled around. "But how could I trust you to remain so? How do I know you wouldn't one day flee my side for some unknown reason and take up with another woman in another clan? Change your name again? You're not even who you pretend to be. You're not a true MacDonald. You're an imposter, lying to everyone who knows you. How can I give up everything I know for a man I know so little about?"

He stared at her long and hard. "I am a true MacDonald, for I have given my oath to Angus and I will never betray that oath. If you don't believe me, then you should go to your fiancé. Walk out of here now and do not look back. I'll be gone by the time you return. You won't ever hear from me again."

Her heart wrenching sorely in her chest, Larena couldn't catch her breath. "Please...I don't want us to part like this."

"What difference does it make how we part? It's a bad ending, no matter how you try to dress it up."

Tears flooded her eyes. "But I don't want there to be bad blood between us. I don't want you to remember our time together with a feeling of ill will. I want to go on dreaming of you, imagining you out there somewhere, thinking of me fondly at least, hoping I am well, as I will always wish the same for you."

The ferocity in his eyes softened and he slowly shook his head. "You're making it worse, lass. Show a man some pity, will you?"

She understood immediately what he was trying to tell her. "You would find it easier to hate me."

"Aye, but I'm not sure that will be possible, because if I think you're dreaming about me or wanting me, I will keep coming back for you. I will return, again and again, over and over, until the day I draw my last breath."

A torrent of desire welled up inside her. She backed away from him, trying to deny it, wishing he wouldn't say such things. "Darach, *please.*"

Despite the words, somehow he read into her soul and recognized the deep chink in her armor. Confidently striding forward, he gathered her into his arms and kissed her hard on the mouth. Her lips parted for him and she fell into the blinding force of his passion. At the same time, she felt as if she were being ripped in two.

Darach swept her up, carried her to the bed, and set her down again. He stood back, massive in the candlelight, looming over her.

"Don't go to him," he commanded. "Stay here with me. All night."

"I can't promise that," she replied.

"Maybe not now," he replied, "but I can change your mind. Do you want me, lass? Do you want to feel my hands on you? My mouth? Will you let me taste you everywhere, touch you and pleasure you for hours on end until you can't even speak? Until you can do nothing but sigh with rapture?"

His provocative words shook her, body and soul, and all at once, the whole world disappeared. Unable to stop herself, she rose up on her knees and kissed him passionately on the mouth, then she sat back on her heels. Her hands moved down to his hips and she stroked his big powerful thighs over the top of his kilt.

The corner of his mouth curled up in a knowing smile of seductive allure, and he spoke in a smooth voice that crushed whatever remained of her resolve.

"Do you want me, lass?" he asked a second time. "Would you like to touch what's under here?" He gestured toward his kilt.

"Aye," she replied, shuddering and quaking in total arousal.

Darach reached down and unbuckled the leather belt at his waist. He tossed it aside, then the plaid came loose and dropped heavily to the floor.

Still standing over her, Darach pulled his loose linen shirt over his head and stood before her, completely nude. She gazed at him in astonishment and he allowed her time to admire the stunning spectacle of his body—the broad muscular chest and shoulders, the impossibly strong arms, and narrow hips below a toned, athletic torso. Lower still, his shaft was thick and firm with passion. It held her attention for a long pulsing moment of trancelike wonder.

He was like some kind of beautiful god standing before her, extraordinary and captivating in every way.

Reaching out again, she ran her fingertips across his chest and over one tight, hard nipple. His stomach muscles twitched and clenched, as if he were struggling to suppress his desires—at least for the time being—while she explored his body with her inquisitive hands.

Lower she went, down to his massive erection, taking him in her hands and stroking the smooth, hot skin…then lower still, where she cupped and stroked his heavy balls. His breathing quickened and she gloried in the obvious power she had over him.

"I want to kiss you everywhere, too," she whispered after a time, bending to take the swollen head of his manhood into her mouth and lick it with her tongue.

She heard him suck in his breath and felt his hand at her cheek, gently touching her face with rough, callused fingertips.

"You're killing me, lass," he said in a low voice that goaded her on.

Too busy to reply, she continued to pleasure him until it seemed too much for him to take. Darach forcefully pulled her up by the shoulder, kissed her on the mouth, then came down on top of her on the bed with reckless resolve.

The weight of his naked body pressed hotly to hers made Larena feel positively feral. She wiggled her hips and tugged at her skirts to shove everything out of the way.

With trembling fingers, she unlaced the front of her bodice. Seconds later, it landed on the floor. Darach wrenched her skirts down over her hips and she pulled her chemise over her head. It all happened very quickly. Suddenly she was naked and sinfully aroused by the touch of the cool night air on her skin.

He came down upon her then, holding her close while he kissed her mouth and neck and shoulders and drove her wild with yearning. His manhood rubbed and stroked against her and she softened for him, parted her legs wider, and welcomed him with her own primal thrusts and urges.

"You're wet, lass," he whispered in her ear. "Your body's ready for me. Tell me you want me, because I want nothing more than to be inside you."

"I want you. *Please, Darach.* Make love to me. I'm yours. I'll do anything you want."

He plunged into her a few rapid heartbeats later with a driving force that stopped her breath. He pushed deep, all the way to the hilt, arching his back and pressing his groin into hers. A searing pain overwhelmed her senses, but with an astounding level of desire, she wanted more of it. She squeezed at his firm, muscular buttocks, pulling him even deeper into her body.

When he pushed in as far as he could go, they both lay still, pausing, as if to comprehend the situation and find their bearings. Larena said nothing. She merely squeezed her eyes shut and felt a tear spill across her cheek, for the pain was intense.

"I know it hurts," he whispered.

But she wasn't sorry, for she didn't care about that. All that mattered was that she'd given herself to him completely, body and soul—*forever*—and she'd never felt more loved and protected.

Her thoughts and hopes flitted to possible ways for them to be together, while she squeezed her arms tightly about his shoulders and buried her face in the warmth of his neck.

After giving her a moment to become accustomed to his size, Darach slowly began to move, gently at first, gliding in and out of her on a slick, sultry wave of eroticism. Her body seemed to melt around him as he drove in deep, all the way to the entrance of her womb and back again.

She wanted to cry out, but was afraid he might stop when she didn't want him to. This was all so overpowering, so achingly beautiful.

Before long, orgasmic sensation rushed to all her nerve endings and she felt as if she were drowning in waves of rapture. Her body quaked and shuddered—for the second time that night. She dug her nails into Darach's back as a fierce climax trembled through her body, then she went weak with gratification, her body drained of energy and the ability to think or entertain any form of logic.

She opened her eyes to look up at Darach, who continued to work in and out of her in a loving embrace.

He smiled at her then and kissed her tenderly on the mouth. It filled her with such joy, she could have wept.

She reached up and held his face between her palms. For a long moment she watched him—so magnificent in the flickering candlelight—until he squeezed his eyes shut and his slick, muscled body bucked like an animal. His erection convulsed and throbbed within her. Then he threw his head back and she felt the hot gush of his seed shoot into her and drench her in his passion.

"Ah, my sweet lassie," he whispered tenderly as he collapsed his full weight upon her and held her close. She felt as if she were floating in a dream.

⚜

Darach had bedded many women in his life, and he'd always enjoyed their pleasures as much as his own, but he'd never wanted a woman as badly as he'd wanted Larena that night. It was a need that went beyond mere physical desire. Making love to her had become a matter of supreme importance, not just to slake his lust, but to claim her as his own and ensure that she belonged to him and no other.

Now, as he lay with her on the soft bed, their hot sticky bodies entwined in a hazy erotic stupor, he had no regrets about taking her virginity. If anything, he was grateful that she'd been brought into his life at a time when Darach was beginning to think there would never be anything left in the world to stir his soul. Nothing to live for outside of endless, recurring scouting missions around the Kinloch perimeter and the continued struggle to bury a shameful secret that would plague him until his dying day.

Until now, no one other than his brother had known the truth and he'd wanted it that way. He'd always believed it was safest, but confessing the truth to Larena had been a release of some sort.

Everything about her felt like home—though it had nothing to do with the stones in these castle walls or the people of the Campbell clan he'd left behind. It was just her alone, and the effect she had on his tainted soul. She had learned the truth about his past and had accepted him apart from it.

Darach wasn't certain what would happen after this—where they would go, how they would live—but he knew it was right and proper, and that he had been meant to find this woman and rescue her that day in the forest. As she had rescued him.

That morning, he had dreamed he was a hawk, flying home to Leathan, and here he was, feeling a connection to another living person that he'd never felt before—not even with his brother. He couldn't explain it. He only knew that it was as real as the scarred flesh on his bones.

He lifted his head to look down at Larena, wondering if she might have fallen asleep, praying he hadn't crushed her with his weight when he'd relaxed on her just then.

Her eyes were closed, but she opened them and smiled up at him sleepily. She was so lovely in the candlelight, he couldn't bear it. It hurt just to look at her.

"I'm still inside you," he whispered, "and I don't want to go anywhere."

"It feels nice," she replied.

"You must be a bit sore?" he asked.

"Aye, but it's oddly exciting."

Chuckling softly and feeling a renewal of his lusty appetites, he laid soft kisses on her cheeks, her nose, and eyelids. "You're the most beautiful woman I've ever known," he whispered. "I'm beginning to wonder if I died and went to heaven. Maybe you *did* kill me with that rock when you tried to bash my head in."

A loud, purposeful knock rapped at the door just then, and Larena's body went rigid beneath him.

"Miss Campbell?" Lieutenant Roberts shouted from the corridor. "It's nearly ten and the colonel is growing a bit concerned. Are you all right in there?"

Darach raised a finger to his lips and calmly whispered, "Tell him you fell asleep."

"I fell asleep," she quickly answered, turning her head toward the door with a look of panic.

Roberts paused. "What should I tell the colonel? Will you still be joining him for dinner?"

Darach looked down at Larena, waiting to hear what she might say.

He was not at all pleased when she pushed at his chest, rolled him off her and quickly scrambled off the bed to her feet.

"I'll be right there!" she called out to the guard. "I just need a moment to freshen up."

Darach sat up and frowned. "Freshen up? You're *going*? After what we just did, you're still going to meet him?"

She grabbed her chemise and gown from the floor and hastened toward the dressing room. "I have to, or my father will die."

Darach listened to the sound of rustling fabrics and water splashing while she remained out of sight.

Eventually, he rose from the bed, picked his shirt up off the floor and pulled it on. He donned his kilt next, buckled his belt, and was sitting on the chair, pulling on his boots, when Larena finally emerged wearing a different colored gown.

She smelled of rosewater—an attempt to mask the fragrance of their lovemaking no doubt. He felt a severe jolt of irritation.

"I thought you'd changed your mind about Chatham," Darach said in a low voice. "Otherwise I wouldn't have...."

He stopped himself, however, because his next few words would have been a lie. He couldn't have resisted making love to Larena, no matter the circumstances. Not when she'd been so willing and open to him.

She shook her head with frantic eyes. "What have we done, Darach?"

He frowned. "What do you mean?"

"I can't simply run away with you and leave my father behind. I can't break my word to Rutherford."

"But what we just did…." He pointed toward the bed.

"I know." She covered her face with her hands. "I don't know what I was thinking. I wanted you so badly. You made me forget."

"Forget about *what*?"

She lowered her hands and met his eyes again. "Everything. Oh God, I must have been out of my mind."

His body stiffened at the insult. "Aye, you must have been, lass. I think you're out of your mind now, too, for you cannot go to Chatham or any other man. You belong to me now."

"I belong to no one," she insisted with a dark and willful glare. "At least, not yet."

"Then what did we do just now?" he asked, feeling confused and infuriated. "What was all that if you intended to marry another? Why did you say the things you did? Touch me the way you did?"

"It was…." Appearing lost for words, she dropped her gaze to the floor.

Darach waited impatiently for her to answer the question.

At long last, her eyes lifted. She strode closer and laid her palm on his cheek. "It was lovely, Darach, and I'll never forget it, or you, but now you have to go. If Chatham finds out—"

"I don't care what he knows," Darach barked as his ire escalated and he had to fight the urge to storm out of there and settle things with Chatham himself.

"Please," she begged, backing away slightly, "don't do anything that will spoil what I was able to achieve for my clan. I must keep my word to Rutherford."

"What about your word to *me*?" he asked, grabbing hold of her arm. "You made promises just now—with your body and with your heart. Don't deny it, lass. You care for me. Tell the truth."

She tried to shake him away. "I do care for you, but I never promised you anything. I couldn't, for I'm already betrothed to Chatham. I'm *his*."

God's blood, she might as well have pierced his heart with ten blades.

With sickening anguish, Darach let go of her and stepped back. "If that's what you want, I'll go."

Tears welled up in her eyes. "Please Darach. This isn't what I want. You have to believe that."

"I don't need to hear your apologies. You've already said more than enough."

A mix of agony and antagonism sizzled in the air between them until she pointed at the bed and spoke ruefully.

"It kills me to ask this, but could you hide back under there, so that I can open the door?"

His eyes narrowed with bitter, pungent loathing. "I'll not crawl under your bed and hide like a frightened mouse."

"You did it before."

"That was different."

She waited for him to at least move behind the door where he would not be seen, then she opened it. Light from the torches in the corridor illuminated her face. She smiled brightly at the guard outside and said, "I am ready now." Then she walked out and shut the door behind her.

With his blood burning hot as it pulsed through his veins, Darach waited a few seconds until the sound of footsteps disappeared down the tower steps. Then he turned, squeezed his eyes shut and tapped his forehead against the wall a few times, praying for self-restraint.

He'd never known himself to be a wild-tempered man. He had never felt anything to stir such intense feelings of rage before—except maybe when Logan was attempting to ravish Larena in the woods. Either way, she was the cause of it, and there seemed to be no cure. All he could think of was Larena doing what she must tonight to charm Colonel Chatham, to make sure he kept his promise to her. She might even offer additional temptations in exchange for more comfortable lodgings for her father, something preferable to the cold dungeon with the rats. She would smile at Chatham and allow him to kiss her hand, hold her in his arms, perhaps take liberties a fiancé might expect to enjoy with a woman he considered to be his property. A woman who owed him things.

Eyes blazing, his breathing ragged, Darach glanced sharply around the room.

How could she have done this to him? Led him on when she fully intended to go through with her marriage to another?

Darach's blood exploded with ferocity. What did he have to offer her after all, but a drifter's life with no true home? It would be day after day spent living in the saddle—or at best, in a small croft somewhere in the farthest reaches of the Highlands, where they would be forced to hide away like fugitives for the rest of their days? Love would never be enough. At least not for her, for she had proven that tonight.

Darach's vision blurred into a sea of red, and he moved to gather up his weapons. He shoved his pistol into his belt and sheathed his sword. Then he whipped the door open, strode out into the corridor, and looked left and right, daring any man, armed or otherwise, to get in his way.

The next thing he knew, he was gathering provisions for the journey. A short while later, he mounted his horse in the stable and trotted across the bailey quickly. The fact that he had to pause at the gate and wait for the guard to raise the portcullis only fueled the fires of his discontent.

Glancing over his shoulder at the light in Chatham's window at the top of the East Tower, he imagined Larena doing what she must to ensure her father's survival.

Darach's gut churned with white-hot jealousy, and he seriously considered storming up there and choking Chatham to death.

When the portcullis finally rose up on the rattle of chains through giant winches, Darach forced himself to kick in his heels and gallop across the bridge without looking back. His duty to his chief and to Larena Campbell was done. Her future and the politics at Leatham Castle were not his problem.

It was time to return home and push her from his mind forever, no matter how hard it would be to do so.

L arena had done the correct thing in sending him away. It
must have been the correct thing because clearly she had
no will left in her heart to resist him.

God in Heaven, she had let him make love to her. How
could she have surrendered to him like that? So completely and
without hesitation or a single thought about her future and the
commitments she'd made?

Yes, oh yes, she was right to send him away, and she must
continue to convince herself of that. Perhaps eventually, her
heart would believe it as well and the agony would recede,
because heaven help her, she still desired him and couldn't bear
to think that she would never see him again.

But despite all her practical, mindful deliberations as she
walked with Lieutenant Roberts through the castle corridors
to meet Gregory Chatham, she had to fight against the urge
to turn around and run straight back to her bedchamber. At
the very least, she wanted to apologize for the things she had
said—because the memory of the hurt she'd seen in Darach's
eyes seemed a punishment worse than death.

She had once believed that nothing could be worse than the
loss of her father, but the despair she felt now over the loss of
Darach matched it equally. Her heart was grieving, as if Darach
had been murdered before her very eyes—and *she* had been the
one to wield the weapon. How would she ever carry on through

dinner and hide her sorrows from Gregory, the man she was betrothed to marry?

Everything felt very wrong suddenly. She supposed it had felt wrong for quite some time, but even tonight, after she had chosen to give herself to Darach, she had somehow been able to deny what she truly wanted.

They reached the top of the stairs and Lieutenant Roberts knocked on the door. Gregory called out from within, "Enter."

The door opened and Larena walked in to find him sitting in one of the upholstered chairs before the fire. He wore his elegant scarlet officer's uniform with ivory breeches and held a glass of red wine in his hand.

He rose immediately upon her arrival and bowed slightly at the waist. "At last."

She was vaguely aware of Roberts backing out and closing the door behind him. There could be no turning back now. She had come to her fiancé this evening and they would dine together, discuss the future, and make plans.

Her weary gaze slid to the candlelit table beneath the window. It was adorned with a white cloth, a vase full of colorful, freshly cut flowers, and the fine gold-trimmed china that had once belonged to her father.

Her father, who was lying in a prison cell at this very moment.

She felt like a prisoner, too.

"I apologize for my tardiness," she said, striving to put on a brave face and get through this night.

"No apologies are necessary." Gregory strode to the table and poured her a glass of wine. "You've had an exhausting day and you've been through a terrible ordeal. I am sorry for everything, Larena. Truly I am."

"Sorry?"

"Yes." He faced her. "I am sorry that you had to witness your father's arrest and face the idea of his execution." He strode toward her, holding out the wine. "I am sorry that you had to ride halfway across Scotland to plead for his life. I am also sorry that you were attacked by rebels upon your return. I wish I could have spared you all of that."

She forced herself to meet Gregory's eyes as she accepted the wine from him. "Thank you, but it's in the past now."

"Indeed," he replied, looking decidedly pleased, "and we must look to the future. Please, come and sit with me by the fire."

Still troubled by the events of the evening and the persevering memory of Darach standing nude over her bed with desire in his eyes, she took a deep swig of the wine and sat down.

"We have a few minutes before supper arrives," Gregory mentioned, "and I am glad. I wanted a chance to tell you how pleased I am that we could come to this arrangement. If you only knew how often I have thought of you—always with the utmost affection—since we parted all those years ago. I have many fond memories of our friendship."

"As do I," she dutifully replied.

"Really?" He sat forward, conspicuously hopeful. "You were so young. What do you even remember of me?"

"I remember that you encouraged me to read," she told him. "I still have the books you gave me."

He sat back, appearing both surprised and delighted. "Which ones?"

"You gave me a book on English manners," she explained, "and a child's book of fables. The last book you gave to me before you left was the tragedy of *Romeo and Juliet*."

The corner of his mouth turned up in a smile. "Ah. Perhaps I fancied myself Romeo and that you were my Juliet."

She took another sip of wine. "Good gracious, I hope not. That play doesn't end well for either of the young lovers."

"No, it does not." He set his glass down on the table beside him and rested his temple on his forefinger. "I was young I suppose, and at the time, I believed it was the end for us. I never would have believed I would see you again, Larena, especially under circumstances such as these. But here we are."

Larena lowered her gaze to her lap. She knew not what to say, for she had been with another man a mere hour ago. She had given herself to him completely and could not purge him from her thoughts.

Everything about this moment in Gregory Chatham's presence felt disastrous. She was both ashamed and devastated by the direction her life had suddenly taken. What was she to do?

"Would you like to know what I remember most about you?" Gregory asked, tapping a finger on the armrest.

Larena looked up, waiting quietly for him to continue.

"I was twelve or thirteen years old," he began, "and you couldn't have been more than nine or ten. I had been backed into a corner of the library by a pack of Campbell ruffians. The lads had taken my book and were ripping the pages out of it, calling me all sorts of names I don't care to repeat. Then you showed up with your bow and arrow, smaller than any of them, and threatened to shoot the leader, straight through the heart."

"Did I? Goodness…Yes, I do remember that now. I didn't actually shoot anyone, did I?"

"No," he said with a laugh. "But you were quite fierce and they all ran out and didn't bother me again. At least not for a long while, anyway." He leaned forward and regarded her with narrowed eyes. "You'd forgotten about that?"

"Yes," she replied with a small smirk at her girlhood mischiefs.

A muscle flicked at his jaw. "Well, I suppose I should consider that a blessing, because it's not how I want you to remember me, Larena, or how I wish you to see me now."

She stared at him, confused. "How do you mean?"

He stood and went to pour himself more wine from the decanter on the table. "I am no longer that timid boy, Larena. I know how to handle my enemies now. Though I was sorry to leave this place years ago, I am grateful that my English father came to collect me. He was very effective, you see, at toughening me up and instructing me in the arts of war. I came back here hoping to meet those bullies again on equal footing, but I was sorry to learn that most of them perished at the Battle of Sheriffmuir, years ago."

Gregory returned to stand over her, slowly raised the glass to his lips, and regarded her over the rim as he sipped it.

Something about the way he looked at her caused a chill to skirt up her spine.

A knock sounded at the door just then.

"Wonderful," Gregory said. "Supper has arrived." He offered his hand to help her rise. She went with him to the table where they sat down and waited for the clanswomen to serve up their dinners.

"That will be all," Gregory said when they were done.

After they were gone, Larena picked up her fork and made a valiant attempt to eat something, despite the fact that she possessed no appetite. How could she possibly think of food when she had been made love to that very night? Yet she had banished her lover forever, and was now dining with another who expected to become her husband.

"You look tired my dear," he said, aggressively slicing his meat. "I cannot imagine you had an easy time of it, traveling all the way from Kinloch with that MacDonald man. I am most concerned about it."

"Why?"

His eyes lifted. "Because I saw the way he looked at you when you walked through this door today. There was something rather sinister in his eyes. He didn't touch you did he?"

"Of course not," she quickly answered. "He seemed very intent upon doing his duty for his laird. That was all."

"*Hmm.* But you would tell me, wouldn't you? If he tried to disgrace you in any way? Because if anything made you the least bit uncomfortable or fearful for your safety or virtue, I would see to it that he was properly punished."

Larena set down her fork. "He was a perfect gentleman and I owe him everything. As do you, Gregory."

Gregory studied her eyes for a tension-filled moment. "Of course. He is gone now, I presume?"

She feigned indifference. "I have no idea. Though I suspect so. Did he not say he wished to leave tonight? I thought that's what I heard."

"*Mmm.*" Gregory slid a forkful of beef into his mouth and chewed vigorously. "There was something familiar about him, though. It put me on edge. I am still trying to figure out what it was."

Larena's heart began to beat faster. She forced herself to speak in a light and casual tone. "He wasn't familiar to me at all."

"No?" Gregory looked up with a hint of mistrust. "But you would tell me if there was anything I should know about him."

"Of course." She smiled and worked diligently to help the smile reach her eyes.

Noticing that her wineglass was empty, Gregory reached for the decanter and refilled her cup. "About your father," he said as the dark wine gushed into the glass. "Did you have a pleasant visit with him?"

"As pleasant as can be expected when father and daughter are reunited in a prison cell."

Gregory set the decanter down again. "Naturally, I understand how you must feel, but I am afraid there is not much to be done about that. He is a traitor to King George and the law is the law."

Finding it difficult to continue her meal, she discreetly pushed her food around on her plate. "I was hoping to speak to you about that, actually. I was wondering if it might be possible to move my father to a more comfortable location for the long term. I understand that he cannot have his freedom, but since he will eventually be your father-in-law, perhaps he could be placed in the South Tower, in a room with a window. Perhaps even with a view of the loch."

Gregory stared at her for a long moment, then he set down his utensils and sat back in the chair. "You must have misunderstood my father's terms," he said with a note of regret. "Surely you realize that it was an enormous concession for your father to be spared the noose at all, considering what he attempted to do. You must content yourself with the arrangements that have already been made, Larena. He will be sent to the Tolbooth at the end of the month."

A scorching heat exploded in her belly. "*The Tolbooth!*"

She knew what sorts of inhumanities occurred in that notorious stone edifice. Prisoners were tortured and starved and displayed callously outside the prison walls in iron collars.

"Please, Gregory, surely you could intervene on his behalf. If you become laird here…." She paused, cleared her throat, and began again. "*When* you become laird, you will be my father's keeper. His jailor, so to speak. Will that not suffice to ensure that no further uprisings ever occur at Leathan again?"

"But he attempted to incite a rebellion," Gregory argued. "The fact that he will be allowed to live at all means he is getting off lightly." His eyebrows pulled together in a frown. "Besides, what sort of example would it set for the people of Scotland if your father was permitted to live a life of luxury in his own home, simply because his daughter married an English colonel? We cannot be perceived to show favoritism. I daresay it would cause tremendous discontentment."

Anxiety rose up inside Larena, but she swallowed hard to keep her emotions in check. "But he will be grandfather to your children."

Gregory slowly nodded. "I realize that, and it is unfortunate, I agree. But have no doubt, our children will be raised as loyal subjects to King George. You and I will be Laird and Lady of Leathan Castle. I cannot risk having your father plant seeds of rebellion in anyone's mind."

"He wouldn't."

"I don't think you are in a position to know what he might or might not do. You were kept in the dark about his Jacobite activities, were you not?"

"He was trying to protect me."

"And thank God for that," Gregory replied, picking up his glass and taking a drink.

Larena bit back the urge to argue further, for she suspected it might do more harm than good and cause Gregory to distrust her. She could not afford to let that happen. Not when she was already at his mercy in so many ways.

She thought of Darach in that moment and felt an excruciating stab of regret over her impetuous decision to send him away. Why had she acted so hastily?

Of course, she knew why—because she had allowed him to make love to her. She had not been able to resist him, which had made her feel powerless and out of control.

And he had made her want to break an important oath.

"I suppose I do see your point," she said to Gregory, working hard to conceal her true thoughts and feelings. "Let us say no more about it." She picked up her wine glass as well. "May I ask if you have given any thought to a wedding date?"

She needed to know all of his intentions. Every last one of them.

"As soon as a proper ceremony can be arranged," he replied, "if that meets with your approval." He reached across the table and covered her hand with his own. "I cannot tell you how eager I am to make you my wife. If you must know the truth, it's why I requested this Scottish commission in the first place, in the hopes that our paths would cross. Speaking of planting seeds, I did suggest an arrangement like this to my father more than a year ago. So when you arrived at Fort William, pleading for your father's life, he must have thought it was fate. What a wonderful blessing that turned out to be."

The effect of his words was shattering to her soul. She could not imagine how any man who claimed to care for her could be so pleased that she had been forced to flee her home and plead for her father's life—as if his imminent death was somehow a stroke of good luck.

"That is very romantic," she said, masking her revulsion. "May I ask another question?"

"Of course, my darling."

"Once we are married, how long will the English soldiers remain here?"

"I cannot say for sure," he replied, sliding his hand from hers and returning to his meal, "though I predict they will remain for as long as there are rebels in Scotland determined to fight for the Stuart pretender."

"But that could go on forever," she mentioned, "for men are always at odds when it comes to politics and crowns."

Gregory wagged his knife at her from across the table. "That is true. Which is why I have made it my purpose in the Highlands to do whatever I must to maintain peace and encourage loyalty to our one true King. I must ensure that there is no threat to the Hanover succession. We must continue to punish those who promote traitorous ideas."

"Like my father," she said, slicing into her meat rather violently.

"Yes, like your father," he replied. "I am glad you understand my position, Larena, and that you do not share his opinions."

"I was raised to support the Hanover succession," she told him flatly, which was mostly true. "But I also understand that the clan has become divided in that regard."

She wanted only to know how Gregory intended to govern over that particular issue.

"Only since your father took over as chief," he agreed. "But I've been asking questions since I arrived, and I have come to the conclusion that most members of this clan never supported your father's ideas. And there are rumors...."

Gregory's eyes bored into hers.

"What rumors?" she asked uneasily as she picked up her glass and sipped the wine.

"That your father had a hand in the former chief's death."

"I beg your pardon?" Darach had mentioned such a thing, but it could not possibly be true.

"So that he could take his place as laird and push his traitorous ideas on the clan," Gregory added.

Larena slammed down her glass. "Those are false rumors, Gregory. Ronald Campbell's death was an accident. He fell from his horse during a hunt and there were witnesses. My father may have been disloyal to King George, but he is no murderer. He is the kindest and most loving man I've ever known."

Gregory raised a hand, as if to calm the waters of disagreement between them. "Of course, of course. I did not mean to imply...."

By now her heart was pounding like a hammer in her chest and she wanted to leave the room immediately.

"I am afraid the wine has made me sleepy," she said. "You were right before. I have been through a terrible ordeal. If you don't mind...." She removed her napkin from her lap, folded it on the table, and began to rise from her chair. Gregory stood up as well. "I must retire for the night. I fear that once I reach my bed, I may sleep for three days straight."

He smiled sympathetically and escorted her to the door. "Shall we dine again tomorrow evening?" he asked. "There are still so many things I wish to discuss with you and share with you. I want to know all about your life here at Leathan since I left. And I am sure you must want to know more about my life in England as well."

"Yes, that would be lovely," she replied, not wanting to arouse any suspicions that she might be having second thoughts about this marriage, among other things.

She waited for Gregory to open the door, but to her utter astonishment, his hand came up to rest on her cheek and he leaned in for a kiss.

Larena gasped slightly in shock as his lips connected with hers—a chaste kiss, thank the Lord, which only lasted a heartbeat or two. But what would come next, after that, she wondered, as the days and nights passed and their wedding feast drew near?

He smiled at her and drew away. "Good night, my dear. I will look forward to our dinner tomorrow evening. Perhaps we can talk more about our nuptials. We must decide upon a firm date."

Her eyebrows lifted as she reached for the door latch. "Yes, we must."

Gregory took hold of it first, however, and spoke to Lieutenant Roberts, who stood outside. "See that the lady is escorted back to her chamber."

"Yes, sir."

Larena thanked Gregory one last time, then followed the guard down the stairs.

As she moved through the arched castle corridors, then across the moonlit bailey to the South Tower where her rooms were located, her heartbeat escalated with every step, for she was secretly praying that Darach had not left the castle as she'd so foolishly asked him to do. She'd been so sure that following through with her pledge to marry Gregory was the right thing to do, but suddenly she was overcome with doubts about everything—her future happiness, her father's survival at the

Tolbooth, and the honor and integrity of her fiancé, whose words had struck more than a few bad chords in her heart as they spoke over dinner.

It was true. He was not the gentle, intellectual boy she remembered from her childhood. There was something about him that unnerved her. She suspected he was a changed man and she was not entirely certain he would be a good chief for her clan—or the sort of husband she could love.

Love....

What did she even know of that? In bed with Darach, she had felt a mad desire like no other. He was a handsome Scotsman she admired, respected, and trusted, despite everything in his past that should pit her against him. She had given herself to him. She had relinquished her precious virginity, for she wanted him—and only him—to be the one.

How could she have been so foolish as to send him away? She felt very alone now, unsure of her future and her father's safety. She had no one on her side.

Unless Darach had chosen to stay....

Perhaps he knew she was making a mistake. He had tried to talk her out of it after all. Perhaps he had predicted she would come to her senses before the night was out, and he would still be there, waiting for her return.

When at last she arrived at her door, she thanked Lieutenant Roberts, sent him on his way, and ventured inside.

She shut the door and locked it behind her, then dashed to the bed where she crouched down to peer under it.

There was nothing there but a dust-covered floor.

Rising to her feet, she searched every corner of her room, including her dressing room and behind the drapes, whispering his name. "Darach, are you here?"

He was gone.

Not yet ready to give up—praying that he had not given up on *her*—she peered out into the corridor to make sure Roberts had departed, then hurried down the steps and ran outside across the bailey.

She discovered that Leathan was a changed place. Redcoats were everywhere—standing around in groups, patrolling the battlements. She felt their curious stares as she walked quickly and impatiently to the stables.

She found a groom who had fallen asleep on a pile of hay with his cap tugged low over his forehead. She shook him hard to wake him. "Have you been here all night, Alastair?"

"What's that?" he asked, jerking upright.

"What happened to the MacDonald clansman who arrived with me earlier at dusk?" she asked. "Is his horse still here?"

"Nay, my lady. The MacDonald rode out of here in a hurry over an hour ago. He was a bit rude about it, too. Not a very friendly man."

Her spirits sank. "An hour ago? Are you sure? Did you actually see him leave?"

"Aye. They raised the gate for him and lowered it afterward. He's long gone."

She turned away from the groom and covered her face with her hands. "Oh, Darach," she whispered.

"What's that, my lady?" Alastair asked, following her.

"Nothing," she replied, lowering her hands to her sides and walking out.

But as she climbed the tower steps to her bedchamber, she had to fight hard against tears, for her heart trembled with remorse and fear for the future. She had never felt more alone or vulnerable in her life. Or so terribly heartbroken.

CHAPTER
Twenty-three

At the approximate spot on the mountainside where Darach and Larena had met up with the Redcoats earlier that day—when Darach had been placed in irons and forced to walk the final distance at gunpoint—he reined in his horse to a skidding halt and turned to look back at Leathan Castle.

It was a mighty and spectacular sight under the star-speckled sky—a high-reaching bastion with windows that glowed like dozens of cats' eyes staring back at him. Even from this distance he could hear the faint sounds of a fiddle playing from somewhere within the walls and the raucous singing of men. Miller pricked his ears and whinnied in the cool breezes rising up from the moonlit loch below.

"*Bloody, bloody, bloody,*" Darach said, shaking his head at himself, for something was holding him back from continuing on his journey back to Kinloch. He'd be a fool to deny what it was—pure carnal lust for the sweet body of the woman he'd just made love to, for he could still smell her provocative womanly fragrance on his hands.

Or maybe it was just the memory of her smile that would be forever imprinted on his brain.

Either way, something was calling to him. All his muscles clenched tight with an inexplicable urge to go back. He felt a burning curiosity. What was occurring in Chatham's chambers at this very moment? What if Larena had discovered he was not the man she'd imagined him to be? What if she needed Darach?

He had been very quick to leave when she'd asked him to. He hadn't given her time to think it through or change her mind. What if the guard had never knocked on her door? Would they still be lying in bed, making plans to be together somehow?

Closing his eyes and bowing his head, Darach thought about all the perfect moments when he'd held her in his arms, and how badly he wanted her, still, despite everything.

How could he leave this place without being absolutely sure?

There it was then. He couldn't ride back to Kinloch just yet. He had been wrong to let his jealousy and anger eclipse everything else. At the very least, he needed to assure himself that Larena was safe and content.

So he kicked in his heels and returned.

This time, he would enter more discreetly.

⋘⋙

Gregory Chatham had long prided himself on the supreme powers of his intellect. As a boy, he had never been the fastest, strongest or mightiest, but he'd always known he was smarter than the others. In time, he had come to realize that he could use his brains to his advantage, even learn how to build muscle, and with the right tools and the body God had given him, eventually learn to fight faster and more efficiently.

He had his father to thank for that. The man had taken one look at him when he collected him at Leathan a decade ago and seen immediately to his physical training. All the while, he had permitted Gregory to nurture his mind as well. It had never been one pursuit at the expense of the other. Gregory spent equal hours with a sword or a book in his hand. And discipline toward either of those ends was, of course, always paramount.

But tonight, after the table was cleared and he sat before the blazing fire with a glass of brandy in his hand, a spark alighted in his mind. He was forced to question his so-called supreme intellect, for why had he not solved this puzzle sooner?

Rising from his chair, he strode behind the desk, then called out to Lieutenant Roberts.

The man hurried into the room and stood at attention on the opposite side of the desk. "Yes, sir?"

"What can you tell me about the MacDonald clansman?" Gregory asked. "Is he still here?"

"No, sir. I was informed that he left the castle a few hours ago."

"You're certain he's gone?"

"I believe so, sir."

Gregory slapped the top of the desk with his open palm. "Dammit. We should have held him here. I knew there was something suspect about him."

"What is it, sir?"

"He's not a MacDonald," Gregory replied with a grimace of disgust. "He's a bloody Campbell. I didn't recognize him at first, but now I remember him, clear as day."

Darach Campbell. He was one of the former chief's younger sons. They'd been a menacing pack of brutes. The worst of the lot at Leathan. A foul bunch of rotters.

How many times had Gregory woken up in a cold sweat during his childhood, suffering from endless nightmares about their teasing, beatings, and threats?

As far as Gregory knew, their father had never done a bloody thing about it. 'Lads must have their fun,' he'd probably said.

"Send troops out to find Darach MacDonald and bring him back here in irons," Gregory said.

"Yes, sir." Roberts hurried out.

Gregory returned to stand in front of the fire and stared down at the dancing flames.

*At last...*some sport to be had here at Leathan after the disappointment of learning that half the clansmen he once knew had perished at Sheriffmuir—most notably the sons of the former chief.

Once Gregory invited Darach into his chambers, he would have a little fun with him. If Darach wound up on the floor, bleeding to death, it wouldn't be a stretch to claim that he'd lunged at Gregory like the filthy savage that he was.

Although a public sword fight might be more satisfying—and a fine opportunity to demonstrate to the clan how he had learned to wield a saber with deadly efficiency. He wished for them to see him as a worthy and capable laird.

More importantly, he wished for Larena to see that. He wanted her to gaze up at him with awe. He had been dreaming of that for years.

He wondered suddenly if she had known about Darach's true identity all along.

No, surely not. The man claimed to be devoted to his laird at the MacDonald stronghold. If she had known, she would have told him. *Wouldn't she?*

Unless there was some sort of secret affection between them.

Gregory sank down onto the chair, disillusioned and forlorn at the possibility that she might be concealing secrets—or worse, improper feelings for the former chief's son. Did they share a history?

No, that could not be the case. Not his darling Larena. She would not do such a thing. Not after agreeing to become his wife. She couldn't possibly know who Darach really was.

Why, then, did he feel such a deep and harrowing ache inside his chest?

He'd been so happy earlier when she sat down across from him at the table and asked about a possible date for their wedding. She was the most fetching creature he'd ever laid eyes on.

Now he felt only disappointment and grief—and a debilitating fear that she might not be his in the end.

But he had come so far. He had waited so long. Everything had fallen into place so perfectly.

Please, Lord, let it not end badly. I've waited too long.

ᏉWENᏉy-ϜOUR

If only one had the power to turn back the clock and do things differently, Larena thought to herself as she trudged up the tower stairs to her bedchamber. If it were possible, she would go back to the moment the guard knocked on her door and she would ask Darach to stay and wait while she dined with Colonel Chatham. She would have assured him that she only wished to buy time until they could figure out what to do. How to be together. How to save her father. Surely there were options.

But when she entered her room and glanced at the clock on the mantle, it was still ticking steadily and showing the correct time. There would be no magic for her today.

With a sigh of resignation, she crossed to the window and looked out at the bailey below. She tried to imagine Darach emerging from the stable and riding to the gate.

Had he paused and entertained any second thoughts about leaving? Or had he ridden out with bitterness and hatred in his heart, without a single look back over his shoulder? Did he hate her now? Or was he in hell, like she was? Was he longing for her touch as she was longing for his?

Burying her face in her hands, she shook her head and uttered a few quiet oaths.

"What are you cursing about, lass?" a deep voice whispered in her ear. She whirled about in surprise.

"Darach!"

Was she dreaming? Or had her prayers been answered and the clock had indeed been turned back?

She threw her arms around his neck and stepped to the side as he slid her along the wall, away from the leaded glass, out of sight of the bailey below.

Suddenly his lips were on hers, crushing her mouth, claiming her with brutal, hungry passion. She dug her fingers into his massive upper arms, then reached up to pull him close.

"You came back for me," she whispered on a sigh as he pressed hot kisses down the length of her neck and thrust his body against hers, anchoring her to the wall.

"But you were cursing just now," he said. "Are you angry with me?"

She pulled back to look him in the eye. "Angry with *you*? For what?"

"For leaving you."

"No," she firmly told him. "It was my fault that you left, and now that you're here, I'm ecstatic. I'm so sorry, Darach. I was wrong to send you away. All through dinner, all I wanted to do was get up from the table and chase after you. I was a fool to think I could marry someone else."

"Aye, lass, you were a fool. So you want me, then?"

"Of course I want you," she said with a laugh. "Can't you tell?"

He smiled down at her with that slow, lazy, heart-stopping smile, and she knew she was done for.

Again, he pressed his lips to hers and kissed her ravenously until she felt as if she were drowning in a sea of happiness. A shiver of need coursed through her and she knew she would never have convinced herself she could live without him. Not in a thousand years.

He ran a hand down over her breast and moaned with desire.

"Take me back to bed," she whispered provocatively, wanting nothing more than to satisfy her own lust when she'd thought she'd lost him forever.

"Nay, lass," he replied, resting his hands on her hips and drawing back slightly.

"Why not? Are you angry with *me*?"

"Nay, it's not that."

"What is it, then?"

Had he only come back to say good-bye? Or to claim one last kiss?

"I cannot stay here," he said. "I'm a MacDonald now and I carry a shameful secret."

"I would never tell anyone," she assured him.

"I know that, and I would trust you with my life, but it's only a matter of time before someone recognizes me. For that reason, I must leave here and return to Kinloch."

"No," she pleaded. "Tonight I thought I'd lost you forever. Now that you're back, I can't let you go again."

"That's not what I'm suggesting," he said.

She inclined her head and regarded him with curiosity. "You have another idea? One that won't send my father to the gallows?"

"Aye, lass, but it's risky and it's dangerous—and I don't even know if it's what you want."

"Tell me," she said, pulling him toward the fire and sitting him down.

Wʜat are you doing here, lassie?" her father asked, leaping off the cot as Larena pushed the prison door open and entered his cell.

She raised a finger to her lips. "*Shh.* There's no time to explain now." Grabbing hold of his hand, she led him toward the door. "We have to go."

"Where?"

"I found out tonight that they're sending you to the Tolbooth," she said, "so we need to get you out of here."

She peered into the passageway where Darach was kneeling before one of the Redcoats, checking the pulse at his neck.

"Is it safe to come out?" she asked.

"Aye, lass, but we must move quickly."

"Who's this?" her father asked, watching Darach rise to his full height in the torch-lit corridor.

"His name is Darach and he's a friend," Larena explained. "He helped me after we were ambushed on the road. Remember I told you about that? He wants to help." She turned to Darach. "This is my father, Fitzroy Campbell."

Her father sized Darach up from head to foot and narrowed his focus on the broach pinned to his tartan. "He's a MacDonald."

"It's a long story," Larena said, "but there's no time to tell it now. If you want to avoid an iron collar at the Tolbooth, you must come with us."

Her father considered it for a few brief seconds, then nodded his head.

"Help me put this man in your cell," Darach said to him. "We'll lock the door and with luck, no one will notice you're gone until the shift changes in the morning."

"There are Redcoats everywhere," her father said as he helped Darach drag the soldier into the cell. "I hope you have a plan for getting us out of here."

"He does," Larena said with confidence, closing and locking the cell door behind them. "Just stay close."

"I don't have much of a choice, do I? Now that we're hiding the bodies of dead soldiers."

"Follow me, this way," Darach said.

With his hand on the hilt of his sword, he led them back up the steps to the south corridor, then through the kitchen, and back down another set of steps toward the surgery.

It was nearly two in the morning so it was quiet in most areas of the castle, but they were careful nonetheless, at every turn, to keep an eye out to avoid any unexpected encounters.

When they reached the end of the arched passageway, Darach grabbed a torch from a wall sconce and used it to light their way across the surgery.

"Where are we going?" her father asked as they ventured through a back door and down a few steps into a lower storage room full of herbs, bandages, and bottles on shelves.

"I know a secret way out," Darach whispered. He swung the torch around, sweeping light and shadows across the walls. "It's right here…."

He passed the torch to Larena and stepped forward to move a wooden barrel out of the corner. It was too heavy, so he waved Larena's father over. "Help me with this."

Together they inched the barrel along the wall, then Darach knelt down to run his hands over the stones. He slid the knife out of his boot and jimmied a large block out of the wall. It came loose and he gently lowered it to the ground. He slid the knife back into his boot and pulled a second block out of the wall, then a third, just below it. "It'll be a tight squeeze but we can all fit, one at a time."

He slid through first and peered out at them from the other side. "Come now. You next, Larena. Pass me the torch."

She handed it to him, then climbed through to the dark space beyond. She rose to her feet but remained hunched over because the height of the space was no more than four or five feet.

She looked ahead at a low, narrow tunnel dug into the earth. "We'll have to crawl out on our hands and knees, I suppose."

"Aye. I hope you don't mind tight spaces."

"Not if it means we all get to live."

Darach peered back out at her father who was still waiting in the storage chamber. "Your turn, Fitzroy. Once you are through, we'll have to replace the stone blocks so no one sees where we went. There's not much we can do about that barrel except to hope no one notices it was moved."

Larena waited for her father to slink through the hole and close it up behind him. When they'd sealed the entrance, her father rose to his feet in a hunched position and regarded Darach suspiciously. "How did you know about this?"

"We'll explain later," Larena whispered, laying a hand on her father's arm. "First we have to get you out of here."

Darach gestured toward the smaller tunnel. "After you."

They studied each other's eyes for an intense moment until Larena tugged at her father's sleeve. "Come on."

She dropped to her hands and knees and proceeded to crawl into the tight channel. "It's dark in here. I can't see a thing."

"Just follow your nose," Darach said. "It's not far. You'll see the moonlight on the lake in a minute or two, and I'll be right behind you with the torch."

"If it's a conduit to our freedom," she replied, "I'm more than happy to lead the way." Putting one hand in front of the other, she felt her way along the cold, damp floor while bits of dirt rained down on her head. "This must be what a worm feels like."

"Who dug this?" her father asked, crawling behind her.

"My brothers and I," Darach replied. "It was our punishment for picking on each other and half the other lads in the clan when we were younger."

"Do you mean the *Campbell* clan?" her father asked with surprise.

"Aye."

"Are you telling me that you're a Campbell, not a MacDonald?"

"That's right," Darach replied. "Though I've lived at Kinloch most of my life."

While listening to their conversation behind her and dreading the moment the whole truth would come out, Larena continued to lead the way through the tunnel, still searching for the moonlight Darach had promised.

"Does Angus the Lion know you're a Campbell?" her father asked.

"Nay. No one knows except for my brother and your daughter. Now you."

Larena spotted a flicker of light up ahead, beyond a curtain of tree roots and vines. "We're almost there," she said over her shoulder. "It's not much farther." Crawling faster, she reached the exit, pushed the stubborn branches aside and looked down over the edge at the rocky beach below. "This looks treacherous."

"It's steep but not deadly," Darach told her. "Roll down like a log if you have to. You may tumble a bit, but you'll survive."

Bracing herself, she climbed out face first, then turned her body and slid down the rocky incline on her behind. Her father tumbled out behind her.

Feeling a bit bruised and chafed in places, she rose to her feet and looked up to see Darach putting out the flame of the torch and leaving it behind before he launched himself out of the hole. He skidded down the bank and landed on his feet on the beach in a surprisingly graceful maneuver.

"Everyone all right?" he asked in a quiet voice.

"We're fine," Larena whispered in reply.

"Who knows about this breach in the castle wall?" her father asked, looking back up at the hole in the mountainside, camouflaged by foliage.

Darach shook his head. "I couldn't tell you that. I haven't been back here in fifteen years. But I'm surprised *you* didn't know about it. Our father made us keep it secret when we were digging it, but he said it was for us and all the future lairds of Leathan and their children. This seemed a good time to use it."

"Who the devil is your father?" Fitzroy asked with dismay.

Darach hesitated a moment, then squared his shoulders and rested his hand on the hilt of his sword. When he finally spoke, there was pride and self-assurance in his voice. "Ronald James Campbell. Your former laird."

They regarded each other with heated intensity on the moonlit beach, while Larena glanced around uneasily, worrying about Redcoats coming after them. "There's no time for this now."

"All of Ronald Campbell's sons were killed at Sheriffmuir," her father argued, completely ignoring her concern. "He had no living heirs when he died."

"My younger brother and I survived that battle," Darach replied, offering no more information than that.

"But why did you not come home?" her father asked. "Did you disgrace yourself on the battlefield? And why did you join the MacDonalds? Are you a traitor to your family, boy?"

Larena stepped forward. "Please, Father. We have to get away from here."

"And you want me to follow *this* man?"

"Aye," she replied desperately. "You must trust me."

He breathed heavily with agitation. "Fine. Which way are we going?"

Darach led the way. "My horse is up the beach in this direction, tethered in the woods."

"I hope you know what you're doing, boy, because this whole area is crawling with Redcoats."

"We'll do our best to avoid them," Larena replied, breaking into a run.

❧❦❧

"You should have planned this better," Fitzroy said, less than an hour later. "We won't get far with only one horse."

"I would have had to steal them," Darach explained, leading Miller by the reins while Larena rode in the saddle. "It would have been too risky and there wasn't time."

"There would have been time if you'd put together a proper plan of escape," Fitzroy said, walking on the other side of Miller. "Why didn't you just return to the castle through the main gate instead of sneaking in through that hole? Larena could have gotten us horses somehow, maybe even enlisted the help of a few loyal clansmen."

Darach was about to defend his actions when Larena interrupted. "There's no point arguing about it now. We got away and we're out of range. They probably haven't even noticed that you're missing yet."

"When they do, they'll sound the alarm and we'll be worse off than three rabbits running from a pack of hungry hounds. This was a foolhardy plan. What were you thinking, Larena?"

"I was thinking of *you*," she replied from high in the saddle.

"You shouldn't have. I don't care about myself. I was as good as dead anyway. I'd accepted that. But *you*…. You had a chance. You could have married Colonel Chatham and remained at Leathan Castle with the clan. I know he's my enemy, but at least you would have had position and security."

"But I don't love him. And the clan is all gone."

"*Ach*! What is wrong with you, lass? You cannot base your decisions on the fickle whims of your silly heart. Beside, you only just met Chatham yesterday. How do you know you wouldn't love him in time?"

Gritting his teeth together in irritation, Darach worked hard to stay silent, for this was a touchy issue, better left alone for the time being.

"I won't ever love him," Larena replied. "I would have been miserable."

"Ah, I see now," Fitzroy replied. "You've taken a fancy to this traitor here. Is that it? When did that happen? What did he do to turn your head?"

"It doesn't matter, Father. I've made my choice and we rescued you from the Tolbooth. What happens next is up to us. At least we're all alive, together and free."

"Free? To do what?" Fitzroy demanded to know. "Are we to disguise ourselves as MacDonalds and live out the rest of our lives as cowards, a disgrace to our clan, like this man here?"

He gestured toward Darach who bit back the urge to draw his sword and demand an apology from Fitzroy—for the man had touched on a raw nerve.

Darach would also like to demand that Fitzroy explain what he knew about his former chief's death. Ever since Darach had locked eyes with Fitzroy in the prison, that question had been burning a hole in his mind.

Did you murder my father?

Darach fought to temper his rage, but only out of respect for Larena.

"Quiet, both of you," Darach said. "Redcoats could be anywhere."

"He's right," Larena replied. "Let's keep going. We'll figure everything out later."

Darach led them to a shallow burn where they could walk in the water for some distance and leave no trail.

⟨⟨✦⟩⟩

They steered clear of the main roads and ventured deep into the forest, traveling the next hour without stopping. They encountered no one, and with every mile gained, Darach breathed a little easier.

Just before dawn, when the birds began to chirp in the treetops and the sky grew a shade or two lighter, Larena asked if they could stop and rest awhile. Understanding how fatigued she must be, Darach found a spot near a babbling brook and helped her dismount.

"We cannot linger long," he quietly told her when her feet touched the ground. "They'll be searching for us by now."

At the stroke of her hand on his arm, he loathed how powerless he felt, thrust into a situation he did not wish to be in—not with her. All he'd ever wanted to do was protect her, keep her safe. *Love her.* Yet here they stood, on the run from the English army with a known fugitive, a traitor to the English Crown. Possibly his own father's killer.

"I understand," she replied. "Do you have anything to eat? He wouldn't say anything, but I've never seen my father look so frail. I'm worried about him, Darach. You don't know what he looked like before. He's so thin now. I almost didn't recognize him when I first saw him."

"He may be thin," Darach replied, glancing over his shoulder at Fitzroy, who was sinking down to the ground to sit with his back against a tree, "but he's still a brawny giant of a Highlander." Darach faced Larena again. "I packed supplies before I left the castle last night. I'll dig something out for all of us."

"Thank you." She gestured toward a grove of evergreens a short distance away. "I'll just be a moment. But first…." Larena glanced at her father to make sure he wasn't looking, then she kissed Darach lightly on the lips. "I need you to know that I have no regrets about escaping with you. I don't care what happens. Even if we die trying, I'd rather die with you than spend the rest of my life married to another man, wishing I could have one more moment with you. And don't listen to my father. He'll come around. I promise. I just need time to talk to him and convince him that you are the man who will make me happy. No one else. He'll understand once he gets to know you. I'm certain of it."

Darach raised her hand to his lips and laid a kiss on her knuckles. "But what about your clan? They have no leader now, except for Chatham, and you know he'll come after you. He won't rest."

"We'll just have to stay one step ahead of him," she replied. "And my clan will survive, as they always have. Maybe some other ambitious Campbell lassie will step up to marry Gregory."

As Darach watched her disappear into the grove, he felt lost in some kind of trance, completely besotted.

Snapping himself back to the present, he dug into the saddle bags for sustenance, for they had a long journey ahead of them.

He intended to take them north, to cross over the Great Glen, then continue traveling until they found shelter where they could hide out over the long winter. Whether or not they would ever return to Leathan or Kinloch remained an unknown factor at present. At least they would have plenty of time to consider their options.

Darach was about to withdraw a loaf of bread from the bag when suddenly his sword and dirk were pulled from their sheaths and he found himself being strangled in a chokehold.

Darach struggled against Fitzroy's grip, but the sharp blade of his own dirk was pressing into his jugular. Fitzroy tossed the heavy sword into the bushes.

"Don't give me a reason to slice your throat," Fitzroy said as he dragged Darach across the forest floor toward the creek, "because you know I want to."

A burst of shock and adrenaline lit in Darach's veins. This was not what he wanted, not what he'd hoped for.

"Like you sliced my father's throat?" he ground out.

"Aye. He was a foul rotter, that one. The clan deserved better. But I didn't slice his throat. I did that with my own bare hands, shoved him into a ravine. It was a fair fight before that, I'll have you know."

God, it was true.

"Why don't you make *this* a fair fight?" Darach suggested, feeling the blade cut into his flesh. "Drop the knife."

"Maybe I will, but first I want to know what you're up to, lad. Why did you save me? Why not let me hang, or let them take me to the Tolbooth?"

"Because I love your daughter."

"*Ach*! You're just using her to take my place as chief. Have you bedded her yet? Is that how you changed her mind about marrying Chatham?"

Darach struggled harder.

"I remember you," Fitzroy said. "You never looked anything like your father, but you resembled your mother, with hair dark as night. I know what you're here for. You're here to have your revenge on me."

"Nay, I'm just here for Larena. I want to marry her."

"*Ach*!" Fitzroy spit on the ground. "I'd rather have a half-English colonel for a son-in-law than the son of Ronald Campbell."

Fitzroy's hold loosened for a split second as he altered his grip on the knife. Internal rage spiked in Darach's blood and he seized the opportunity to flip the man onto his back. Fitzroy landed with a heavy thud, the knife fell from his grip, and all the air puffed out of his lungs.

Darach grabbed the knife and backed away, holding it out, hoping Fitzroy would yield, but the powerfully built warrior rose to his feet and ran at Darach like a crazed bull. Fitzroy hurled his body forward and shoved Darach up against a tree.

Suddenly, Fitzroy's eyes grew wide and he went still. It took a few seconds for Darach to realize that he'd dirked Larena's father in the belly.

"Oh, Christ...." Darach ground out as Fitzroy slid to the ground and pressed a hand to the blood gushing through the fabric of his shirt.

Heart racing, Darach knelt over him.

"*Darach!*"

The sound of Larena's voice caused him to swivel on his knee. There she stood, at the edge of the glade, staring at him in horror in the pale light of the advancing dawn.

His gut clenched. "It was an accident," he tried to explain, holding the bloody knife out for her to see.

She ran to her father and dropped to her knees beside him.

Just then, Darach heard a distant sound in the woods.

Voices, hoofbeats....

He rose to his feet and listened.

Miller's nose lifted from the grass and his ears twitched. He began to back away and tug at the leather line as if wanting to bolt.

Glancing around in search of his sword, Darach spotted it at least ten paces away. Making haste to reach it, he drew the pistol out of his belt, but he was not quick enough, for all at once, the glade erupted into a deafening cacophony of musketfire.

Larena screamed, but there was nothing Darach could do. It was too late. Everything spun out of control. The soldiers had come. There was shouting, heart-pounding chaos, and madness. There were too many of them.

God help us.

Larena…!

Another shot was fired and pain exploded in the center of Darach's back. *Please, God! Not this! Not now!*

The world turned white before his eyes as he fell forward onto the forest floor. Then the chaos receded and there was only a calm sea of silence.

arena cradled her father's head in her arms as she looked up at the English officer in the saddle, trotting around the glade on his massive black warhorse. "Stand down!" he called out to five other mounted soldiers.

Reeling with shock and horror, she looked toward Darach who was lying immobile, face down in the grass. "*Darach!*"

He made no move to rise. Feeling dizzy and disoriented, she lowered her gaze to her father who was bleeding profusely from the belly.

"I'm sorry," he said. "I should have kept my wits about me, lass. I should have known."

"Known what?"

"That the Campbell lad wanted me dead."

"That's not true," she argued, glancing toward Darach again, wanting to go to him, but her father grabbed her by the chin and forced her to look down at him.

"He accused me of murdering his father."

"*Did* you?" she asked, not knowing what to believe.

"Of course not, lass. You know me better than that. The lad was full of vengeance. I shouldn't have challenged him, but he said he seduced you to spite me. I couldn't let it go."

The officer in charge dismounted and stood over them. "Are you Larena Campbell? Is this your father, Fitzroy Campbell?"

"Why should I tell you anything?" she bit back.

He scoffed. "Because you're under arrest for coming to the aid of a convicted criminal."

"This one's dead!" another of the Redcoats shouted from the far side of the glade. He kicked Darach with his boot and rolled him over onto his back.

"*No...Please...*" Tears welled up in Larena's eyes. Her heart was pounding so hard, she could barely breathe. She felt as if all the trees in the forest were closing in around her.

"Seize that horse and get this prisoner onto his feet," the officer in charge ordered. "Can you ride?" he asked her father.

"Aye."

"Good. We'll take him back to Leathan!" he shouted at the others.

"But he's hurt," Larena argued with a note of pleading in her voice.

"All the more reason to get him back to the garrison, miss. We'll have him tended to there."

"But why? So you can hang him in front of the clan or ship him off to the Tolbooth?"

"I don't make those decisions," the officer said with an infuriating note of indifference.

Two Redcoats surrounded them and hoisted her father onto his feet. He cried out in agony.

"Please, be careful with him!" she shouted, following at his side.

"Larena, you must go back to the colonel and plead with him," her father said to her over his shoulder as they dragged him toward Miller. "Tell him the truth about what happened here—that this rebel Highlander wanted vengeance against me and he seduced you to get it. It wasn't your fault, lass. Chatham loves you. He'll forgive you. You can still save yourself and the clan. They'll need you in the coming years."

She turned toward Darach, still lying lifeless on the grass. Her chest felt on fire and a sickening wave of nausea rose up in her belly. She tried to go to him, but one of the other soldiers grabbed hold of her arm and clamped irons around her wrists.

"What are you doing?" She struggled to resist but he shoved her toward a horse.

"You'll be riding with me, miss," he replied, "so I can keep an eye on you."

"What about him?" she asked the officer in charge, gesturing toward Darach. "You can't just leave him here."

"We can do whatever we bloody well please." He turned to one of the others—the one who had kicked Darach with his boot. "You're certain he's dead?"

"Yes, sir."

"Then confiscate his weapons and we'll leave him for the crows."

Larena let out a sob of protest as she was dragged toward a horse and forced up onto the saddle.

Darach…

Dear God…

What had happened here?

Her father, clearly in pain, was pushed up onto Miller's back. They tied a line to Miller's bridle to lead him along.

"Father…." She turned to make sure he was all right.

"Don't worry for me, lass," he assured her, hunched over. "I'm a Campbell. I've survived worse than this."

But with one look at the dark bloodstain on his shirt, she knew his prospects were grim.

As they moved in a single column out of the glade, Larena glanced back at Darach, unmoving in the grass. Every piece of her soul ached with grief—an incomparable agony that felt worse than any pain she'd ever experienced in her life.

How could it end like this? How was it possible that he had put a knife in her father's belly when he'd claimed that he loved her?

The promises he had made....

What had gone wrong? Was it all lies? The entire time?

She thought suddenly of Logan, and wondered what had become of him. Had he returned to Kinloch Castle as Darach had ordered him to do?

God, oh, God....

Her emotions tumbled into a sickening downward spin that left her numb and frozen inside. She felt as if she were breaking apart. Then the flood of quiet, agonizing sobs began as they departed from the glade and left Darach's dead body behind.

B y the time they reached the castle and the iron portcullis lifted on giant, rattling chains, Larena's father was long dead. He had fallen out of the saddle many miles back.

There was no hope when they all dismounted and looked him over. He'd lost too much blood and was stone cold.

The officer in charge suggested that he'd probably been dead for quite some time when he tumbled to the ground. The soldiers then proceeded to ponder how long he had been riding upright without a pulse. They'd even wanted to set a wager about it, but they let the game go when they realized there was no way to prove a winner.

So they hauled her father up off the ground and tossed him over Miller's back like a worthless sack of grain. Then they resumed their journey back to Leathan.

From that moment on, Larena felt as if the innermost core of her heart and soul had died, too. A heavy cloak of misery descended and she wallowed in unspeakable despair, torturing herself for all the mistakes she had made over the past fortnight and all the things she could have done differently to prevent this horrific unfolding of events.

Was she being punished for succumbing to the temptations of the flesh? Had her sinful, self-indulgent desires for Darach MacDonald—or Darach Campbell—caused all of this misfortune?

Perhaps her instincts had been correct all along and she should have placed duty above desire. If she had insisted that Darach return to Kinloch and leave her behind to fulfill her pledge to Lord Rutherford, then Darach would be alive today and so would her father. He would still be in his prison cell, awaiting his removal to the Tolbooth. Darach would be... *somewhere.*

Who knew what might have transpired if she had accepted her fate or maintained some caution where Darach was concerned? She could have continued to plead with Gregory to allow her father to remain at the castle. Perhaps she might have used her feminine wiles to wield a greater influence over him.

'He loves you. He'll forgive you,' her father had said.

Would Gregory forgive her now, after what she'd done?

Did she even care, when her heart felt completely dead and all happiness had been sucked from the earth?

⋇⟡⋇

As soon as they entered the bailey, the soldiers pulled her off the horse and escorted her down to the prison, where she was thrust into the same cell her father had occupied. The guard removed the irons from her wrists and walked out. He slammed the door shut behind him and locked it.

Larena sat down on the bed and stared at the wall.

She had no idea how much time had elapsed before the heavy clang of metal caused her to lift her weary gaze. The door slowly opened.

A different guard entered, instructed her to stand, and escorted her back up the stairs to the bailey and across to the East Tower. People stared at her in silence—a few fellow clansmen she knew and members of the English army—but she didn't care. Nothing seemed to matter.

When she reached her father's former chambers—now occupied by Gregory Chatham—she had no memory of climbing the curved staircase. She had been thinking of something else. She knew not what.

The guard knocked on the door. A second later it opened. She gazed in a numb stupor at her betrothed.

"I didn't believe it when they told me," Gregory said.

She offered no reply. What was there to say?

"Come in." He signaled to the guard to leave them alone, then he led her inside to the upholstered chair before the hearth that had recently been swept clean. There was not a single speck of ash. Her eyes lifted at the sound of a clock ticking on the mantle. It was not yet noon. How odd. It felt like it should be evening.

A glass of claret was presented to her. Feeling strangely disconnected from everything, she looked down at the hand that held it, then her eyes followed the red sleeve up to the gold shoulder epaulets and she took in the white neck cloth in a tidy knot. Finally she regarded Gregory's face.

He stood over her, watching her with concern. "You've had quite a morning." He gestured for her to take the drink.

"Aye," she replied as she accepted it.

"I'm sorry about your father."

With trembling hands, she raised the glass to her lips and sipped thirstily.

Gregory took a seat in the chair across from her, leaned forward, and rested his elbows on his knees. "They tell me it was painful for you. Your father was already wounded when they found you?"

She nodded her head.

"They also told me that the Highlander was running off after he stabbed your father. Is that what happened?"

"So they say."

He leaned back. "I'm so sorry you had to suffer through all of that, Larena. No doubt you are terribly distressed."

She nodded and swigged more of the claret.

He sat in silence, watching her for a moment. "I'm not clear about why this happened," he finally said, "or how you escaped the castle walls. Reports say the gate hadn't been lifted since last night and I have guards patrolling the battlements at all hours. How did you get your father out?"

"We escaped through a window on the east wall," she lied. "Darach lowered a rope."

"No one saw you?"

"It was dark and very late. Luck was on our side."

"I see." He paused. "So you admit you played a part in your father's escape. Was it your idea?"

She was not calculated in her responses. In fact, she hardly cared what came out of her mouth, for the future mattered not at all. She had no hopes or dreams left in her heart. The world seemed like some sort of waking nightmare.

"It was Darach's idea," she told Gregory. "He suggested it, and it seemed like a good idea at the time."

"I had been led to believe that he had passed through the castle gates last night and was on his way back to Kinloch. Yet here you sit, telling me that he returned. How did he get back inside?"

She shrugged. "I don't know. All I can tell you is that he knocked on my bedchamber door after I said good night to you and told me that he could rescue my father. Because of what I knew was in store for my father at the Tolbooth, I agreed."

"So it was not something you plotted before you arrived at Leathan," he said.

"No. It was completely spontaneous. And foolish, I now realize."

"Indeed." Gregory rested his temple on a finger and continued to regard her with meticulous scrutiny. "May I ask you something, Larena?"

"Yes."

"Are you in love with that Highlander? Or rather, *were* you in love with him?"

She took a deep breath and let it out. "I suppose I must be honest with you, Gregory. *Yes*. I don't know how it happened. It just did. I didn't plan it."

"I want to believe you," Gregory replied, "but I need to know the truth. How long have you known him? Were you betrothed to him before you accepted the proposal to become my wife?"

Larena looked up. "Goodness, no. I assure you that I entered into that arrangement in good faith. I only met Darach for the first time after the ambush," she explained, "when he came to my aid."

Gregory cocked his head to the side. "You don't think it's possible that he played a part in organizing that ambush, so that he could get his hands on you and ultimately your father?"

"I don't think so," she replied, her attention sparking. "He didn't even *want* to escort me back here. He made it very clear that he didn't like Campbells—and that is putting it mildly. Angus had to command him to do it. I didn't even like him at first. I thought he was an arrogant bully, but eventually I came to rely on him and...." She paused. "He gained my trust."

Gregory inhaled deeply, stared at the empty hearth for a few seconds, then he sat forward again and laid his hand on her knee. "May I tell you something about that Highlander?"

With growing unease, she nodded.

"When I first met him here in this very room yesterday," Gregory said, "I knew there was something familiar about him, but I couldn't put my finger on it. After dinner, when you left, it came to me."

Larena's stomach began to burn. "What was that?"

"The fact that Darach MacDonald was not a true MacDonald," Gregory explained. "He was an imposter. How and when he adopted that identity, I cannot be sure, but this much I know: He was a Campbell by blood and a son of your former chief, Ronald Campbell."

Larena's eyes lifted with apprehension.

"You might not remember him," Gregory continued. "You were only six years old when he and his brothers went off to the battle at Sheriffmuir. He would have been much older than you. Fourteen or so. He had shorter hair then. He was thin and lanky." Gregory's eyebrows pulled together with frustration. "But I should have noticed the resemblance when he first walked in, for he once chased me up a tree and sat there on the branch for a full hour, not letting me come down. I should have remembered those dark, sinister eyes. I was distracted, I suppose. Then I recalled all those days in my youth when I was persecuted in the worst way. He and his brothers were the foulest of the bunch. They were cruel and violent. Did you see that side of him at all?"

She shook her head. "No. He was very kind to me."

Although that was partly a lie, for she had seen a dangerous side to him at first. He had been most intimidating in the early days of their acquaintance, and she had seen him snap the bone in his brother's arm without the slightest hesitation.

In addition, she had seen the bloody knife in his hand that very morning. The knife that killed her father....

Nevertheless, she still didn't want to believe what Gregory was saying. Heaven help her, she didn't want to believe *anything* about this day.

"He was kind to you," Gregory explained, "because he wanted to use you to seek vengeance upon your father."

Good Lord, what else did Gregory know about this?

He sighed and noticed that her glass was empty. He rose to his feet, went to fetch the decanter and poured her another drink. As soon as he was seated again, he crossed one leg over the other and said, "Do you remember what we discussed during dinner last night? I told you about the rumors surrounding Ronald Campbell's death—that your father murdered him during a hunt."

"And I told you that they weren't true. There were witnesses who saw what happened. He fell from his horse and that is all. My father is innocent."

"The witnesses were Jacobites who supported your father and wanted him as chief, so I wouldn't trust their word. But you see, that is why I believe Darach was using you—to seek out his own justice against your father. An eye for an eye, so to speak."

Larena bowed her head and shook it. "This has been a trying day, Gregory. I cannot think straight anymore. It all feels like a terrible nightmare from which I cannot wake."

Gregory touched her knee again. "None of this is your fault," he said. "I believe you were taken advantage of in the worst possible way by a villain and an enemy. Do you see that now?"

Her eyes lifted and she saw compassion in Gregory's eyes. "I don't know."

He sat back. "Obviously you need time to recover."

"Yes." She set the claret on the table and wondered when she would ever be able to *feel* anything again, when all her emotions seemed to be made of cold clay.

"You must go back to your chamber and rest," he added, rising to his feet. "I will have a bath arranged for you and supper sent up later. All I want to do is ease your pain, Larena, and protect you. I hope you know that."

She frowned up at him with dismay. "How can you say that when I just admitted that I loved another man?"

He shook his head. "It wasn't love. How could it be after such a short period of time in his company? You didn't know the real man. Surely you must see how you were misled and seduced."

She tried to make sense of it all, but couldn't.

"You and I have known each other all our lives," he continued, brushing a finger across her cheek. "I have loved you devotedly for years and there is nothing I wouldn't do for you. I only hope that you can find it in your heart to remember why you agreed to this marriage in the first place. You knew it was the best thing for your clan, and for *you*. I will do anything to make you happy, Larena. Give this a chance and I will say no more about what happened between you and the Highlander."

"But...I don't understand how you could forgive me. You don't even know what happened."

"I don't want to know," he firmly told her.

Larena swallowed hard. "But I am under arrest for aiding my father—a convicted criminal. The officer put me in irons and locked me up in the prison."

Gregory cradled her chin in his hand and cupped it, hard. "You were a victim in this, Larena, nothing more. You were practically abducted. Darach MacDonald—or Campbell, whatever you want to call him—was your enemy and that is what you must accept. In terms of your arrest, I have already wiped that slate clean."

She swallowed uneasily and looked up at him. "I should... thank you."

He laid both his hands on her shoulders and squeezed firmly. "No thanks are necessary. You are the love of my life and always will be. I will do whatever it takes to make you my wife."

Suddenly, he pressed his mouth to hers in a rigid, invasive kiss that caused her eyes to fly open in shock. He pulled her tight against him and thrust his tongue into her mouth.

Larena's stomach exploded with revulsion. She pushed him away and wiped at her mouth with the back of her sleeve. "What are you doing? My father just died."

Gregory blinked at her with confusion, then he squared his shoulders. "I suppose that was ill timed. Clumsy of me."

The intensity in his voice and the manner in which he wet his lips sent a shiver down the length of her spine. It was not the same sort of pleasurable shivers she'd experienced with Darach. This was something else entirely. She felt only anger and disgust, which was unfortunate, since Gregory seemed genuine in his affection for her and in his desire to ensure that she was safe and protected.

But would she ever truly feel safe and protected? Could she love him? Did she want to marry him?

No, most assuredly not, which left her in a difficult position indeed, for where else did she have to go? And what did she know about love anyway? Clearly nothing.

According to her father, she had a duty to hold onto the castle for the good of the Campbell clan, despite the presence of the English army.

But her father was gone now. Her clan had scattered.

She had never felt so completely alone in all her life. She was surrounded by blackness.

She curtsied respectfully to Gregory and walked out.

In the dream, Darach was riding Miller bareback across a lush green valley. Miller galloped gracefully, almost as if they were flying. He was white in the dream.

The scent of meat filled Darach's nostrils and suddenly the dream changed. He found himself dashing through dark, stone corridors in an unfamiliar castle, rushing past flaming torches on the walls. For a moment he thought he was being pursued, then he realized he was the pursuer, chasing after that familiar hawk from other dreams. It had become trapped and was searching for a way out. Darach wanted to guide it, to free it from the castle interior, to thrust it upwards toward the sky.

He woke with a start and sat up. He was in a dark room with a curtain over the door. It was nighttime.

His back and shoulder throbbed with pain, so he lay back down on the pillow, fatigued by the sudden movement.

Where was he? More importantly, where was Larena?

Closing his eyes, he searched through his hazy mind for the last thing he could recall. *Ah yes….* He'd been running for his sword in the glade while Larena tended to her father.

Darach had stabbed him. He remembered all too clearly the shock in Fitzroy's eyes when he realized the knife had stuck him in the belly.

Then the soldiers had come….

Larena?

Darach tried agonizingly to sit up again. He glanced at the curtain across the door. There was a strip of light under it.

He was in a cottage.

Whose cottage? Where? Were these friends or enemies?

Sitting all the way up, he carefully put his feet on the floor and took a moment to find his breath. He was just beginning to feel like he might be able to stand when the curtain swept open and he found himself staring into the eyes of a small, red-haired child. She stared at him in shock, then let the curtain fall closed and called out, "Ma! He's awake!"

The sound of voices and chair legs scrapping across a plank floor provided some warning that others would soon appear to gape at him. Sure enough, the curtain was thrown open again.

It was a woman this time. She was small and plump with red hair like her daughter. She wore the Campbell tartan as a sash.

A man stepped into view behind her. He was much taller, fair-haired, and lean. He also wore Campbell colors. "We weren't sure you'd live," he said.

"I was shot," Darach explained, "by English soldiers."

"We figured as much. We heard the musketfire from here. Then we saw the soldiers riding across the field with two prisoners, but they left you behind for some reason."

"I can't imagine why," Darach replied, hunching forward as a fresh wave of pain erupted at his back. "I gather you brought me back here? How long have I been out? And did you see which way the soldiers were heading? Was it in the direction of Leathan Castle? Was there a woman with them?"

The Campbell clansman held up a hand. "One question at a time, friend. Aye, they were heading in that direction, and aye, there was a woman, along with a bearded Highlander. They were a fair distance away so we couldn't make out much else."

Darach tried to stand but felt woozy and sat back down.

"You must stay put," the woman scolded as she tied the curtain back to let more light into the room.

"What day is it?" he asked. "How long have I been here?"

"We picked you up this morning," she told him. "I reckon you would have bled to death if we hadn't found you when we did."

"My wife's good with a needle and thread," the clansman offered.

"The ball was lodged in your shoulder blade," she explained. "I had to dig it out. No doubt you'll be sore for a while."

"Thank you," Darach replied, nodding his head in gratitude.

"You're not out of the woods yet," the woman said. "You need time to heal, and we must keep an eye on it. Pray it doesn't fester."

Another wave of dizziness washed over Darach, so he lay back down on his side to take a few deep breaths and wait for the nausea to pass.

"You'll need something in your belly," the woman said. "I've got a pot of soup simmering over the fire. I'll fetch you some broth."

He wanted to thank her again but he felt so weak and dizzy, he couldn't manage to get any words out.

⚜

"What are your names?" Darach asked a short while later when he was able to sit up again and take some broth. The little flame-haired lassie had crawled into the room and was now sitting on the floor behind her mother's skirts.

"I'm John Campbell," the crofter said, "and this is my wife, Mary."

"It's good to meet you. I'm Darach MacDonald. From Kinloch." He ate a few more bites. "You must be seeing a lot of commotion around here lately, ever since the English invaded at Leathan."

"Aye," John replied. "But the commotion began long before that, friend. It began the moment Ronald Campbell passed away and our new chief took his place. That was when we thought it best to leave Leathan. It's a good thing we did, too."

"Why is that?"

John shrugged, as if to make light of the situation. "Clan politics were changing. We didn't wish to get involved."

"You must be referring to Fitzroy's plot to raise a Jacobite army," Darach suggested, curious to learn more.

John's eyebrows lifted and he shifted uncomfortably. "You heard about that?"

"Aye. News travels fast throughout the Highlands when a Campbell chief is sentenced to death for acts of treason against the English Crown." Darach thought he should probably keep his mouth shut about the whole situation, but these people had saved his life. Besides, he wanted to know what they knew. "That bearded Highlander you saw with the Redcoats this morning? That was him. Fitzroy Campbell."

"Are you sure?" John asked.

"Aye, because I was trying to help him escape." Darach dipped his spoon into the bowl. "Obviously that didn't work out very well."

John and Mary regarded each other with apprehension. "You're a friend to him, then? Are you a Jacobite?"

Darach shook his head. "Nay, I'm nothing. I was just trying to help his daughter. I wanted her to come away with me."

"So it was true love, then," John suggested, glancing knowingly at his wife. "Now *that* I understand. Nothing else in the world can make a man do more foolish things."

"Truer words were never spoken," Darach replied, finishing his soup. "Which is why I need to leave here tonight. I have to return for her."

"Return where?" Mary asked. "To Leathan Castle? *Are you mad?* You just broke Fitzroy Campbell out of the prison. There will be a price on your head, to be sure."

"Not if they think I'm dead," Darach argued, "which they must, otherwise they would never have left me behind."

He only wished he knew what was happening to Larena. He had to make sure she was all right and, God willing, get her back in his arms. At the very least, he needed to explain what happened in the glade. He needed her to understand that it had never been his intention to murder her father.

Was Fitzroy even alive?

"Maybe so," Mary said, "but if they see you again, they'll realize their mistake and arrest you."

"They won't see me," he assured them, setting the empty bowl on the bedside table and laboring to rise.

"How will you manage that?" John asked. "Because you're no ghost, Darach MacDonald. You're true flesh and blood. Wounded, for that matter."

"You must at least wait another day," Mary added. "You were shot in the back this morning. You're not fit to travel."

Darach set his feet on the floor and tried again to stand. *"Ach,"* he whispered as a searing pain exploded in his shoulder blade. He winced and sat down again.

"What did I tell you?" Mary scolded. "If you run out of here now—all fired up and wanting to rescue your beloved—you'll open that wound and end up dead before you get anywhere near the castle walls."

Mary was right and Darach knew it. He had to heal before he could return, or he'd be no good to Larena at all.

With a groan of pain and frustration, he lay back down on the bed and struggled to catch his breath.

Larena was grateful that Gregory had left her in peace after their meeting that morning and the disturbing kiss she had not enjoyed in the least. Keeping to his word, he arranged for a bath to be sent up to her room, after which she fell asleep for many hours. By nightfall, a supper tray arrived. She spent the rest of the evening lying in bed, blinking up at the ceiling, grieving for her father and reliving those last few moments in the glade just before the soldiers arrived.

She couldn't erase the images from her mind: Darach holding out the bloody knife, her father lying on the ground beneath him, bleeding from the stomach.

It was an accident...

Those were Darach's final words, the last thing he'd said to her before the world exploded into a hellish firestorm of musket balls.

He wanted me dead. The lad was full of vengeance. He accused me of murdering his father, her father claimed.

She didn't want to believe it, yet Gregory had suggested the same thing, and Darach's brother Logan had made no secret of his own desires for vengeance.

By midnight, Larena felt as if her heart and mind had frozen over with ice. Then she realized she hadn't shed a single tear since her arrival through the castle gates that morning. All she could do was stare up at the ceiling in a daze.

Maybe she didn't want to believe what happened.

Or maybe she truly was dead inside.

Nevertheless, nightmarish images persisted to haunt her mind. She saw the Redcoats bursting through the trees on their horses. She smelled the gunpowder from the muskets, saw the blood staining her father's shirt and the English soldier kicking Darach's lifeless body and rolling him over onto his back.

Oh, Lord…Darach. His remains had been left behind to rot. She squeezed her eyes shut and covered her face with her hands. Despite what he might have done, it was too ghastly to think of.

Suddenly she found herself recalling the tender moments in his arms when he had gazed down at her in the candlelight—the feel of his warm, naked flesh pressed to hers, his thick firm muscles beneath the stroke of her hands.

Sweet Mary and Joseph, how could all the pleasure and joy have been severed from her life so quickly and completely?

And how could she be thinking of Darach's tender touch when she felt so utterly betrayed?

Was it true? Had he been using her all along to seek an opportunity to kill her father with his own bare hands? She didn't want to believe it, not after everything they'd been through together. He had protected her from Logan, who confessed his own twisted need for vengeance. Darach had broken his brother's arm and sent him away. Had he only done that so that he could seize that opportunity for himself?

And what of the warmth and love she'd felt whenever Darach looked into her eyes or touched her?

He would never touch her again.

He was gone from this world.

He no longer existed.

Tears, at long last, spilled from her eyes and she curled up in a ball, hugging the pillow. If she could have had one wish that night, it would have been to turn back time. If only it were possible. If it were, she never would have broken her father out of the prison. What happened in the glade would never have occurred. She would not feel betrayed by Darach. She would not be wondering if what existed between them was real. He would be alive tonight, and her father would be alive, too.

⚜

Larena wasn't sure what woke her, but it caused her to sit up straight in bed and hug the blankets to her chest. There was a noticeable chill in the air which caused the skin on the back of her neck to prickle. Her heart was racing and she was overcome with fear.

"Hello?"

She hadn't felt a night terror like that since she was little girl. Back then, she would dash up the stairs to her brothers' chambers and crawl into bed with one of them. They would always comfort her after a bad dream, but there was no one left at Leathan to comfort her now. Everyone was gone.

Except for Gregory.

But he could never comfort her. No matter how hard he tried or wanted to. The kiss that afternoon had been unpleasant and she was still inexplicably disturbed by it.

The drapes fluttered in the dimly lit room and sent a burning rush of anxiety into her belly. Determined to set her mind at ease, she rose from the bed, wrapped a blanket around her shoulders, and padded cautiously across the floor to peer behind the curtains.

There was nothing there of course—except for the moon, high in the sky outside the window. Nevertheless, she felt a presence. Gooseflesh erupted across her skin. She felt restless and agitated.

Perhaps it was Darach's ghost. Perhaps he had come back to haunt her for allowing the soldiers to leave his body behind.

She still couldn't bear to think of his cold corpse lying on the ground in the forest.

Someone had to give him a proper burial. Logan needed to be informed of what had happened.

Pulling the blanket more snugly around her shoulders, she returned to bed. She remained sitting up against the pillows, however, feeling terribly unsettled as she hugged her knees to her chest and stared into the emptiness.

A powerful yearning to see Darach again nearly smothered her with its power. She couldn't keep herself from dreaming that he would come back, that he wasn't dead after all. In her fantasy, he surprised her by sneaking up on her and speaking softly in her ear, just as he had done before, even when she'd believed he was gone forever.

In the fantasy, he had not killed her father.

All at once, she knew what she had to do.

Rising from the bed, Larena hurried into her dressing room. Part of her knew it was morbid madness to feel such a need to return to where Darach was shot and see for herself that he was truly dead, but she couldn't wait until morning to ask for Gregory's permission to leave the castle. He would never allow it. He would convince her that she must leave it to the army. He would promise to arrange Darach's burial and he would advise her to put it all behind her.

But she needed to see Darach. If she didn't, she would go out of her mind, always dreaming of his return, or feeling the presence of his spirit in the night, haunting her.

A short while later, dressed in a simple dark skirt and bodice, she entered the storage closet beyond the surgery and pulled the heavy blocks out of the wall.

⊰✧⊱

The sun was just coming up when Larena reached the shallow burn where they had walked in the water to cover their tracks. It was a miracle she'd found it, for everything looked vague and shadowy in the forest at night. But she knew these lands like the back of her hand, and she remembered which way they had gone.

A flock of starlings flew in a circular pattern overhead. She stopped to look up and catch her breath. Not ravens circling death.... Her feet were wet with dew and stinging with blisters, but at least there was light in the sky now. It wouldn't be long before she found the clearing where the soldiers had come upon them and shot Darach in the back.

The idea of it caused a severe pounding of dread to begin in her core, for she wasn't sure she was prepared to look upon Darach's pale corpse. It was a strange and macabre quest she had begun, and she had to wonder if she was half mad to have come here.

Something drove her on nonetheless, albeit with a degree of hesitancy. She picked up her skirts and waded into the water.

⊰✧⊱

Larena's heart nearly quit beating in her chest when she emerged from the woods and beheld the place where her father had lain on the ground, bleeding to death. Her frantic gaze darted around the clearing, searching for the exact spot where Darach had fallen, but the glade was empty.

Was she in the right place?

Yes…yes she was. She recognized everything from the giant juniper on the other side, to the chips in the tree trunk where the musket balls had found their marks.

She ran toward the patch of grass and knelt down where she was certain Darach had fallen. Indeed, there was a bloodstain on the ground. But where was Darach?

A spark of hope lit in her veins.

Rising to her feet, she looked around again and listened for any sound that might alert her to the presence of others, but she heard only the rapid tattoo of a woodpecker in the distance.

Turning her attention back to the ground, she searched for some evidence of tracks. Was Darach alive? Had he walked out of there? Or had someone carried him off? Her stomach turned over with dread at the possibility that Gregory had already sent soldiers back here to confirm that Darach was dead and they were the ones who had carted him away.

Within seconds she identified a single boot-print, then another.

Through the chilly, shifting haze of the early morning light, she followed the tracks through the woods until she emerged from the trees, onto the valley floor where a crofter's cottage came into view. Her heart burst with hope.

Picking up her skirts, she sprinted toward it.

CHAPTER

THIRTY

D arach woke to a loud, violent pounding on the front door of the cottage. His first thought was that the English soldiers had learned of his survival and come to arrest him.

Sitting up, he searched the room for his weapons. Then he remembered that he'd lost them during the attack. He had nothing with which to defend himself. Not that he could, since he would be outnumbered against a battalion of Redcoats at the ready. Besides that, he had a hole the size of an acorn in his shoulder blade. He doubted he could lift a sword if he had one.

His ears alerted to the sound of John answering the door.

Voices....

A woman...?

Larena!

Within seconds, the curtain across the doorway was thrust open and he found himself staring in openmouthed shock at the woman he loved more than anything in this world.

"What are you doing here?" he asked. "How did you get here? Where's your father?"

Larena covered her mouth with her hand. "My God. You're alive."

"Aye."

Though he was stiff and sore from the waist up, nothing could keep him from touching her and holding her in his arms. He tossed the covers aside and rose to his feet.

Larena crossed the tiny room in a few swift strides, wrapped her arms around his waist, and rested her cheek on his chest. He stroked her hair and kissed the top of her head. "Ah, lassie," he softly said. "I was going to come back for you. Just as soon as I could walk out of here."

"I thought you were dead," she whispered. "They said you were."

"Nay, lass. Nothing could keep me from you. Not even a musket ball in the back."

Loosening her grip, she stepped away and looked up at his face with a frown. "I don't know what to say. I didn't expect this."

His heart squeezed like a fist, for he saw a haunted look in her eyes that he'd never seen before. Then he understood.

"Your father?"

"Dead," she replied, regarding him with reproach. "It happened on the way back to Leathan."

Darach bowed his head and shook it. "I'm so sorry."

"Are you? How could you be, when *you* were the one who put the knife in his belly to begin with?"

God, oh God…

Darach lifted his gaze to regard Larena in the dawn's pink light. The disappointment he saw in her eyes was worse than a stinging slap across the face.

"Not on purpose," he replied.

"You expect me to believe that? Your brother made it clear how he felt about my father, and Gregory informed me that he remembered you from his youth. He said you were one of the bullies who taunted him. And he heard the rumors—that my father had murdered yours. He suggested that you wanted revenge."

Darach's hands clenched into fists. Why was everyone giving her this false information? And why was she believing it?

"I asked my father about it before he died," Larena continued. "In the glade, after you were shot, when they were taking us away.... I asked him if he killed your father. He assured me that he didn't. He gave me his word. What do you have to say about that?"

"I'll say that he was lying, because he admitted it to me."

Her mouth fell open and tears filled her eyes. "But why would he lie to me when he must have known he was going to die?"

Darach spoke gently. "Because he didn't want you to know the truth about what he'd done. Because he *did* kill my father." Darach didn't want to add more pain to her grieving condition, but she needed to know the truth. The future—*their* future—depended on it. "He admitted it to me in the glade."

Her eyebrows lifted. "And that's why you killed him?"

"Nay! He's dead because he came at me, full of hate and aggression. He hated me because I was the son of his enemy—a man he despised enough to kill. And he's dead because I was forced to defend myself."

"I don't believe you." Something darkened in her eyes and her cheeks flushed with color. She stepped back.

"Wait. Please listen...." A wave of desperation crashed over Darach. He couldn't let her go. He needed her to believe him. "The minute you were gone, he approached me from behind. He stole the knife from my boot and held it to my throat. Look."

He raised his chin and pointed at the abrasion on his neck. "Then he accused me of seducing you just to spite him. He said I was using you to reclaim my right to be Laird of Leathan. I denied it, of course, but just like you, he didn't believe me."

She stared at him with stricken eyes. "Part of me wants to believe you, but how can I believe a man who has lived his whole life as an imposter?"

Darach's heart broke into a thousand jagged pieces. "I told you that in confidence, Larena. I trusted you to understand and see me as I truly am. I thought you did."

"And I trusted you to save my father from the Tolbooth, yet he ended up dead."

"I told you...that was an accident," Darach explained again. "When I got hold of the knife, he lunged at me. I didn't intend to kill him. Sweet Mother of God! I had just rescued him out of the prison for you. I did *everything* for you."

"But why?"

"Because I love you, dammit!" he told her. "Nothing else mattered to me. Not my brother or my clan. Not even what your father did to mine."

She stared at him for a long moment, and he felt sick to his stomach at the look of mistrust in her eyes. The wound at his back throbbed like a son of a bitch and he wasn't sure if he could continue standing. He needed to sit.

Down he went. He squeezed the edge of the mattress in his hands and gave himself a moment to recover.

"Are you all right?" Larena asked.

"Just a bit dizzy."

Neither of them said anything for a moment.

"I still can't believe you're alive," Larena said, more calmly now.

Darach wet his lips, then looked up at her. "Do you believe me about what happened?

She hesitated. "How can I? He was my father and I loved him. He was always good and loving to me. Yet you are telling me that he was a liar and a murderer. Why should I believe you when your whole life has been a lie?"

"Your father didn't tell you about his Jacobite plots either."

She sank onto a wooden chair behind her. Covering her face with her hands, she wept quietly.

Darach stood and crossed the small room to kneel before her. "I'm sorry," he whispered. "I know how much you loved him."

She nodded and lowered her hands to her lap. "It was awful," she said, "when he fell off the horse. I knew he was gone, but the soldiers were so cruel about it. They wanted to place wagers about how long he had been riding without a pulse. It was all I could do not to spit in their faces."

Darach took hold of her hands and held them in his.

"I wish we had never broken him out of prison," she continued. "I shouldn't have listened to you. I should have kept my promise to Lord Rutherford. I wish you had never returned."

"Don't say that," Darach replied. "All you wanted was happiness—for yourself and for your father. You tried. We both did. But sometimes things don't work out as we hope. We must simply make the best of it and go on living."

"Make the best of it! My father is *dead*!" She shook her head at him. "And how can I go on living when I am pledged to marry a man I don't love—and for what? Nothing can save my father now."

"Then come away with me," Darach said. "We'll leave this place. Today. You can put all this behind you."

"But I don't *want* to put it behind me! I can't simply move on as if this never happened. I don't want to forget my father."

"You don't have to, but you shouldn't have to marry Gregory Chatham."

"I promised Lord Rutherford I would."

"Whatever contract you had with Rutherford can no longer be enforced because your father is dead. Neither Rutherford or Chatham can fulfill their end of the bargain, so you should not be expected to fulfill yours."

She was quiet for a long moment. "How could I go with you, Darach? You killed my father." The anguished tone in Larena's voice cut him to the quick. "You say it was an accident, but how will I ever know for sure? And even if it *was* an accident, it still happened."

"What are you saying?"

"That I don't think I could ever look at you and not think of that moment when I saw the bloody knife in your hand. I would always remember that you were responsible for my father's death. That you hated him because of what you believe he did to your father. Our fathers were *enemies*, Darach."

"Just because our fathers were enemies does not mean we have to be. That has nothing to do with us."

"Perhaps not, but yesterday…." She stopped. "I should hate you for what happened."

"*Do* you hate me?" He felt as if all the blood in his veins had drained to his toes.

"Yes. Part of me does. Part of me wishes I'd never met you. Never cared for you. But another part of me is glad that you are alive, and I find that very confusing."

His heart began to pound riotously in his chest. "It's confusing because you still care for me, Larena. I know you do. And if I could undo what happened with your father, I would. But I cannot. All I know is that I need to be with you." Darach took hold of her hands and raised them to his lips. "I pray to God you can forgive me for what happened. Your father's death was not what I wanted. Believe me. I'm so sorry."

She watched him kiss her hands, then she pulled them away and wiped a tear from her cheek. "Stop it. I can't simply fall into your arms and forget all this. It *did* happen. He was my father and now he's dead."

Darach bowed his head and nodded. "Perhaps…in time…."

"I don't know." They sat in silence for a drawn out moment. Then she stood. "I need to go back before they discover I am gone."

Darach stood up as well. "Go back? Nay, you will not be going back there. And you won't be marrying Gregory Chatham either."

"It's not up to you," she told him. "It's my life."

"But you don't love him," he practically growled. "You love *me*."

"I did," she replied, "but now everything is cloaked in shadow. I don't know what I feel."

"But you cannot go back there," he insisted. "I don't trust the colonel. I cannot explain it, but I saw a streak of cruelty in him."

She scoffed. "Says the man who used to taunt and bully him?"

"Aye, I bullied him. I admit it. But I was a just a childish lad following the lead of my reckless older brothers—and they bullied me just as much, if not more. We were all punished for it. Our father saw to that. I spent the better part of a year thinking about all that I'd done wrong while I dug that hole out from under the castle. I left Chatham alone after that."

"Still," Larena said, turning away, "I need to go back. If I don't, he'll search for me. He'll find the tunnel and he'll know you're alive."

She made a move to leave, but Darach grabbed hold of her arm. "Let him search. Come with me now and he won't catch us."

"Like they didn't catch us in the glade yesterday morning?"

Darach dropped his hand to his side. She might as well have kicked him in the guts. "I would have heard their approach if your father hadn't been holding a knife to my throat. We could have gotten away. There would have been time."

She let out a sigh, as if she were disappointed that he was blaming this on her father.

But it *was* Fitzroy's fault, damn him. If it had been just the two of them—Darach and Larena—they would be halfway to the Great Glen by now.

"Come with me," he firmly said, his eyes boring into hers with desperate intensity.

"Where?"

"Kinloch. Angus will help us. He'll hide us. You won't have to marry Chatham."

"But my clan...."

"They're already scattered and divided," he said. "Maybe in time, another leader will rise and take Leathan back from the English, but until then, it's not your responsibility to provide an heir—and certainly not a half-English one."

She considered this. "What makes you think Angus will help us?"

"He owes me a debt."

"What sort of debt?"

"I saved the life of his young son a few years back."

She inclined her head. "What happened?"

He shook his head quickly as if there wasn't time for this, but then he explained. "The lad was misbehaving and wanted to avoid being punished, so he ran off with another boy. They were missing for three full days in the dead of winter. I didn't stop searching until I found them huddling in a cave, half frozen to death. I brought them both back alive, but just in the nick of time. One more night in that cave and they wouldn't have survived."

"I see." She closed her eyes and shook her head as if to clear it. "All that aside, this is madness. You're asking me to give up everything I know."

"It's all gone now anyway, lass. Your home is occupied by the English army and your father and brothers are gone. Everything that was important to you is gone. Except me. I am still here and I want to protect you. Forever."

She sat down again. "That's exactly what Gregory said to me."

"But you don't love him," Darach replied. "You know it's true."

She sighed heavily and said nothing.

"Just *trust* me," Darach persisted. "Trust your heart."

She thought about it for a long moment, then looked up at him. "I *don't* trust you, Darach. I can't. But you're right about one thing. I don't want to marry Gregory."

All the tension sailed out of Darach's lungs. It was one small concession, at least.

"Then let us go," he said. "We'll travel on foot until we can purchase a horse in one of the villages north of here."

"Fine," she said, rising uncertainly to her feet.

Overcome with relief, Darach straightened, and though he was in significant pain, he knew that the loss of this woman would have been far more excruciating than any fatal wound.

He took her by the hand and they walked out to the main room of the cottage where Mary was hanging a pot over the fire.

"Thank you for your care," Darach said to her. "I owe you my life."

"You owe us nothing, Darach MacDonald. Or is it Campbell?" She cocked her head to the side.

He swallowed uneasily. "You were listening."

"Aye, but if you are our former chief's son and you must go into hiding, your secret is safe with us. Now you be careful. Take care of each other."

"We will. And please, for your own protection, say nothing to anyone about my presence here. You mustn't reveal that you ever saw me."

Mary quickly set about packing up a sack of food and other provisions.

Larena turned to John. "There were tracks in the woods where Darach was shot. It's what led me here."

"I'll take care of that straightaway," he assured her. Then he moved quickly to pull a basket down from a high shelf, and rifled through it. "Take this." He held out a knife in a leather case. "I cannot let you leave here without some means of survival."

Darach reached for it and slid it out of the leather casing. "This is a very fine blade," he said, running his fingers over the decorated ivory handle. "I cannot take this from you, John."

"Do not be daft," he said. "Take it. Maybe someday you can return it, if we are fortunate enough to cross paths again."

Darach thanked John and Mary, who escorted them into the yard. Darach fastened the leather sheath to his belt, then said good-bye and wished them both well.

A few minutes later, as Darach was leading the way across the narrow valley toward the forested hill on the other side, Larena stopped.

"Darach," she said, "just because I am going with you doesn't mean I've forgotten what happened. I feel as if I don't know you at all."

He stared at her a moment and realized with despair that no matter how badly he wanted to be with her and protect her, he'd never be able to erase what happened in the glade or shield her from the pain of all she had lost.

Not yet ready to give up, he glanced around to scan the horizon for Redcoats. "I understand that, lass, but I hope that one day, you will."

She looked down at the grass and followed him across the glen.

When Larena did not respond to Gregory's dinner invitation that evening, he grew concerned and went himself to the South Tower where her rooms were located.

Climbing the curved staircase, he worried that she might have become inconsolable over the death of her father and not risen from bed all day. She had no one to talk to, after all, here in the garrison. Most members of her clan had chosen to leave, even though he'd invited any and all loyal British subjects to remain. Perhaps they feared guilt by association?

Either way, he would need to remedy that situation when Larena became his wife. What he wanted was for the loyal subjects to return and discover him to be a generous and benevolent laird. Some soldiers would have to remain for a time, of course, but eventually, as the Jacobite cause was stamped out, the gates could open up again. Life, as it was, could resume and become similar to what it had been like when he lived here as a boy.

He reached the top of the stairs and found Larena's door closed. He knocked firmly upon it.

No answer came so he knocked a second time.

Then a third.

"Larena? It's Gregory. May I come in?"

Still, no answer came, so he took the liberty of opening the door and peering inside.

The bed was in shambles with the covers strewn about. A strange feeling of foreboding tingled down his spine as he slowly moved closer and walked to the window, which looked out over the bailey below.

The room was silent as a grave, and he wondered with increasing unease where Larena had gone.

Striding out of the room with purpose, he ran down the stairs, entered the hall where the officers were eating supper, and approached the long table upon the dais. "Has anyone seen Larena Campbell today?"

All the men stood. "No colonel," the highest ranking officer replied.

"You haven't seen her at all…heading to the stables or the kitchen? The gallery perhaps?"

"No, sir."

He strode quickly out of the hall and descended to the kitchen—the one place in the castle where a few Campbell women still presided. "Has anyone seen Larena?" he asked.

The clanswoman who was kneading bread dough at the worktable looked up and wiped her brow with her forearm. "Not since yesterday, Colonel Chatham, when we sent up her supper tray."

"She didn't have any breakfast?"

The clanswoman hollered over her shoulder. "Did any of you lassies take breakfast to Larena's chamber this morning?"

"No, ma'am," they each replied.

Gregory walked out and returned to his private chambers. He went straight to the drink tray and poured himself a brandy. He tossed it back in a single gulp, then poured another.

"Roberts! Come in here!"

The young lieutenant hurried into the room. "Yes, colonel?"

"Larena Campbell has gone missing. Was the gate lifted today?"

"A few times, when the men were coming and going."

"Did she leave? Did anyone see her?"

"I haven't heard, but I can enquire about it."

"See that you do, and report back to me immediately. Then I want you to assemble a few men and search every nook and cranny of this castle."

"Are we to search for the lady, colonel?"

"Yes, and if you find her, you will politely and persuasively invite her to join me for supper in my chambers. She will not refuse you. Do you understand?"

"Yes, sir."

Roberts walked out and left Gregory alone to obsess about that dirty Highland imposter whom he'd presumed to be dead.

Gregory imagined for a moment that Darach might not be dead after all and might have returned for Larena. He could have snuck in somehow when the soldiers were coming and going.

If that is what occurred—and Larena left with him willingly—Gregory wasn't certain if he'd be able to forgive her. Especially when he had done everything possible to show her patience and kindness.

What had she given him in return?

An appalling betrayal. A shocking lack of respect.

There would have to be consequences.

He downed the rest of the brandy and moved to sit in the chair in front of the fire. While he envisioned what the appropriate consequences might be, he noticed a long-legged spider on the floor and considered crushing it with his boot, but instead he gently scooped it up onto his palm and watched it crawl toward the tips of his fingers. Eventually, he couldn't resist plucking off one leg at a time until there were none left. He then tossed what was left of the spider into the fire and returned to his thoughts about consequences. What he did to Larena would all depend, he supposed, on whether or not there was still going to be a wedding.

He hoped to God there would be. Surely there was still hope.

Thirty-one

"We'll stop here for the night," Darach said, dropping the food sack on the ground and sinking to his knees on the forest floor.

"Dear Lord, are you all right?" Larena rushed to his side. "It's nowhere near nightfall. You must be at death's door if you want to stop now."

"I'm fine. We just need to rest awhile."

"But you're white as a sheet," Larena said with concern and a heated rush of dread. She may have been angry over what happened, but she didn't want him to die. "Let me check your wound."

Heaven help them both if it was festering.

She tugged at his shirt and pulled it out from under the belt at his kilt. Rolling it up, she found the bloody bandage, which was wrapped diagonally across his back, and gently lifted it. The wound was raw and had been sewn closed, but it did not appear to be blighted.

"My word, how did you ever survive such a shot? You should be dead, Darach—or at least in bed, not crossing half the Highlands on foot."

"I didn't see that we had much choice, lass. And the soft ground will serve just fine as a bed for this evening."

She glanced up at the angry sky beyond the canopy of leaves overhead. "Normally I would agree with you, but it looks like rain. We need to find shelter for the night." She lowered his shirt and patted him on the arm. "Stay here while I go and see what I can find for us."

"Do not get lost," he replied as she walked away. "And tread lightly. Keep your eyes and ears open for Redcoats."

"I will say the same to you." With that, she ventured out on her own.

⚜

When Larena returned a short time later, she found Darach asleep on the ground, lying on his side. Kneeling over him, she laid a hand on his shoulder. He startled awake, sat up with wild eyes, and grabbed her by the throat.

Searing adrenalin sparked in her blood as he glared at her with murderous eyes. Gasping for air, she slapped at his hand. Within seconds, he realized she was not his enemy and released her. Larena fell back onto her hands.

"I'm sorry," he quickly said, sitting up and taking hold of her by the shoulders. "Are you all right? I was dreaming."

"About *what*?"

"About Chatham coming after us. He had me in irons and was beating me to a pulp with a horsewhip while you watched."

She shook her head at him. "It was just a dream."

"I know that now, lass. Are you sure you're all right?"

Larena rose to her feet. "I'm fine," she said, but she was *not* fine. She couldn't help but wonder if that was how Darach had looked at her father in the glade—with those same murderous eyes just before he lost control of his senses and struck out with the knife.

Heaven help her. What was she doing here? She was still so uncertain of Darach and his true intentions. Why had she thought this was a good idea?

Pushing those thoughts aside, for there was nothing she could do about it now, she started off. "I found a place for us to set up camp for the night. We should go now, before the rain comes."

Darach rose to his feet as well and followed her through a patch of trees and down a gradual slope to a wide, slow-moving river. "There's a large weeping willow up ahead," she said. "It's not far. We can hide underneath it."

A fat raindrop struck her nose, followed by a few more upon her cheeks. "Hurry." She ran ahead, found the tree, and passed through the drooping foliage into a tent-like shelter beneath.

Darach was much slower to arrive. She had to wait for him. Clearly he was in pain.

"This will do nicely," he said as he finally entered behind her.

Rain began to patter heavily on the leaves. They sat down, huddled close to the wide trunk and she dug into the pack to find something for them to eat.

⟨≋⟩

"Do you think, by now, he's noticed that I'm gone?" Larena asked much later as they lay down to go to sleep.

"Probably," Darach replied. "And when they don't find my body where it's supposed to be, they'll search for us. We'll need to keep to the forests and stay off the main roads."

Fighting an onerous wave of apprehension, Larena hugged her arms around herself. "Will we even be able to reach Kinloch? It seems impossible from here."

"Aye, lass, we'll do whatever it takes."

"And you're sure Angus will help us? What if Logan has already returned and told him what you did?"

"I trust Angus to see that I was fulfilling my oath to him, no matter what the cost, even if it meant I had to snap my brother's arm in two."

She thought about that for a moment—the violence of him breaking his brother's arm—then shook that thought from her head, like all the others. "But Angus might not be quite so pleased to learn that we helped my father escape from the English prison. He may resent you for causing trouble and raising the ire of the English, and bringing his own clan into the fray."

"We'll cross that bridge when we come to it, lass."

"If you say so." She lay back down and struggled to find a comfortable position on the uneven ground. Saying nothing more, she tried to sleep, but it wasn't easy when she felt as if her whole world and everything she'd ever loved had been ripped away from her in the most tragic way.

⊰⟡⊱

Not long after he fell asleep, Darach woke to the sound of a sniffle. He opened his eyes and saw Larena sitting against the trunk of the tree, hugging her knees to her chest, weeping quietly.

He leaned up on an elbow. "What is it, lass?" he gently asked.

She shook her head and wiped under her nose. "I was just thinking about my father, remembering happier times."

Darach sat up. "He was a good father to you. I'll give him that."

She wiped a tear from her cheek. "How can you say that when you believe he murdered yours?"

Darach paused. "Whether he did or didn't, all I know is that I don't want to spend the rest of my life carrying a grudge against any man—especially one you care for so deeply."

She rested her chin on her knees and seemed to be taking time to consider his words.

The nearness of her in the darkness caused a painful shot of longing deep in his core. His heart began to beat fast and he hungered to move closer, to touch her, to take her into his arms and comfort her.

"Would you like me to lie beside you?" he carefully asked. "I could hold you and keep you warm."

"No, Darach," she somberly replied. "Your touch is what got us into all this trouble to begin with. I should never have lain with you."

The cold, sharp edge of her tone and the harshness of her words caused a throbbing ache to begin inside his chest, for she spoke as if she loathed him with every inch of her being. It broke him in two, and he feared that she would never forgive him for what happened.

God help him, he had murdered the love that existed between them in that moment her father fell upon his knife.

"Don't say that," Darach said. "You cannot regret it. I touched you because I loved you, and you loved me back. I know you did. What happened to your father was no one's fault. It was an accident."

At least he thought it was. Maybe Fitzroy had done it on purpose just to spite Darach and prevent Larena from ever surrendering her heart to him.

If that had been his plan, it appeared to be working. As far as Darach was concerned, there could be no worse torture, no worse punishment than what was happening here. It was the ultimate revenge, even from beyond the grave.

"Do not presume that I loved you," Larena said. "I don't know what it was. Lust, perhaps. But it couldn't have been love."

"Why not?"

"Because I hardly knew you. I still don't."

"Yes, you do," he replied. "You're just angry."

It was too dark to see her expression, but he heard the soft sound of her frustration. "Go back to sleep," she said, lying back down on the ground. "I'm sorry I woke you. I'm fine now."

But she wasn't fine and he wished he could ease her pain, yet he knew that he couldn't. All he could do was stay by her side and give her enough space to nurse her anger and blame him for what happened. If that's what she needed to do, so be it. He blamed himself, in many ways, but he prayed there would come a day when she would be ready to go on living and forgive him for what happened.

Because he had no intention of never touching her again. He loved her and desired her. His was a passionate, bone-deep need and he would do whatever it took to help her remember what they'd shared in those intimate moments when she had given herself to him completely.

He would do everything in his power to make her see the man he truly was—and realize that she loved him.

Thirty-two

Gregory Chatham sat down at his desk and listened to the faint rattle of the chains lifting the heavy iron portcullis at the main gate. Setting down his quill pen, he pinched the bridge of his nose, for he suspected that Larena had not been found. It had been three days since her unexplained disappearance, and every night, a battalion of soldiers returned to the castle with no news of her.

It was becoming increasingly vexing. If Gregory didn't find her soon, he might go mad. And it was not simply jealousy that rankled him—although that was more than half of it.

There was also the additional problem of reporting these awkward circumstances to his father, who was not a forgiving man by nature. Gregory had already sent word to him that Fitzroy Campbell had escaped from a locked prison cell while under Gregory's command, and had died shortly thereafter in an alleged knife fight.

His father would not be pleased. Evidently, elaborate plans had been made for the Scottish laird's arrival at the Tolbooth in Edinburgh. Fitzroy was to be used as an example for other traitorous rebels in Scotland, and it was intended to be a gruesome and memorable spectacle for the people of Scotland.

But because of Gregory's failure to keep the Campbell laird imprisoned, the pageantry would have to be called off, which would shine a very poor light on Gregory as a commander. He was a colonel in the British army, yet he had no control over the prisoners under his watch, or his future bride.

In light of that, how the devil was he to send a second report to his father and explain that his fiancée had also escaped his grasp? He didn't even know if it was her choice to leave the garrison, or if that dirty Scottish rebel had returned, scaled the walls somehow, and abducted her against her will. Truth be told, Gregory didn't even know if the man was dead or alive for his body had gone missing.

Either way it was an embarrassment.

And Gregory suspected the abduction theory was just wishful thinking. Larena had admitted openly that she had become infatuated with Darach during her journey from Fort William to Leathan.

There was a sudden pounding in Gregory's ears as he thought about that. What exactly had happened between them? Had that despicable savage touched her? Defiled her? Had she welcomed it?

Fire burned in Gregory's guts, and he wanted to smash something. *Damn!* How witless could he have been?

He'd foolishly presumed that if he didn't push Larena too hard—if he was patient, gentle and understanding—she would appreciate his kindness and eventually forget about Darach and accept her position here in the garrison as First Lady of Leathan.

Gregory pounded his fist on the desktop, stood up, and with a bellowing roar, swept all the papers, the crystal wine glass, and inkwell onto the floor with a resounding crash.

Bloody hell. He had not been aggressive enough. He should have bedded her right then and there after dinner that first night. He shouldn't have allowed her to push him away when he kissed her. He should have staked his claim. Branded her as his own.

It was a constant battle, to become the sort of man his father wanted him to be. His polite decorum had always been his greatest shortcoming.

He had to get her back, and he had to deal with Darach—if he lived. Gregory had to prove to everyone—his father as well as every last member of the Campbell clan—that he was not to be underestimated and that he was fit to rule over them. They needed to know that he was not the timid boy he used to be. He had grown into a man deserving of their fear.

A knock sounded at the door just then. "Is everything all right, colonel?"

Gregory strode to the door and opened it. "What news is there?"

Roberts took one look at the papers and shattered glass on the floor and swallowed uneasily. "The men are back, sir. They found nothing."

Gregory winced. "She couldn't have disappeared into the clouds." He turned his gaze toward the fireplace. "If that wretched Highlander is alive and has taken Larena with him, there is only one place they would go. One place where they would seek refuge."

"Kinloch?" Roberts suggested.

"That's right." Gregory returned to his desk. "As it happens, the famous laird of Kinloch, Angus the Lion, is the son of a Jacobite traitor himself, and if he is sheltering the man who broke a known criminal out of an English prison, he must face the consequences. Don't you agree?"

"Yes, sir."

"Good. Make the necessary arrangements and we will squeeze that Lion around the neck until he squeals. I'll need at least twenty good men and we will ride out first thing in the morning. If we couldn't make an example out of Fitzroy Campbell, I will bloody well capture a few other prestigious Scots and provide an even better show. I want both Darach and Angus the Lion, and needless to say, my fiancée needs to be rescued from their clutches."

Roberts bowed and hurried out while Gregory strode with purpose to the fireplace.

There now. That is how it must be done. I only wish I hadn't waited so long. This time I won't be gentle. This time I will force my hand, and Larena will finally see that I am a man to be respected and feared.

ᚈᚺᛁᚱᚈᚤ-ᚈᚺᚱᛖᛖ Thirty-Three

"I didn't expect to ever return here," Larena said to Darach as they crossed the drawbridge and rode through the castle gates at Kinloch on the spirited gelding they had acquired along the way.

It had been a trying journey, for she had spent most of it grieving over the death of her father, while at the same time struggling to make sense of her feelings for Darach.

She had asked him on that first night to keep away from her, not to touch her. She had told him she wished they'd never lain together, and she had recognized the hurt in his eyes every moment since.

He'd been correct when he'd accused her of being angry. She was most certainly that. There were times she wanted to physically lash out at him with her fists and pummel his chest repeatedly. She suspected that if she tried, he would let her. He would simply stand there and take it.

Other times, when he wasn't looking, she found herself watching him, studying the handsome, chiseled lines of his face and those dark eyes that communicated so much and yet so little. Whenever he gazed at her, she felt as if she meant a great deal to him and that he wanted her to know it.

Yet at the same time he was circumspect about the events surrounding her father's death. He did not push her to talk about it or to forgive him. He did not try again to explain his actions or defend himself. Most of the time, it felt as if there were a giant wall between them.

Nevertheless, her body could not forget the passion they had shared. Whenever he lay down across from her at night and drew his tartan about his shoulders, she longed for the comfort of his arms. Her mind turned to memories of their lovemaking. Desire fluttered through her belly and her flesh grew warm as she recalled the pleasures of his touch.

She was lonely and heartsick over the loss of her father, but also from the lost intimacies with Darach, which at one time she had imagined would last forever. But that was all gone now. Shaken apart by violence, death, and loss.

Darach reined the horse to a halt in front of the stables.

An older groom approached. "Darach! Good to have you back, laddie!" He took hold of the gelding's bridle. "Where's Logan?"

Darach stroked the gelding's smooth muscled neck. "I thought Logan would have returned by now. He's not here?"

"No, sir. We haven't seen hide nor hair of either one of you since you left." He glanced curiously at Larena in the saddle.

Darach dismounted and helped her down as well, then Haggis led the gelding toward an empty stall.

"Haggis…?" Darach followed and spoke to him in hushed tones for a moment. When he returned, he led Larena toward the entrance to the Great Hall. "I told him not to mention to anyone that we've returned. We need to see Angus right away."

An attractive, dark-haired woman appeared under the archway to the Great Hall and regarded them both with concern. "Darach, welcome home." Darach approached her and she kissed him on the cheek. "You're not alone, I see." She turned to Larena and studied her up and down, from head to foot.

"May I present Larena Campbell of Leathan Castle," Darach said. "This is Gwendolen MacDonald, Mistress of Kinloch."

The Lion's wife. Larena dipped into a curtsy. "It's a pleasure to meet you, madam."

"And you as well," Gwendolen replied. They all stood in awkward silence for a few seconds. "Well, then. You both look as if you've been through a war, and I suspect that's not far from the truth. Won't you come in? Angus will want to see you immediately."

Immediately? As Larena followed Gwendolen into the Great Hall—an impressive room with high arched ceilings, tapestries hung on the walls, and heraldry carved into the stones in the hearth—she sensed that the Lion and his Lioness already knew what was afoot, and they were not pleased.

Gwendolen walked quickly ahead of them, her heels clicking purposefully across the stone slabs on the floor. Perhaps she resented the fact that they had come here as fugitives and would put her husband in a difficult predicament and perhaps even risk the safety of the clan. If the English decided to exact vengeance upon the MacDonalds for harboring two criminals, it could be a dark day for those at Kinloch, especially their laird.

Larena followed the Lioness through the vaulted stone passageways and up curved tower steps to the same room where she had met Angus the first time, which seemed a hundred years ago now. So much had occurred since she woke up in this fortress with a bump on her head and was forced to beg for her freedom and the chance to return to Leathan to save her father's life.

The Lion had been merciful that day. She prayed he would be equally so today.

They reached the top of the stairs and entered the solar, which was brightly lit, but empty.

Gwendolen gestured toward the center of the large room. "Please wait here. He will see you shortly." With that, she walked out.

Larena's heart began to race. She turned toward Darach, and he regarded her with a look of unease.

❧❦❧

There were no chairs to sit upon in the massive, open space, so Larena strolled to the window to look out over the moat and meadow beyond. Further in the distance, she could make out a village with a market square and numerous cottages spread out over the landscape.

"We shouldn't have come here," she said, remembering that she was a Campbell, a longstanding enemy of the MacDonalds. "You should have left me behind. It's not right that I am putting all of you in danger."

She felt a hand come to rest upon her shoulder and realized that Darach had followed her to the window, quiet as a whisper. Her body tingled with awareness, for it was the first time he had touched her since she'd told him to keep away. He had respected her wishes over the past few days and kept his distance, to the point where she'd almost regretted ever asking for that.

"I couldn't leave you behind, lass," he whispered. "No matter what you think of me, I'll be devoted to you until I draw my last breath."

His words touched something deep inside her and she turned around to face him. "I can't imagine why. I've told you

I am aggrieved, that I cannot pledge my heart to you. Not after what happened. I am still grieving for the father I realize I never truly knew. I am a lost soul, Darach. You shouldn't have brought me here. You should have left me to find my own way."

He laid a hand on her cheek. "Now you're just speaking nonsense, lass, because I'll never give you up."

She was shocked by his declaration, for she'd thought she'd made herself clear that night under the willow tree. She had told him she regretted ever loving him, yet now her eyes were drawn to his soft, full lips and she felt the same stirring of attraction she'd felt the first moment they'd met. *Did he know it? Could he feel it?*

She didn't *want* him to feel it. She needed him to stay away because how could she ever love the man, or accept love from a man who had struck her father down and ended his life? Darach claimed it was an accident, that he had not been seeking vengeance all along, but how would she ever know the truth?

The sound of heavy footfalls up the tower steps caused them both to turn. Larena stepped back. Her belly careened with nervous dread, for the Lion's reputation alone was enough to intimidate anyone.

Angus walked in and strode menacingly to the center of the room, where he paused before them with his big hand on the hilt of his sword. His golden hair appeared windblown, as if he'd just returned from a brisk ride, and there was mud on his boots. His pale blue eyes narrowed in on them. Larena gulped.

"I heard what happened," he said. "They tell me you broke Fitzroy Campbell out of the English prison, and for some reason I cannot comprehend, you decided to dirk him in the woods the next day." His gaze slid to meet Larena's. He tossed a look toward Darach, beside her. "You're still speaking to him?"

She shook her head. "Not really."

"I see," he replied with a strangely disturbing nod that did not relax her in the slightest.

Slowly, Angus strode closer until the light from the window illuminated his face and reflected in the wintry blue of his eyes. "What happened to Logan?" he asked Darach. "I sent the two of you out of here to escort the lady home to Leathan, then all hell breaks loose and only one of you returns."

"I don't know where he is," Darach replied. "We had a disagreement along the way."

"You didn't dirk him, too, I hope."

"Nay," Darach said. "But I did break his arm."

Angus shook his head and paced around in a circle. "Let me guess. It had something to do with this bonnie Campbell lass. I should have known better than to send the two of you together. And I should have sent a maid along as well. What was I thinking?"

Angus turned away and strode to the far end of the room where he stood with his back to them, gazing up at a large tapestry on the wall. It was a peaceful, rustic scene of a stone bridge over a river which led to a small hamlet in the distance. He stared at it for a long moment, then he turned.

"But here we are." He spread his arms wide. "All of us in a difficult position because without a doubt, a certain half-English colonel will be wondering what became of his fiancée. And I expect he'll want to beat you to a pulp, Darach, for what you did."

"I suspect so, too," Darach replied. "Which is why we've come. We need your help."

"To do what?" Angus coolly asked.

"To stay hidden."

Angus scoffed. "You hardly need my help to do that. If anyone is an expert in that area, it's *you*."

Darach shook his head, as if he didn't understand the implication.

Angus raised an eyebrow. "You think I don't know that you're a Campbell?"

Darach's head drew back in surprise. It took a moment to find words. "How long have you known?"

"Since the day my father took you in, you bloody fool."

"But if he knew we were Campbells, why did he treat us like his own sons? Why did he let us pretend?"

Angus shrugged. "I often wonder that myself. I suspect he intended to use you as pawns initially, but then he grew fond of you and enjoyed knowing that you deserted your clan, knowing that you preferred us over them. He always hated the Campbells, except for the two of you." Angus regarded Larena. "No disrespect to you or your clan, lass, but you must know how things are."

"I do," Larena replied. "And I hold no grudge against you for it. My clan has no love for yours either."

Angus turned to Darach and inclined his head. "She has a good sense of perspective, this one."

With that he turned away and strode to the window where he looked out over his lands, as if contemplating what to do.

Darach slowly approached him. "I'll understand if you do not wish to help us. We will go if that is your command."

Angus faced him. "Where, Darach? Where would you go?"

Darach shrugged. "I don't know. We'd figure something out."

Larena waited uneasily in the center of the room, watching them both consider the situation. With his hand still on the hilt of his sword, Angus paced.

"The obvious choice would be to head north," he said. "I did that once myself—traveled as far as the Western Isles and spent two years in exile. But it's a hard life, Darach. If you would prefer to stay close, I could arrange for you to be absorbed into the MacLean clan, under the protection of the Duke of Moncrieffe. He is like a brother to me and he knows what you did for my son. His land and property holdings are vast. He could find a place for you—but I will not ask him to arrange for your pardon. The way I see it, you're guilty as sin for helping Fitzroy escape."

"I am," Darach agreed. "I won't deny it. And that sounds like a generous offer that we should accept."

Angus faced him. "Very well then. I will send you both to Moncrieffe with a letter of introduction, explaining things. I will provide you with supplies for the journey and whatever else you might need. You will leave tonight, after dark. But if I do this for you, Darach, we are square, you and I. Once you leave here, you cannot ever return. Do you understand?"

"I do."

They shook hands, then backed away from each other. The Lion turned to address Larena. "Gwendolen is preparing rooms for you both in the East Tower. You must remain there until dusk. Do not go roaming about the castle. No one must know of your presence here. Now go and get yourselves cleaned up. I wish you luck."

"We are indebted to you," Larena replied, dipping into a curtsey. As she rose, she took one final lingering look at Angus the Lion, then turned and walked out with Darach.

"Are you sure this is what you want?" Darach asked.

She considered it carefully as she descended the stairs. "I have no idea *what* I want, Darach, and I'm not certain this is the best path. The future feels like a dark hole to me."

"Then I suppose you'll just have to trust me to shine some light into it," he replied. "I will fetch you at dusk."

She sighed with resignation and followed him to the East Tower.

A short while later, a party of maids arrived in Larena's chamber with a copper tub and buckets of hot water.

She felt much better after she'd bathed.

Gwendolen also paid her a visit to deliver a clean gown for her travels that night—as well as something appropriate for an introduction to an illustrious Scottish duke in two days' time.

"Moncrieffe is a charming and honorable man," Gwendolen said about him. "He will do his best to secure your safety, and his duchess is the most enchanting Englishwoman you could ever dream to meet. There is no need to be nervous. They will treat you well."

"Thank you, Gwendolen," Larena replied, turning the gown over in her hands, feeling rather absentminded as she looked down at the fine, dark blue fabric. "How can I ever repay you for your kindness?"

"No need." Gwendolen nodded somberly. "I was very sorry to hear about your father. I cannot imagine how difficult this must be for you."

"It has indeed been difficult," Larena agreed, letting out a deep breath.

"But at least you have Darach," Gwendolen added. "He appears to be very protective of you."

Larena turned away and laid the gown on the bed. "Yes, he is doing all he can to assure me of that. I am not sure if it's because he feels guilty over what happened, or if there is still a chance he might be entertaining some secret agenda to gain control over me. Everyone has been warning me about that relentlessly."

Gwendolen shook her head with bewilderment. "Why would he wish to do that?"

"Because he despised my father. Darach believes that my father stole Leathan from his after murdering him during a hunt. Darach's father was our former chief."

"I know who he was." Gwendolen approached Larena and took hold of her hand. "My dear. You haven't known Darach very long, but I can assure you that he would never try to use you or anyone else as a pawn in some elaborate revenge scheme. He is one of the kindest men I know and I owe him everything. His brother, on the other hand…." She paused. "Logan was always an ambitious lad, rather broody if you ask me. I didn't know him as well. But Darach was protective of Logan all his life and protective of others as well—especially those who were younger, smaller, and weaker. My son was one of those people."

"That's strange to hear," Larena replied. "Gregory Chatham described him as quite the opposite. He said Darach was a terrible bully in his youth."

"Perhaps he was, as a boy. I didn't know him then. But he is not that way now." She turned to go. "You should get some rest, Larena. I suspect it will be a long night for you."

Larena thanked her and waited until she was gone before she climbed onto the bed to lay for a while, staring up at the ceiling. Eventually her eyes fell closed and she drifted off.

It seemed like only a few moments had passed when a knock sounded at the door. She sat up with a jolt and shook herself awake, then noticed the windows were dark. She must have been sleeping for quite some time. "Yes?"

"It's me," said the voice on the other side of the door, which she recognized as Darach's.

"Come in." Dressed only in her shift, she tossed the covers aside and stood.

The door swung open and he walked in wearing a clean white shirt and his familiar MacDonald tartan. He stood at the threshold with saddlebags slung over his shoulder and a new weapon belt that housed a claymore, a pistol and powder horn, and the knife John Campbell had given him. "You're not ready," he said.

"I'm sorry. I fell asleep. Just give me a moment. It won't take me long."

He closed the door behind him to wait while she reached for the gown on the bed. Without modesty—for they'd been travelling together for many days—she stepped into the skirt, tied the ribbons, and donned the bodice. "How late is it?" she asked.

She realized he had turned his back while she was dressing and he was now facing the wall. "It's almost ten. It's full dark now so we should be able to gain some distance by midnight. Angus is giving us two of his best horses."

She finished fastening the ties on her bodice and crossed the room to sit on a chair and pull on her shoes. "That was good of him. How long will it take us to reach Moncrieffe Castle?"

"It's a two-day ride."

"You can turn around now." She stood up and reached for her cloak.

He faced her and his broad shoulders rose and fell with a resigned sigh.

"What is it?" she asked.

"You look pretty, lass."

"Pretty?" she replied with astonishment. "I just woke up."

"Aye, and your hair is tousled, your cheeks are flushed. Good thing it's dark outside, otherwise you'd be a terrible distraction. I might ride straight into a tree."

She couldn't help but warm to his words and the friendly, open tone of his voice. She responded in kind. "Hasn't anyone ever told you that flattery will get you nowhere?"

"I'm only speaking the truth. And a man can always dream." He turned to the door and put his hand on the latch, waiting for her to follow. "We must leave the castle quickly," he said. "Don't stop to talk to anyone. The horses are saddled and waiting for us just outside the gate. We'll head for the western forest." He paused before he opened the door. "But I must ask you again, lass. Are you sure this is what you want?"

"I'm afraid my answer hasn't changed," she replied. "I'm still not sure of anything."

Darach accepted that and opened the door, but he drew back at a most alarming sight.

Gregory Chatham stood in the corridor with his fist in the air, as if he were just about to knock. His eyes grew wide. "*You....*" he said, frowning at Darach.

In a lightning flash of movement, both men drew their swords. Gregory was a split second faster.

Thirty-four

Whipping his slender blade through the air, Gregory came crashing into the room. Larena scrambled to get out of the way while Darach backed away defensively, blocking blow after blow as they traveled across the floor.

Another soldier in a red uniform entered behind Gregory and also drew his sword, but Gregory shouted at him. "Stay out of this, Roberts! He's mine!"

Gregory's quick and nimble technique took Larena by surprise. He was a lean and feisty swordsman. Though Darach was bigger and stronger, his weapon was twice the width of Gregory's, which was not an advantage when he was still recovering from his wounds. It slowed him down considerably.

Darach knocked over a small table and threw it between them to deflect Gregory's forward motion. Gregory leaped over it.

"Shut the door, Roberts!" Gregory commanded while he lunged forward and sliced Darach across the upper arm. "I don't wish to be interrupted by some other meddlesome Scot!"

Darach winced in pain.

"Stop, Gregory!" Larena pleaded. "You'll kill him!"

"With any luck!" Gregory replied, slicing Darach across the chest and drawing more blood. "Though it appears luck has nothing to do with this. Clearly I am the superior man."

Darach swung his heavy claymore through the air, missed Gregory and struck the bedpost. The oak splintered into bits that flew onto the bed. Gregory lunged at him again and struck fast, forcing Darach to retreat around the upholstered chairs in front of the fire. Darach fell over one of them and landed on his back with a roar of pain.

Gregory kicked the claymore from his hand and stood over him with the point of his sword at his throat. "Do you see this, Larena?" Gregory asked. "I have subjugated him. What do you say to that, Darach Campbell? How does it feel to be humiliated in front of the woman you love?"

"Stop, Gregory," Larena pleaded, moving closer. "Don't do this. You have caught us. Is that not enough? Arrest us if you must, but please put your sword down."

"And give this prisoner a chance to escape again?" Gregory replied, his eyes flashing with bloodlust as he glanced across at her. Then his eyes narrowed and his thin lips tightened. Returning his attention to Darach, he pushed the point of his sword into Darach's neck until blood began to seep from the puncture point. "I cannot decide whether I should kill you now or save you for the guards at the Tolbooth. Maybe I should just break your leg, or cut off your thumbs."

At some point, the guard named Roberts had drawn his pistol and moved closer to aim it at Darach's head.

Larena took a step forward but Roberts immediately turned his pistol on her. "Stay where you are, miss."

She halted and raised her hands in the air.

No one moved. The silence was suffocating. A slow, diabolical smile spread across Gregory's lips. Then suddenly Darach swiveled and kicked Gregory's legs out from under him. Gregory dropped like a heavy stone.

Roberts fired the pistol at Darach—but missed. The ball pierced a hole in the window glass. He fumbled to reload and dropped his sword.

A flashing second later, Darach stood over Gregory with his boot pressed hard upon Gregory's wrist, his claymore pointed at his heart.

Darach withdrew the pistol from his own belt and tossed it across the room to Larena. She caught it and aimed it at Roberts.

"Hands in the air, soldier," Darach said to him.

Gregory squeezed his eyes shut and put his hand in front of his face, defensively. "Please don't kill me. I beg of you. If you let me live, I will let you both go. I promise, I can make all of this go away."

Darach's pressed the sword harder upon his chest. "You expect me to trust your word on that? I suspect as soon as I lower my weapon, you'll call in your men and put me back in irons. Lord knows what you'll do to Larena."

"I won't do anything," he replied, curling into a squirming position. "I'll tell them you were never here, that we didn't find you. Just please, don't kill me!"

A muscle twitched at Darach's jaw. He glared down at Gregory with dangerous malice and raised the point of his sword to Gregory's throat.

Gregory cried out. "Please!" He began to weep, which only served to add fuel to the fire of Darach's wrath.

Larena's heart raced with fear. Only once had she seen such a look of fury in Darach's eyes—on the night he rescued her from Logan, just before he broke Logan's arm. But this man was not Darach's brother. He was his enemy.

Darach squeezed the handle of his sword until his fist turned white.

"Darach," Larena said. "Please don't do this. You mustn't."

His dark eyes turned slowly to her and he regarded her with a mixture of dismay and derision. "What did you say?"

"Don't kill him. I can't let you. I won't." She pointed the pistol at him. Her hands trembled.

Darach's eyes narrowed with dark, calculating resolve. "You disappoint me, lass." Then he turned his attention toward Roberts, whose hands were still in the air. "Did you hear what your colonel just said about letting us go?"

Roberts quickly nodded.

"Colonel Chatham, you will release Larena from your betrothal," Darach added, "unless of course she wishes otherwise. Tell everyone that she was my victim. All this was my doing, alone. I wanted revenge against Fitzroy Campbell and I used her as a pawn for that purpose."

"Yes," Gregory replied.

Darach removed his boot from Gregory's wrist and resheathed his sword. "Then it is as you say. I was never here tonight. Do not come after me and I give you my word that you will never see me again."

Larena stared at Darach in shock while Gregory rose shakily to his feet, picked up his sword, and hurried out.

"That was too easy," Larena said. "I don't trust him not to come after us."

"Nor do I," Darach replied, shutting the door behind them. "Which is why I'll not be staying here. I still plan to ride to Moncrieffe," he whispered. "You can do whatever you please, lass. You're free of me now."

A sudden coldness hit her core. "*What?*"

Darach moved about the room, righting the furniture and setting it back in place. Then he faced her and shook his head. "Did you really think I was going to kill him?"

She stammered. "I-I don't know."

"Like I killed your father, I suppose. In cold blood. For revenge. Or maybe you think I simply can't control myself, that I'm a bully, or an animal at heart."

"No, I don't think that," Larena replied, feeling baffled and confused as he approached her, took the pistol from her hand, and shoved it back into his belt.

"You could at least *try* to sound convincing." He turned away and looked around the room, spotted the damage to the bedpost and moved closer to run a finger over it. He peeled off a splinter of wood and tossed it into the fireplace. "Gwendolen won't be happy about that," he said.

Larena's stomach rolled with nausea. After everything that had just occurred, her head was spinning. "What did you mean when you said I'm free of you? Do you intend to leave me here?"

"I think that's best. Don't you? You'll be fine here at Kinloch. You're an innocent victim, remember?"

"But we're *both* supposed to go to Moncrieffe territory."

"That was before."

"Before what?"

He faced her squarely. "Before I realized how little you truly think of me." He started for the door.

Larena followed. "Wait...Darach, you cannot blame me for that. You killed my father."

"Aye, and I'll never be able to live that down. Nor can I change it. You will always see me as your father's murderer. And we cannot change the past." He stopped, turned and strode purposefully, ominously toward her until she backed up in fright and hit the bed. "But you need to know one thing, lass."

"What is it?"

He hesitated briefly while his eyes focused on her lips. She felt the heat of his breath and was overcome by the sheer force of his presence before her.

"Over the past few days," he finally said, "I've been as sensitive as I could possibly be because I care for you and I know how much you loved your father, but the truth is...." Darach inhaled deeply. "He deserved what he got. He was an imprudent fool to attack me that morning. I had no choice but to defend myself. And yes, I *do* believe he killed my father during that hunt, beyond any shadow of a doubt, and I am not sorry your father is dead. There, I've said it." He paused. "Though I didn't intend to, I'm glad I killed him because he confessed to killing my father and he bloody well had it coming." Darach backed away. "So now you finally know who I truly am."

He picked up the saddle bags, raised his tartan over his head like a hood, and opened the door. "Good-bye, lass. And good luck to you."

Shocked and horrified by what had just passed between them, Larena followed him into the corridor. "Wait...please...."

But before she could voice a protest, he was gone, vanished down the staircase like a ghost.

CHAPTER

ᏖᏂᎥᎡᏖᎩ-ᖴᎥᏉᎬ

One month later

D arach checked one last time to make sure the cellar
door was locked, then he strode up the narrow stone
staircase to the main hall of the distillery where the
office was located.

It wasn't a bad appointment. As warehouse master for the
most famous whisky distillery in Scotland—the duke's very
own brand—Darach had been living onsite for the past four
weeks. He kept an eye on the casks and stills during the night
and mostly slept during the days. It was a lonely occupation
at times, but it allowed him to stay hidden, undetected, until
the scandal of Fitzroy Campbell's escape and subsequent death
blew over. How long that would take, Darach had no idea. Not
much longer, he hoped, for he was beginning to grow impatient
and restless.

There were days he longed desperately for his old life as a
scout for Angus the Lion, free to roam the Highland forests and
glens on horseback with his brother.

His brother....

There was still no word from Logan, which left Darach
deeply concerned and beleaguered by guilt. He was beginning
to believe that he might never see his brother again—if Logan
was even alive. No one seemed to know anything, and every

day, with no news, Darach struggled more and more to resist the urge to return to Campbell territory and search every cave and croft himself.

This wasn't an easy life. Darach had lost his brother, his home, and the woman he loved. And what was it all for? He'd never imagined a woman would come between him and Logan. Despite their differences and many arguments over what was right and wrong, they'd always been as loyal to each other as two brothers could be, but now Darach was alone. He had no brother, nor did he have Larena.

Did he even want her? After all that had happened? She was the daughter of the villain who had killed his own father years ago and tried to kill Darach as well. She blamed Darach for everything and saw him as a bully and a murderer. He should despise her with every last breath in his body.

And yet....

Surely there must be something wrong with him because he continued to wake each day with her image emblazoned on his brain, her womanly scent fresh and clear in his mind, as if she were lying next to him, naked in his bed.

Heaven help him, he did love her—still—even though she did not see him as the man he truly was. She could not have loved him the same way he loved her, or things would have turned out differently.

The sun was just coming up to brighten the pre-dawn sky, so he sat down at the desk in the office to await the day manager's arrival. He would then retire to his own bedchamber and sleep for the day—and he would try not to think of her again.

‹◊›

Darach woke with a start when the manager arrived. He lifted his head off the desk and realized he had fallen asleep in the chair.

He'd had the dream again. This time, the hawk was flying out over the water, swooping freely down just above the waves, then back up again. The last time he'd dreamed of the hawk, it had turned out to be a premonition regarding his return to Leathan Castle, and later, of his escape. Sadly, his home had turned out to be nothing that it once was. The Leathan he knew as a boy was all gone now, taken over by the English. There was no one left to return to.

After handing the keys off to the manager, Darach crossed the courtyard to the south building where his room was located on the second floor. He climbed the outdoor steps and laid a hand on the knob, but hesitated to push it open when he noticed the door was ajar.

Half expecting to find a Redcoat inside rifling through his belongings, he reached for his sword, quietly withdrew it from the scabbard, and gently pushed the door open with the toe of his boot.

The room appeared to be empty, but he moved silently nevertheless. Adrenaline coursed through his veins as he tiptoed across the floor.

He sucked in a breath and lowered his sword when a woman popped into view, rising to her feet from the floor on the opposite side of the bed.

Larena....

"Oh. You're here," she said with surprise, smoothing out her skirts.

"Yes," he flatly replied, though on the inside, he was bursting open with a sudden rush of exhilaration. "I live here."

What was she doing in his apartments? And dear God, she was more beautiful than he remembered. He couldn't breathe. It was a miracle he didn't collapse.

"I hope you don't mind," she explained. "His Grace let me in. I dropped my earring just now." She gestured toward the floor.

"The duke was here?" Darach asked. "In this room?"

Darach had only met the duke once—on the day he'd arrived with Angus's letter of introduction. The duke had immediately assigned Darach to this position in the distillery on the outskirts of the village to guard over his whisky. Darach had not set foot on the castle grounds since.

"Yes," Larena replied while Darach re-sheathed his sword. "And Gwendolen was absolutely right. He is a charming man and his duchess is stunningly beautiful. Did you meet her?"

"No." Confused by all of this, Darach closed the door but remained just inside the threshold. "How long have you been here, Larena?"

"I arrived yesterday afternoon with Angus and Gwendolen. They brought their children as well. We had dinner with the duke and duchess last night. What an experience that was."

"How nice for you," Darach said with a frown, not entirely sure what her purpose was in coming here. He certainly hadn't invited her. He had been working so hard to forget….

"It was indeed," she replied, moving around the foot of the bed. "I feel very blessed to have met them, but that is not why I came, Darach. I have traveled here for quite another reason."

The closer she came, the faster Darach's pulse pounded beneath the surface of his skin. She was everything he remembered from the first moment he'd laid eyes on her in the ravine, when she'd sat up and struck him on the head with a big rock.

Perhaps it was time he simply got down on his knees, surrendered completely, and allowed her to finish him off.

"I owe you an apology," she said, and all at once, Darach's passions ignited into a flurry of conflicting emotions, for he could not forget why he'd left her at Kinloch a month earlier—because she had not trusted him enough to believe that he would never use her for revenge. She had not understood that he'd loved her. She had not loved him enough, in return, to see the truth.

"Yes, you do," he coolly said.

She appeared startled by the iciness in his tone, but proceeded nonetheless.

"I was wrong to treat you the way I did," she softly said, gazing up at him with clear, determined eyes. "You are a good man and I'm sorry I didn't believe you before about what happened."

"Which part?"

She swallowed uneasily. "All of it. I've had time to think about it, and I've replayed everything in my mind a thousand times over."

"And?" he asked, still frowning.

"And...I don't believe you killed my father on purpose. I *do* know you better than that, Darach. I believe it happened exactly as you said it did—that he came at you from behind and took your knife."

A flood of relief washed over Darach, yet he was still angry with her for all the days she had *not* seen the truth.

"What changed your mind?" he asked.

"I don't know. *Everything.* The way you showed mercy to Gregory Chatham that night at Kinloch when he begged you not to kill him. I was wrong to assume that you would. And the look on your face in the glade when I saw you kneeling over my father with the knife in your hand. You told me it was an accident and I should have believed you. And the mark you showed me at your neck when I found you in the crofter's cottage. That was solid, tangible evidence, and yet I refused to accept it. I'm not sure why…." She strode a little closer. "Or maybe it's just how I feel about you, which is not a factor of reason, but a factor of the heart. Also, what I know about my father—or rather, what I *didn't* know. The fact that he kept me in the dark about his Jacobite plots is unsettling and astounding to me. You were right about that. I don't believe I ever really knew him—at least not that part of him."

Darach's shoulders relaxed slightly and he took a step toward her. "You did know him, lass. You knew the man he was, as your father, and that side of him was worthy of your love."

She wiped away a tear, then bowed her head. "Oh, Darach. How is it possible, after everything I've said and done, that you can be so forgiving—of both me and my father? You make me feel ashamed."

His heart split in two. "Why?"

Her eyes lifted. "Because I was not forgiving toward you when you deserved so much more. You risked everything and gave up everything for me—your brother, and even your freedom—yet I was ungrateful. Untrusting."

"You were grief-stricken," he said.

She smiled with melancholy. "You have no idea what you're doing to me."

He laid a hand on her cheek and felt all his anger slowly draining away. "What do you mean, lass? I'm not trying to hurt you."

She let out a sob that was half laughter, half tears. "You're not actually hurting me. You're making me want you even more when I am so afraid that you'll never want me back."

"Why in the world would I not want you back?" he asked.

"Because of how I treated you," she replied with disbelief that he couldn't understand why she was so forlorn.

Darach nodded his head. "Aye, lass, you were a bit of a shrew, but I was not perfect either. I, too, owe you an apology for the things I said about your father the night we parted. I was very harsh. I didn't mean it."

"Yes, you did," she replied, "and you were justified. I cannot blame you for that. But you once told me that just because our fathers were enemies didn't mean *we* had to be. I don't want to be. None of that matters. It's in the past. I know you for the man you are today and that is the man I love and respect. The man I want to be with." She cupped his face in her hands and gazed into his eyes with passionate purpose. "Please, Darach, if you could only love me again. I would give anything…."

"Love you *again*? My darling lass, I never stopped."

A tear spilled from her eye and Darach wiped it away. She gazed up at him with those big weepy eyes and he was done for.

At last, he pressed his mouth to hers and gathered her into his arms with fierce, unruly desire. It took every ounce of self-control he possessed not to toss her onto the bed right then and there, because he wanted all of her, all at once. He could hardly believe she had come back to him.

Her lips were so soft, so deliciously sweet, he wished he could devour her whole. Running both hands down her slender back and over the curve of her hips, he held her captive while he drank in the delectable taste of her.

"Oh, Darach," she sighed into his mouth, "I missed you so much. I don't care where we are or who we claim to be, as long as we are together. Please don't send me away. Let me stay."

Scooping her up into his arms, he carried her to the bed, set her down, and crawled onto the mattress to lay down beside her. "I wouldn't let you go now if you begged me to."

"I won't," she replied, "but perhaps I will beg you for something else."

She gave him a look of sensual allure and reached up to pull him down on top of her soft, warm body. As she wrapped her legs around his hips, he kissed her deeply and wished he was inside her already.

"I'll never stop loving you," she whispered, "not as long as I live."

"Nor I, you," he replied, "and I still want to marry you, lass, if you'll have me."

"Of course I will."

He drew back slightly and spoke with regret. "But you'll be married to a fugitive."

"I don't care," she said. "And there are ways around it. I spoke to the duke last night about our situation. We could still have our freedom."

"How?"

She inched up on the pillows.

Curious, he sat up beside her.

"Do you know what I admire most about you?" she asked, as if changing the subject.

He shook his head.

"You know when to let go, and when to move on, and you don't get mired in the past. You tried to teach Logan that, but he was built differently than you. I believe, Darach, that you and I are similar that way. I don't want to be mired in the past either. I want to spread my wings and fly, somewhere new."

Darach raised her hand to his lips and kissed it.

"Did you know that His Grace has family in France?" she continued. "That's where his mother came from."

"I wasn't aware."

"Well, it's true, and the duke is very generous. He has offered to send us over there with a letter of introduction. We would have to take the MacLean clan name of course, but we wouldn't need to stay in hiding or live our lives on the run. Gregory would never find us there."

He stared at her, transfixed. "Are you sure you would want to do that, lass? To leave your homeland?"

She smiled. "You were always asking me if I wanted what you were offering, and I always told you I didn't know *what* I wanted. But I know it now. I want *you*, and that is all. Where ever we end up will be my home, as long as you are with me."

With a surge of greedy lust, Darach kissed her again and eased her down onto the mattress. "Does this bed count?" he asked, "even though you just arrived and I haven't even shown you around?"

"Why don't you show me around the bed right now," she suggested with an inviting grin that caused his romantic intentions to increase sizably.

Not wanting to disappoint his future bride, Darach did exactly that for the rest of the morning. He showed her every nook and cranny of that big soft bed...until she cried out in ecstasy and begged to see more.

❧

*Read on for an excerpt from
the next book in this series:*

TAKEN BY THE HIGHLANDER

Logan's Story

Available December 2015

One

Scotland 1730

By the time Logan Campbell emerged out of the dark forest onto a wide river valley, the full moon was high in the sky. The pain in his arm was so severe, he passed out for a few seconds in the saddle and toppled off his horse. Landing with a heavy thud on the grass, he immediately regained consciousness, curled up in agony, and hugged his broken arm close to his ribs.

God, have you no mercy? Logan knew that if he didn't set the bone back in place soon, the swelling would make it impossible to do so. It might never heal properly. This was his sword arm. He couldn't afford to lose it.

He was kicking himself now. He shouldn't have ridden away from the camp in such a fury. He should have stayed long enough to allow his brother, Darach, to tend to him, but Logan's pride hadn't allowed it—not when Darach had been the one to break his arm in the first place.

Logan supposed he'd had it coming. As usual, he'd started the fight. Over a woman, of course. He had been first to draw a blade.

Ach! The pain was insufferable. He couldn't put it off any longer.

Sitting up carefully on the grass, Logan reached into his boot for his knife and slid the well-worn, wooden grip between his teeth. He then felt along the length of his forearm, pressing as gently as possible with his thumb to locate the break, but he couldn't find it through the rigidly swollen flesh. He had no choice but to press more firmly.

Suddenly, an acute pain exploded just above his wrist and he knew he'd found it. The crunching grit of bone rubbing against bone nearly caused him to vomit.

Bloody hell, what he wouldn't give for a cup of whisky....

Biting down hard on the handle of the knife, he rammed all his strength into the bone to set it back in place.

Snap!

Pain shot through his body like a cannon ball, from his wrist straight up to his brain where it reverberated against his skull. His thunderous, agonized roar echoed from one side of the glen to the other, then he collapsed onto his back, where he lay a long time in a stupor, blinking up at the stars, waiting for the pain to pass. He wondered what he would use to bind his arm in place—if he could ever stand up again.

What was his brother doing now? Logan wondered groggily.

Darach had probably packed up the camp and taken their hostage somewhere safe—a place where Logan couldn't find her or use her as a pawn to gain entry into Leathan Castle, the Campbell stronghold that had once been Logan's home.

Their home, as brothers.

Logan closed his eyes for a few moments and tried to drift off, but as luck would have it, the sound of a pistol cocking in front of his face got in the way of that goal.

It was the second occasion that night where he'd been approached by someone with a gun. Last time it had been his brother, and all hell had broken loose.

Pray God this would yield different results, for Logan was in no condition for fisticuffs.

Opening his weary eyes, he found himself gazing up at a woman. A rather lovely-looking woman with dark hair and ivory skin that appeared to gleam in the moonlight.

"I see you're a MacDonald," she said matter-of-factly, taking in the colors of his tartan and the polished brooch he wore.

Nay, he was not a MacDonald. He was a Campbell by blood, but if anyone ever discovered that he was alive, there would be a price on his head to be sure. So he did what he always did. He lied.

"Aye. I come from Kinloch Castle. I'm a scout for Angus the Lion."

"What are you doing in Campbell territory? Or maybe I should ask why you were shouting so loudly in the middle of the night."

"My arm is broken," he explained, feeling exceedingly weary. All the fight was gone out of him. "I just set the bone back in place. It hurt."

Still keeping the pistol trained on his face, she glanced down at his bruised and swollen arm, which he held close to his chest. "No doubt." She calmly released the hammer and lowered the weapon. "But you still haven't told me what I need to know. What's a MacDonald scout doing on Campbell lands? More importantly, what are you doing on my father's property?"

"Who's your father?" Logan asked.

"No one important," she replied, "and I'll be the one to ask the questions."

For more information about this book and the author, please visit Julianne's website at www.juliannemaclean.com. While you're there, be sure to sign up for her newsletter to be notified about new releases and special giveaways. You can also contact her directly through the site. She loves to hear from readers.

Julianne is also on Facebook and Twitter.

OTHER BOOKS IN
THE HIGHLANDER SERIES

Book One

Captured By The Highlander

Lady Amelia Templeton would rather die than surrender to a man like Duncan MacLean. He is the fiercest warrior of his clan—her people's sworn enemy—and tonight he is standing over her bed. Eyes blazing, muscles taut, and battle axe gleaming, MacLean has come to kill Amelia's fiancé. But once he sees the lovely, innocent Amelia, he decides to take her instead...

Stealing the young bride-to-be is the perfect revenge against the man who murdered Duncan's one true love. But Lady Amelia turns out to be more than a pawn of vengeance and war. This brave, beautiful woman touches something deep in Duncan's soul that is even more powerful than a warrior's fury. But when Amelia begins to fall in love with her captor—and surrenders in his arms—the real battle begins...

Book Two

Claimed By The Highlander

NIGHT OF CONQUEST

With his tawny mane, battle-hewn brawn, and ferocious roar, Angus "The Lion" MacDonald is the most fearsome warrior Lady Gwendolen has ever seen—and she is his most glorious conquest. Captured in a surprise attack on her father's castle, Gwendolen is now forced to share her bed with the man who defeated her clan. But, in spite of Angus's overpowering charms, she refuses to surrender her innocence without a fight...

PRISONER OF PASSION

With her stunning beauty, bold defiance, and brazen smile, Gwendolen is the most infuriating woman Angus has ever known—and the most intoxicating. Forcing her to become his bride will unite their two clans as one. But conquering Gwendolen's heart will take all his skills as a lover. Night after night, his touch sets her on fire. Kiss after kiss, his hunger fuels her passion. But, as Gwendolen's body betrays her growing love for Angus, a secret enemy plots to betray them both...

Book Three

Seduced By The Highlander

IN LOVE AND WAR

The fierce and powerful Laird of War, Lachlan MacDonald has conquered so many men on the battlefield—and so many women in the bedroom—that he is virtually undefeated. But one unlucky tryst with a seductive witch has cursed him forever. Now, any women he makes love to will be doomed for eternity...

IN DANGER AND DESIRE

Lady Catherine is a beautiful lass of elite origin—or so she is told. Suffering from amnesia, she is desperate to find the truth about who she really is...or, at the very least, meet someone who inspires an intense memory or emotion. When she first lays eyes on Lachlan MacDonald, Catherine has a sixth sense that he can unlock the key to her past—and maybe even her heart. But how could she know that the passion she ignites in this lusty warrior's heart could consume—and destroy—them both?

Book Four

Return Of The Highlander

A SCOTTISH PRISONER

Nothing means more to Scottish heiress Larena Campbell than saving her father from the gallows. While on an urgent mission to deliver his pardon from the King, she and her English escorts are attacked by a pair of fierce Scottish rebels. When she is dragged unconscious back to the stronghold of Angus the Lion, a powerful and dangerous Scottish laird, she is furious with her captors and determined to escape at any cost…

CAPTOR AND PROTECTOR

Highland scout, Darach MacDonald, is suspicious of the beautiful and defiant heiress who clocked him in the head during the skirmish with the enemy Redcoats. He suspects she will stop at nothing to win her freedom. When he is assigned the task of shepherding the heiress back to her home, he quickly discovers that spending countless nights on the open road with a lassie as temptingly beautiful as Larena Campbell is enough to drive any hot-blooded Scot mad with savage desire. Suddenly he is overcome by a need to claim her as his own, but when they arrive at her father's castle, all may not be what it seems…

Book Five

Taken By The Highlander

A WARRIOR WITH A SECRET

Logan MacDonald, fierce warrior and bold scout for Angus the Lion, hides a shameful secret. When he arrives injured at a crofter's cottage in Campbell territory during a secret mission for his laird, he is immediately roped and bound....

A WOMAN WITH A VISION

Mairi Campbell has dreamed of a powerful Highland warrior who will rise up to rescue her clan from oblivion and reclaim their castle from the English. When she stumbles across the mysterious wounded Highlander in a moonlit glen—a member of an enemy clan—she is strangely beguiled and cannot resist the desire to unearth the secrets of his darkened soul. Soon, Mairi surrenders to forbidden passion in his bed, which thrusts her into the middle of a war—in a battle for Scottish freedom, and in a battle against the true desires of her heart....

About the Author

Julianne MacLean is a *USA Today* bestselling author of over twenty historical romances, including the Pembroke Palace Series and her popular American Heiress Series with Avon/Harper Collins. She also writes contemporary mainstream fiction, and *The Color of Heaven* was a *USA Today* bestseller. She is a three-time RITA finalist with Romance Writers of America, and has won numerous awards, including the Booksellers' Best Award, the Book Buyer's Best Award, and a Reviewers' Choice Award from *Romantic Times* for Best Regency Historical of 2005. She lives in Nova Scotia with her husband and daughter, and is a dedicated member of Romance Writers of Atlantic Canada. Please visit Julianne's website at www.juliannemaclean.com for more information about the author and her books, and to subscribe to her email newsletter to stay informed about upcoming releases.

Made in the USA
Lexington, KY
16 June 2017